Pahulu Hale

Haunted House

Lacey Orazd Gordon

HEAR OUR
VOICE
PUBLISHER

Hear Our Voice LLC

Published by Hear Our Voice LLC
www.hearourvoicellc.com

Edited by Holly Hill Mangin

Cover Design by Hear Our Voice LLC utilizing Canva

Pahulu Hale
Haunted House
(puh-HU-lou HA-lay)

By
LACEY CRAZD GORDON

This book is dedicated to my cheering team. To my amazing husband, Ryan, and my two beautiful daughters, Kierra and Cara. Girls, never give up on your dreams. The world is waiting for you and whatever amazing things you do. Kierra, Cara, mommy and daddy will always be your cheering team. I love you all so much.

Chapter One

L eilani stands outside a beautiful two-story Victorian in
the early afternoon sun, eyeing the house in awe. She
moves closer to the wrap-around porch and front steps, eager
to walk up to the elaborate wooden front door. What treasures
is the old house hiding? There's a voice behind her, but she
hardly hears, her attention riveted on the house in front of her.
Her stormy gray eyes twinkle in the sunlight in anticipation.

"It's beautiful," Leilani says as she walks up the front stairs.
"I can't wait to see the inside."

Gentle laughter follows her, and another woman, clutching
a manila folder to her chest, appears at her elbow. "Well, you
wanted something more Victorian, so here we are, Leilani."
The realtor holds up a pair of keys and jingles them as she
walks over to the front door. Her painted ruby red lips part in
a smile as she slides the key into the keyhole and unlocks the
front door.

Leilani claps her hands as the realtor pushes the door open,
and as they tour the house, the house sits silently around

them. Leilani lightly runs her fingers across some of the pretty furniture and instantly falls in love with the place.

"This place comes fully furnished and is close to the beach and shopping," the realtor says, showing Leilani the lush backyard. "Plus, it's not too far of a drive to Waikiki, where you work."

"Oh, Nalani, this place is perfect! I mean, look at all this living space. And the backyard is perfect for our gatherings, no?"

Nalani brushes strands of her long, straight black hair away from her cheek with her smooth brown-skinned hand, chuckling. "Yes, the backyard would be perfect." She taps Leilani's shoulder before moving once again into the house and towards the stairs.

Leilani lets the blinds fall back over the sliding door and follows Nalani up the slightly curved stairs. She runs her hand along the smooth wooden banister, enjoying the feeling of the polished wood. Leilani originally wanted to only look at single-story homes, but when Nalani had shown her this house on her computer, she decided to give the house a chance. They walk into the master bedroom at the top of the stairs and Leilani drops onto the Queen-sized bed, her eyes scanning the room. Already, she could imagine waking up each morning within these walls.

Nalani steps up to the bed, a smile on her face as she enjoys her friend's excitement over the place. Nalani opens the folder to review her notes about the house. "Like I was saying, all the furniture comes with the house, so you can keep, sell, or get rid of whatever you want if you buy this place. Close to shopping, beaches, excellent schools, and close to the highway, so your trip to work won't be too bad. Plus, it's a great neighborhood." She lifts her gaze from the paperwork to look at Leilani, a hint of sadness in her eyes. "But—"

Leilani nods, "I know . . . the military family who was murdered in the house by their crazed neighbor 20 years ago. That story still haunts the island, but I love this place, Nalani. It's a perfect fit for me. And maybe you can move in so we can be roommates like we've always wanted." She smiles, silently pleading with her best friend.

Nalani sighs as she thinks about Leilani's offer. She doesn't believe in ghosts or vengeful spirits, not really, but she still feels uneasy about what happened to the poor military family twenty years ago. "Well, if you make an offer on the house, I can push it along, but it isn't fully up to me for the owners to accept."

Leilani listens to her friend, Nalani's tone if not her exact words, telling Leilani that she'll move in if Leilani puts in an offer and buys the house. Jumping up from the bed and squealing in pure delight, Leilani grabs Nalani and hugs her tightly, causing her to drop her folder.

"Ugh! Leilani." Nalani pushes her way out of the bear hug and kneels in her black skirt, her smile belying her words. She scoops up the fallen papers.

Leilani quickly kneels and helps gather them up. "Sorry, I just got excited."

Nalani gratefully accepts the papers and lays them out on the bed. She shifts through them, placing them back in order while Leilani walks around, looking in the closet and master bathroom.

"It's a big house for just you and me, Leilani. It has five bedrooms," Nalani says, as she places the papers back in the folder.

"I know . . . I'm thinking of taking the master bedroom for myself, letting you pick the next biggest bedroom, then we could rent out the rest of the rooms to some students that go to the local college."

Nalani laughs, "Well, let's continue the tour, shall we? We can discuss what we want to do with extra rooms later." She exits the master bedroom with Leilani at her side, and they walk into the next room.

It's a smaller room. Leilani notices a worn bunny sitting on the closet floor staring up at her blankly. Part of its tail is half gone, it no longer has a smile, it's missing an eye, and the left ear has a rip in it. She scrunches her eyebrows together as she looks down at the dirty bunny, surprised that someone has left behind such a visibly well-loved toy. Retrieving it, Leilani turns to face Nalani, holding it out for her friend to see. "I think the last people who rented this house left something behind or it could belong to the owners. I bet a little boy or little girl is missing their cute bunny friend."

Nalani eyes the ragged-looking toy. "The owners' children are grown and gone, with no kids of their own yet. I doubt the bunny belongs to either of the owners. And I am not sure about the family who rented the house." She pulls out her cell phone from her side pocket and quickly snaps a picture of the bunny. "I'll send them this and see what they say about it." She types a few lines in her message under the picture, then hits send as she eyes the bunny again, wrinkling her nose. "Why does it look like there's blood on it?" She shakes her head and walks out of the room.

As the women are making their way down the stairs, Nalani's phone dings. Nalani unlocks her phone and silently reads the owner's response about the bunny, her eyebrows knitting together in surprise. Leilani watches her friend's face cloud with a troubled expression and moves closer so she can read the message over Nalani's shoulder.

Thank you for contacting us, Nalani, but that bunny toy does not belong to us or the last people who rented our house. Supposedly, the youngest daughter of the Navy chief and his wife, who was murdered there, had a stuffed rabbit that looks like that one. But that's just a rumor. We hope the client you are showing the house to loves it. We enjoyed renting it out to others. Talk to you soon. The Kahunas

Leilani reads the text again as she processes the information and returns her gaze to the ripped rabbit. "The little girl that was murdered in the house had this toy?" Her voice shakes a little. "Do you think she just wants to play or eat our brains?" She laughs as she places the rabbit on the table by the front door.

Nalani locks her phone and slips it into her pocket as she looks at Leilani, making a face. "First, no, I don't think she wants to play with us. It must have fallen from the attic after the last family moved out. Second, zombies eat human brains, not ghosts. And third, I doubt you have a brain she would want to eat even if ghosts ate brains. Mine she probably would go for." She grins at her friend as she opens the front door and steps out onto the porch.

Leilani laughs. "You are a riot, my friend, a real hoot," she says as she joins Nalani on the front porch, closing the door behind her. She catches one last glimpse of the tattered bunny as she shuts the door and turns to walk down the porch steps as a warm Oahu breeze brushes her long, dark golden-brown hair around her face. Quickly brushing it back, she follows Nalani off the porch to Nalani's sleek black Kia Optima.

Nalani unlocks her car and slides in behind the wheel, slipping the key into the ignition. Leilani opens the passenger door and sits down, taking the folder from Nalani and letting it rest in her lap. As Nalani pulls out of the driveway and onto the quiet street, Leilani peers outside and watches as they pass other beautiful homes with their nicely kept yards and one or two cars parked in the semi-long driveways. Leilani rests her elbow on the door, taking in the serene neighborhood.

"I want to put a bid in for the house, Nalani," Leilani says as she turns away from the slow stream of houses. "Rumors, ghosts, or whatever else, I don't care. That is my dream house." She looks at Nalani, half expecting her best friend to tell her no or that she won't put in a bid for her for whatever reason; instead, Nalani nods. A smile spreads across Leilani's face, and she sits up straighter in her seat. "Well, then let's hurry back to your office and get started on that paperwork."

They drive in silence while calming Hawaiian music fills the car and tropical air blows past their open windows. Nalani drives the five miles from the house to her office that sits just on the outskirts of Waikiki, pulling into her spot in front of Aloha

Homes Real Estate. The music disappears once she turns off the car, and the two women sit in silence for a moment, their eyes staring at the building.

Nalani turns in her seat and faces her friend, her eyes serious as she asks, "Are you sure that you want to put a bid in for that house? I don't want to get your hopes up and you don't get it or if you get it and move in, it's not the house of your dreams like you thought."

Leilani unbuckles herself and pats her friend's hand. "I'm positive I want to put in a bid. A ghost story will not scare me away, and I won't get my hopes up too high, I promise. I know the owners never lived in the house and only rented it out, but *I* want to live in it, not rent it. That house has a sad history and needs new life in it to lift the cloud it has hovering over it. We'll rent out some of the other rooms, but I will own the house and I will live in it, too." She smiles at Nalani before she climbs out of the car and heads for the front door.

Minutes later, Nalani sits at her desk, all the paperwork Leilani will need to sign or initial before her. Pulling out her phone, she thanks the owners for the information about the toy via text. She pauses, studying her friend, who has been meandering around the room looking at the pictures on the walls. The smile on her face and bounce in her step are convincing. Putting in an offer is what Leilani wants. Nalani adds to the text, informing the owners she has a client ready to put in a bid for the house.

"Okay, let's get this paperwork done, yeah?" Nalani asks. She opens the top desk drawer and pulls out three black pens, setting them beside the paperwork, and looks up at Leilani. "Are you ready?"

"I am beyond ready," Leilani says as she watches Nalani highlight the paperwork where she will have to either sign or initial. While she waits for the paperwork, Leilani thinks about something. "Why didn't the owners live in the house?"

Nalani sighs and stops what she's doing. "There have been a lot of stories stating that if anyone who owns the house lives in it, bad things will happen." Nalani returns to working on the paperwork. "Because of the stories, anyone who has ever bought the house only rents it out and never lives in it. But again, those are just stories. No one wants to test the theory so none of the past owners ever lived in the house. You will be the first."

Nalani pushes everything in front of Leilani, jumping a bit when her phone vibrates. Leilani rests the tip of the pen on the first box she must initial and raises her eyebrows as Nalani reaches for her phone to read the new message from the Kahluas.

She smiles as she reads the message, then looks up at her friend. "They are glad you love their old house and will look over your paperwork and bid immediately after I send it to them," she says. She taps the desk with a nail as she sets her phone back down. "So, get to it, Leilani, so I can send it to them today."

Leilani's eyes widen as she returns to signing and initialing, only skimming what she reads since she knows the lingo from Nalani always telling her about it.

While she waits, Nalani looks up houses to rent or buy for other clients and sends out emails, asking the realtors of those houses when a suitable time would be to show the property. Leilani sets the pen down on the desk and slides the paperwork over to Nalani once she finishes. She nervously chews on her lower lip while she waits for Nalani to look the paperwork over to double-check Leilani hasn't accidentally missed anything in her rush to get everything signed. Folding the paperwork, including the extra papers where Leilani has stated her bid for the house, she places them all in an envelope.

"I will drop you off at work and then head over to hand this to the owners' realtor. I'll call you as soon as I hear anything back from them, okay?" Nalani taps the envelope on the desk before she stands up and turns off her computer.

Leilani stands up quickly as well. "That sounds good to me." She grins at Nalani as they walk out of the office.

Nalani walks down the hallway behind Leilani, envelope in hand. "Hopefully, the traffic isn't too bad right now with the lunch crowd," she says as they exit the building.

The two chat during the drive, making plans for the weekend since neither has to work. Soon, Nalani pulls into the parking lot of the Sunny Shores hotel and stops near the entrance. She gives Leilani a quick hug before her friend jumps out of the car. "Fingers crossed!" she shouts out the window. Leilani turns back with a huge grin, crossing digits on both hands before she walks into the hotel lobby to get to work.

Leilani walks through the lobby to a small room close to the reception desk where she slips her timecard into the machine and gets it punched for work. She heads to the locker room next and changes into a nice pair of black slacks and a long-sleeved dark green collared and buttoned shirt. Storing her shorts, tank top, and sneakers inside her locker, she closes it before slipping on a pair of black heels. Leilani pins on her name tag and walks to her office so she can start her day.

Another marketing manager sits behind his desk and glances up as the door opens. He smiles as soon as Leilani steps into the room.

"Leilani, aloha, how is the house-hunting going? Any good ones today?" asks Koa, a handsome brown-haired man with cunning amber eyes.

Leilani sits down at her desk, eyeing some paperwork that sits in her inbox. "Koa," she says, setting the paperwork down, "I found my dream home. It's a cute two-story Victorian house about five miles away from here." She picks up the first packet of stapled papers once again and looks it over. "The furniture is included so I can pick what I want to keep and sell the rest and then do the same with my stuff."

Koa finishes what he's working on and looks up at her, interested. "That's a great deal! So, I take it you've already put in a bid then?"

She grins and nods as she turns on her computer. "I have, and Nalani is on her way with the signed paperwork as we speak." She quickly types in her password and waits for her home screen to pop open before she clicks on the web browser icon. Her fingers fly across the keyboard as she says, "Let me show you the house. It's amazing."

Koa moves to stand beside her, leaning on the desk to look over her shoulder. "Hm, what will your house look like, I wonder."

Leilani glances up at him once the house appears on the screen. "Ta-da! Koa, here is my house . . . well, it will be once the owners accept my bid."

Koa steps back when he sees the house. "Funny," he says with a smirk, but when he sees Leilani is serious, he looks at her incredulously. His voice catches in his throat for a moment. "Are you crazy? That's the house where that family was murdered by their insane neighbor twenty years ago. You know that, right? The spirit of the neighbor haunts it. People have left in a hurry because of the ghost. You can't seriously want to buy, own, *and* live in that house."

Leilani clicks through the pictures to see the house again. "This is it, Kao, my dream home, and as I told Nalani, I won't let some supposed ghost stories run me off from buying it."

Koa shakes his head and returns to his desk to get back to work. Leilani closes the window on her computer before turning her attention back to the pile of papers on her desk and shuffles through them. She scans them quickly to see which pack of papers needs to get done first and what she can work on later. The two work in silence, though Leilani continues to check her phone to see if she has received anything from Nalani about the house. An hour slowly ticks by with no phone call or text, causing Leilani to grow anxious.

Koa glances over at her and chuckles. "Watching your phone won't make Nalani call or text any faster. I remember when I bought my house. It takes time for the agent and owner to go over your bid. And they might come back with a counteroffer if they aren't pleased with it. It took two weeks of negotiating before they finally accepted me over two other bids."

Leilani sighs, her lips hitting each other and making an exasperated sound. "I know that, but I thought she would at least tell me she gave them the paperwork and maybe see if they could read the bid right away."

"As I said, you can't rush these things, Leilani. Same goes for how we produce our marketing strategies. Ideas sometimes pop into our heads quickly and the number-crunching benefits us. Other times, the number-crunching doesn't benefit us, and we have to rethink the ideas so everything comes together," Koa says, his tone kind and his eyes sympathetic.

"If they rush into the bid, they could lose out on the house, or you could lose out on something. So, they need to take their time, and you need to be patient." He picks up an accounting book since he also helps with the financial side of the hotel and crunches some numbers. The clicking of his calculator comforts Leilani's racing mind.

Leaning back against her chair, Leilani sighs again. She knows Koa's right, but it's hard to be patient when something this big is on the line! She twists in her chair, first moving to the left, then back to the right as her eyes wander back to the papers scattered around her computer. She stops swinging her chair around and picks up a paper that has caught her attention, making a few changes with a red pen.

Once she gets into the groove of working, another hour slips by without her realizing it, and after what seems like an eternity, her phone finally vibrates. Leilani turns away from her work when she sees the screen light up, her breath stopping in her throat. She drops her pen and snatches up her phone so fast that she nearly drops it, unlocking her phone.

"Nalani? Hello?" Her voice squeaks into the phone.

Nalani giggles at her friend's enthusiasm. "Aloha, Leilani, I have some wonderful news to tell you."

"But?" Leilani asks.

"They are wondering if you could raise your bid up by $300 since you have bid a lot lower than their asking price. If you can't, I can always lend you the money," Nalani says.

"You'll lend me the money? Oh, Nalani, I will totally pay you back when I can, I promise. Please, tell them we can up the bid $30000 more, and I will pay you back from my future paychecks until you have the full amount." Leilani squeals, unable to contain herself at the news, but she takes in a deep breath to calm herself down. "Will you call me back as soon as you know when we close and can move in?"

"Okay, you need to slow down, Leilani, and let's get over this hurdle first. We need to make sure they will take the bid, and then we will move forward. After, we can discuss the closing date and when you can move—I mean, when *we* can move—into the house." Nalani's voice calms Leilani's anxiety. "Let me call them back and let them know you will put in the extra money, and I'll find out when they can fill out the paperwork. I'll bring over a check made out to you so you can either cash it and give them cash or add it to your account so you can give them a money order or check with the rest of the amount. Be ready with it so we can give it to them as soon as everything is signed.

I hope that sometime this week or next, we'll move to the next step.

"Why don't we meet up for dinner tonight? We can celebrate our new home!" Leilani says.

"Sure! Let's meet after work at Hula Grill Waikiki, and I can bring whatever paperwork that needs your signature to help push the sale through faster," Nalani says, Leilani's enthusiasm rubbing off on her.

The two finish making their plans before they say their last goodbyes and hang up.

"Congratulations!" says Koa, smiling warmly.

"Thank you!" Leilani responds.

They talk for a few minutes more about the house before getting back to work. When it's time to leave for the day, she files the paperwork she has finished and collects her belongings before departing, waving goodbye to Koa.

Chapter Two

Twenty years ago

"Oh, honey, the house is beautiful! I'm going to enjoy being stationed here if this is our home," an eager female voice exclaims as footsteps move closer to the freshly painted Victorian house.

"Well, sugar-pie, it's going to be ours not just for this tour but after too. I will retire in three years, and I thought Oahu would be the perfect place for us and the kids to settle down in." The twang of a country-accented male voice responds as a silver key jingles into the lock of the front door.

A loud click echoes through the empty house and the front door swings inward, letting sunlight shine in and casting two long shadows from the figures standing on the other side of the threshold onto the wooden floor before them.

A tall, tanned man walks into the new home, his chestnut brown eyes gazing proudly around the empty room. Brushing his fingers through his brown and speckled gray hair in need of a military barber's touch, he moves to the side so that his wife can take a peek inside. A beautiful woman with light rosy skin steps through the doorway, pushing up her rose-colored glasses while her glass-green eyes roam over the front entryway. She pushes a strand of her straight auburn hair behind her ear as she walks into the house and tours another room that sits off to her right.

A small boy of about eight years old with tanned arms and legs, short brownish-blonde hair, and ice-blue eyes runs past his dad's leg and into the house. Chasing behind the boy is a ten-year-old girl with curly blonde hair, rosy skin, seafoam green eyes, and a brand new stuffed bunny trapped under her left arm. Straggling behind her are the family's sixteen-year-old twins, one a female with bored hazel eyes, long wavy black and pink dyed hair, and a natural tan, and the other a boy with shaggy plain brown hair like his father's, light rosy skin tone like his mother's, and slightly curious honey brown eyes that scan the houses next door and across the street.

"Tony and Tina, please slow down. We've just gotten here and we don't need a trip to the base's hospital ER already," their mom yells from the stairs as she climbs them to go look upstairs.

The loud footfalls continue from one empty room to the next, laughter ringing through the house from the two playing children as their older sister closes the door. Their father pulls out his cell phone to check if the movers have called, but there are no new messages.

He shrugs a bit and slips the phone back into the front pocket of his jeans before he growls at his running children, "Tony! Tina! Listen to your mother!"

Seconds later, the footsteps slow down until they finally stop in front of the stairs, and the two young children look sheepishly at their dad. "You two, along with Lucas and Lindsey, need to go upstairs with mom because it's time to choose your bedrooms. Remember to fight fairly though," he jokes as he tussles Tony's hair with one hand.

"Thomas, don't say that," his wife says from the top of the stairs.

Thomas looks up at her grinning with puppy dog eyes. He puts his hands together and says, "But Annie . . ."

"No buts, mister!" She laughs. "Let's go, kids. You need to pick out your rooms before the movers get here with our things. We'll also need to discuss what color paint you want for your walls."

"Do we actually get to paint the walls here?" Tony asks while bouncing on the balls of his feet.

"That's right, son. This is going to be our new home for many years to come. No more renting, no more plain white walls, and no more moving after this tour," Thomas says as he slowly follows his four children up the creaky wooden stairs.

Lindsey quickly spins to face her dad on the fifth step. "Are you serious? We don't have to move after this? We get to stay in school here until we graduate?"

Lucas, also turning to look at their dad, pipes in. "We get to live in Hawai'i?"

"I am serious, dead serious. We don't have to move anymore after this tour is up and yes, we get to live in Hawai'i, right here on Oahu," Thomas says as he points from Lindsey to Lucas, answering their questions. "Of course, we'll travel to the other islands to visit them and fly back to Texas to visit family, but we can now call Oahu our home."

Tina squeals excitedly, clapping her hands as she looks from her mom to her dad. "So cool!"

"Awesome!" Tony says.

"Yes, super cool and totally awesome," Annie replies.

Thomas starts up the stairs again. "Come on, move it, slowpokes. Go pick out your rooms already, or maybe I should pick them out for you."

Lindsey runs up the stairs before any of her siblings can react, pushing in between Tony and Tina. Lucas, Tony, and Tina quickly race up the stairs after her, yelling and screaming as they head off to check out the bedrooms to claim one as their very own. Annie hangs onto the banister as she watches her children scamper off in different directions. Thomas climbs the stairs and grabs her hand, dragging her to safety in their master bedroom. They hug each other as they stand in the doorway and watch Lucas shut one door at the end of the hallway. Lindsey closes her door next to Lucas's room. And Tony and Tina run back and forth between their bedrooms, the rooms connected by their own bathroom.

Annie turns to face Thomas and slips her arms around his neck. "This place is perfect." She kisses him, and he wraps his arms around her waist and returns the kiss.

Thomas' cell phone rings, breaking their kiss, and he quickly lets his wife go to answer it. He walks away from her and puts the phone to his ear, eager to see if it's the moving company.

After Annie closes the door to give Thomas privacy, she walks down the hallway and knocks on her children's bedroom doors, each child poking their head out. She smiles at them. "Let me see your rooms."

The children each lead their mom on a tour of their rooms, talking excitedly as they each discuss the colors of paint they want for their walls and where they want to put their furniture. The first room she walks into is Tony's, then Tina's, crossing over to Lindsey's, then lastly Lucas' room, laughing at their eagerness to decorate their bedrooms.

"Okay, okay, hold on. Let me get my pad of paper and pen from my purse so I can write all of this down. I want your father in on this discussion, too," Annie says as she holds up her hands to fend off her excited children.

At the sound of a door opening, Annie turns to see Thomas exiting their bedroom with a huge grin on his face. She waves for her kids to quiet down when she sees him, and the children follow her gaze to see their dad's grinning face. They walk out of Lucas' room and surround him, their faces eager to hear what he has to say.

"Good news, then?" Annie asks.

"That was the moving company. The movers are almost here," Thomas announces. "That means that we can get everything off the truck today, since it's still early, and start unpacking."

"Yes, sir!" came the answer as the kids danced around their parents.

Several hours later, the moving truck is leaving, free of its load, and the Thornton family is opening boxes. Lindsey and Annie work in the kitchen while Tony and Tina unpack the boxes for their bedrooms. Lucas and Thomas move from room to room, double-checking that the movers put together their furniture correctly since there had been issues with other moves.

Several hours later, the family troops out of their new house, chatting about what they want to eat for dinner. It is their first night on Oahu and they found a close restaurant that serves authentic Hawaiian food. As they pile into their red Kia Sedona, Tina notices a man standing on the small porch of a slightly rundown house that sits directly across from theirs. The man is keeping to the shadows of his house. She waves at him, but the man quickly turns his back on her and retreats inside, disappearing into the darkness of the house. The door slams and the lights turn off on the porch.

Tina pauses in her step and regards the neighbor's house with sadness and confusion. He didn't return her wave. Weren't neighbors supposed to be friendly? And why did the man seem angry with her family? She didn't understand. Shrugging it off, she climbs into the very back of the van with Tony, her bunny clutched in her hands. As she watches the houses slip by, she listens to her mom give her dad directions to the restaurant. In the seat in front of her, the twins are tapping away on their cell phones, texting their friends in Virginia. Next to her, Tony plays his hand-held game. Her game sits beside her leg, untouched.

Present Day

Leilani groans as she carries another full box up the stairs. The past month was a whirlwind of exchanging money, signing more paperwork, and packing up her things from her old apartment. But it was all worth it. She has the keys to the Victorian and is finally moving everything into her dream house. She sets down the box on her bed that the movers carried in for her and runs her hand over the mattress.

The week before she moved in, she went through all the furniture and other items to see which items to keep, which items to sell, and which items to donate. She sold the queen bed and bedroom set in the master bedroom. She even sold her old bedroom set and quite a few pieces of furniture from the apartment to have some extra money for updates and renovations.

She looks at her new bedroom set, which was handmade on Kauai, and smiles. But the smile melts away as she notes all the scattered boxes in the room and thinks about the scattered boxes in all the other rooms that will need unpacking. She wants all her boxes unpacked and stored in the garage or broken down and recycled before Nalani moves in, which wouldn't be for another month.

Leilani heads out of her room and stops before the door of the bedroom Nalani picked. Placing her hand on the doorknob, she pushes open the door to look into the empty room. Leilani smiles, happy she will live with Nalani finally. They had always talked about living together while growing up, but they never had the opportunity. She steps out of the bedroom and closes the door behind her before heading back down the stairs to grab some more boxes that go into her bedroom.

As she picks up a box, a knock on the front door startles her and she nearly drops the box. Grumbling under her breath, she balances the box in one arm and opens the door quickly. The box topples forward into the person standing at the door.

"Oh no! I am so sorry about that," Leilani exclaims, embarrassed. "Let me get the box out of your face."

Someone laughs from the other side of the box as it shifts, and Koa's friendly face appears. Leilani gasps when she sees who it is and tries to retrieve the box, but Koa brushes past her. Following Koa is a small group of their marketing team, looking around nervously.

"Leah, Larry, Koa, and Nani, what are you all doing here?" she asks, letting them in. "I thought you had plans today."

Koa smirks as he heads up the stairs with the box still in his arms. Larry, a shorter brown-haired, brown-eyed mainlander who moved to Oahu five years ago, spies the last box marked Master Bedroom and grabs it, heading up the stairs after Koa. Leilani turns to see Nani and Leah move boxes from the living room into the kitchen. She grabs another box and follows them, the three opening their boxes and putting items away.

"Leah, Nani, thank you guys so much for coming over to help me," she tells them.

"Not a problem, Leilani," Leah says as she turns to look at her boss and friend with seafoam green eyes as she opens the drawers. "With our help, you'll be done in no time. Plus, I've always wanted to see the inside of this house. It's beautiful yet very creepy being in here after . . . well, you know." She pulls open the box and with a steady pink hand, she retrieves the knives that are packed inside.

Nani grins, wrinkles forming in her light brown skin around her russet brown eyes as she opens the box she brought in. "You shouldn't be doing this on your own anyway, Leilani. You would be unpacking for years! We know how slow you move, girl. We see it at work." Nani chuckles when Leilani rolls her eyes at her friend's joke.

The three chat as they unload the boxes, placing the kitchen items in drawers and cabinets. Larry and Koa work in the office next, unpacking books, and placing them on the built-in bookshelves.

The girls finish the kitchen in an hour, then move to the upstairs to unpack Leilani's bathroom and bedroom. Downstairs the office is coming together with the books shelved, the computer and printer placed on the enormous desk and hooked up, and notebooks and other writing materials stored in the desk drawers.

Several hours later, the kitchen, master bedroom and bathroom, office, and half of the living room are unpacked. The group breaks down the empty boxes, stacking them by the door that leads out to the garage. The morning has gone, and the afternoon greets the five friends with grumbling stomachs and lunch delivered. They sit around the cherry wood dining room table, eating delicious sandwiches, chips, salad, and sipping on sodas. They talk about the move, the house, and the rumors that surround the house.

Leah tosses her trash in a black trash bag before she and Nani return to the living room to finish unpacking. Larry and Koa follow Leilani into the garage, taking the pile of flat boxes with them. In the garage, there are also a few more boxes sitting beside a new refrigerator, dishwasher, washing machine, and dryer that she and Nalani have bought together to replace the old appliances.

"Can you get these inside for me, please? The company that delivered them already took away the old ones, so you don't have to worry about those," Leilani asks as she places the pile of flat boxes off to one side.

"Not a problem, Leilani. We'll get these put in and hooked up in no time," Larry says as he walks over to the dishwasher first. With Koa's help, he lifts the dishwasher and they maneuver it inside the house to get it in place in the kitchen.

She thanks them before she moves over to some boxes, opening them to see if she needs the items now or can keep them packed for later. Not needing anything, she repacks the boxes and carries them into the house and upstairs to the attic. She pulls on the cord in the ceiling and carries each box up into the dark dusty attic, being careful on the rickety ladder. Once the last box is in the attic, she reaches up to the naked light bulb's cord to turn it off but stops when she sees the old bunny rabbit sitting on the dusty ground beside the last box. It hadn't been there before!

Leilani grabs the toy, her eyes straining to see farther into the darker areas of the attic, half expecting to see the little girl who owned the bunny. But she sees nothing until she looks back down to see a faded blue toy car by the boxes where the bunny had been. She reaches for the car, hesitating with her fingertips only inches away before she grabs the car. Turning off the light, Leilani scurries carefully down the ladder and pushes the ladder back up into the ceiling, both toys clutched in her hand.

Chapter Three

Twenty years ago

The family sits at a booth in the restaurant, laughing and talking to their waitress. The waitress pets Tina's cute bunny toy before she takes down their drink orders and leaves them to look over the menus. Tina makes her bunny hop around in front of her before she places it beside her in the booth and turns her gaze from the bunny to her children's menu. She hears grumbling and looks up to see if it came from Lindsey, who isn't fond of trying new foods. Seeing the twins chatting as they point down at the menu, she turns her attention to those sitting around the restaurant. Her gaze stops when they reach the slightly wrinkled face of an older gentleman who looked like their neighbor she had seen when they left their home.

He sits two tables away, alone, glaring at her parents with menacing honey brown eyes. He wipes his brow with a slightly wrinkled brown hand before he slaps his hand down on the table on his menu. Tina makes a small squeak in the back of her throat that catches the older man's attention, and his hateful gaze turns to her. She stares unblinkingly at the man until their waitress returns with their drinks. With her view blocked, she forces herself to look at her menu to decide what to order. She tells the waitress what she wants to eat, then grabs her bunny and holds it tight as the waitress walks away. The man is talking to his own waiter, pointing down at the menu, and nodding his head as he asks questions. A few seconds later, the waiter walks away, and the man is back to glaring at her family. She keeps her head down so that he can't see her watching him, but her eyes never leave his devilish-looking face.

She leans closer to Tony and whispers in his ear about the man, telling him where the man is sitting, and to look back at him but not to let the man see him looking. Tony pretends to stretch a bit and glances over at the man, studying him quickly before he turns back to Tina. He nods, letting her know he has seen the man and has committed him to memory. Tina moves closer to Tony, stroking her bunny's ear as she does her best to ignore the angry man, her stress-stroking ripping the ear a bit at the seam. Tony gently rests his tinier hand on hers to calm her down and to stop her from rubbing her bunny so hard. They exchange a look before they take sips of their chocolate milk.

Soon their table is full of plates covered in delicious Hawaiian food. Forks clank against plates and silence falls over their table while the family tries the new tasty delights their new home state offers. When Tina looks over at their neighbor once more, she sees he has received his food and is eating slowly. Thankfully, he's no longer staring at her family either. Tony also monitors the man, but he enjoys his food and the food that he takes from his parents' and siblings' plates.

The waitress takes away the plates and brings back the manager at the request of Thomas. Thomas and the manager hit it off instantly. Thomas and Annie ask questions about good picnicking areas, which beaches are a must-visit, and where the best hiking trails are located. Annie also asks about the schools that the kids will attend and the waitress vanishes abruptly. The manager apologizes since he sent his kids to a different school. However, he goes into details about other places they had asked about, Annie writing the names of the places to visit in the notebook she carries in her purse. Two more waitresses join them at their table and talk about the schools. One of the waitress's husbands is the principal of where Tina and Tony will be going. The other waitress is currently sending her teen daughter to the high school where Lindsey and Lucas will go, and her adolescent son goes to where Tony and Tina will go to school.

Before the meal has finished, the Thornton family has four new phone numbers logged into their cell phones, new friends, and a couple of potential new friends for their kids. They finish eating their meals and Thomas pays, thanking the manager along with the waitresses for their time. The Thorntons walk out of the restaurant to their car, full from the hot meal. They still need to go on base to do school shopping and food shopping, but the warm meal made them a little sleepy.

Tina clutches her bunny as they walk outside, her other hand clinging to Lucas' hand. She glances over her shoulder just in time to see their neighbor, beer gut and all, saunter out of the restaurant and just stand at the door. Everyone buckles up and soon they are on their way to the exchange and commissary. Annie digs into her black purse for the school lists, retrieving them along with the list for the commissary.

Annie sits up and looks in the side mirror, spotting a beaten-up old green truck racing towards them. "Dear?" her voice cracks with concern as she turns in her seat to look back at the vehicle as it slowly drives closer, but keeping far enough back they couldn't see who is driving.

Thomas looks over at his worried wife before glancing in the rearview mirror to see the truck. He reaches over and gently pats Annie's leg reassuringly as he moves further to the right so that the speeder can go around them. The truck comes up close, the driver flashing the headlights and honking the horn while swerving back and forth behind them. All eyes in the van swivel back to watch the maniac behind them except for Thomas, who keeps his eyes trained on the road ahead of him. He keeps the van at the same speed, 35 mph as posted. He holds the wheel with his right while sticking his left arm out of the car window and waves his arm to let the driver know he can go around them; however, the driver continues to stay close, almost touching the bumper of the Thorton vehicle, while honking and flashing the lights before backing off. The two cars drive around the curve, the truck still honking at the van. Then, as suddenly as the dangerous game had started, it ends when the driver flew past them and disappears around the next bend in the road.

Thomas slows down as they take the next curve, not wanting to run into the psycho driver again. Concern flashes through his eyes as he scans the area ahead of the car and any side streets they pass, but the old green truck is nowhere to be seen. Thomas speeds up and doesn't slow until he turns on the street that takes them to the exchange and commissary, where he hopes they will be safe. He shows his military card at the front gate and drives down the road until he comes to a red light. He surveys the road still on high alert and turns the car at the light into the parking lot in front of the giant exchange and commissary buildings. Thomas pulls into a parking space as close to the front doors as he can before he turns off the van and quickly troops his family safely inside the exchange. He excuses himself so he can go back outside with his cell phone in hand as his eyes wander over the parking lot.

Annie pulls a cart free and hands each child a list of what they need for school, along with smaller baskets for them to carry while her eyes dart around the exchange. She walks to where the school supplies are before she talks to them about what had happened. She stops at the end of the aisle and waits until her kids are standing in front of her.

"I know what just happened was very scary, but it's over now. We still have a lot of shopping to do for school supplies, food, and maybe a few new things for the new house. We need to push what happened out of our minds for now and concentrate on what needs to get done. We can talk about it more when we get home, but for now, we need to keep our minds on our shopping," Annie says to her nervous children, giving each a tight hug. "I have given you all your supply lists, so now go! Meet me in the clothes department once you finish getting your school supplies."

The kids head down the aisles with lists in hand and small shopping baskets. Hands grab items they will need as they walk down one aisle and up the next. Once all four baskets are full, they make their way to the kid's clothing department. They turn the corner and spot their mom and dad leaning close together as they whisper to one another. Their mom is visibly shaken and upset as they walk closer to their parents.

Tina and Tony hold hands as they step up beside their parents, their eyes looking upwards into their parents' upset faces. Thomas puts on a strained smile as he sees his four worried children join them. Annie turns to look down at Tina and Tony, forcing a smile as to stop them from worrying too much. She brushes back a few of Tina's blonde curls back from her face before she glances over at the clothes.

"Okay, we all need at least two new outfits for school and work. Have fun picking out your clothes and we will meet up at the check-out lines." Annie smiles as her children run off together to find new clothes.

An hour later, the Thornton family stand in the check-out line with a full cart. Tony and Lucas pretend to be wrestling one another while Lindsey took a picture with Tina to post it on her Friend Chat account as her new profile picture. Thomas tells the boys to quit playing around as soon as it is their turn to check out. Lucas makes a face at the back of Thomas' head, causing his siblings to laugh. Annie glances back at them, smiling as she places the items up on the counter for the cashier to scan. She waves them through, and they head past her to stand at the other end to wait for their parents.

As they walk to their car, Annie grabs Thomas' arm when her eyes spot a green truck parked only a few spots away from them. Thomas clenches his jaw and he ushers his family to the car. He makes sure everyone is safely inside before he packs the trunk and gets in behind the wheel. A man walks over to the truck, gets in, and drives away, not even glancing once at the scared family. Annie sighs in relief when she realizes it isn't the same truck as before, this one being new.

Thomas smiles a tight smile before he pulls out of the parking lot and drives back towards home. Lindsey and Lucas are busy on their cell phones while Tina and Tony play together in the backseat with her bunny. Annie's eyes scan the road around them as she keeps a lookout for the beaten up old green truck. Thomas reaches over and squeezes her hand as he, too, keeps an eye out for the truck. They make it back home without seeing the truck. Annie hops out of the car and heads to the back, meeting her kids there. She pops open the trunk and hands them bags while Thomas unlocks the front door. They unpack the Sedona, and fill the kitchen with food, snacks, and drinks, then put away their new clothes and school supplies in their rooms. The tired family drag themselves up the stairs to their bedrooms, get ready for bed, and collapse into their warm awaiting beds.

Present Day

"Hey Leilani, there you are."

A voice drags her out of her trance, and she looks away from the two toys sitting awkwardly in her hands. She spots Koa

31

watching her from the top of the stairs, his eyes narrowed at her questioningly.

He walks over to her and asks, "Hey, are you okay, Leilani?" His eyebrows scrunch together, and concern replaces the questions as he looks into her eyes.

"Oh yea, Koa, I'm fine. I just thought that Nalani had tossed out this toy the other day, but..." She looks back up at the attic, then back down at her hands. "I found the bunny before in a closet while I toured it a few months ago. This time it was hiding in the attic with an old car toy," she says as she holds the toys out to Koa, who takes them curiously from her hands.

He turns the toys over in his hand, "That is strange." He shrugs and his curiosity disappears as he hands them back to Leilani. "Well, just toss them in the trash bag downstairs and I will take it out later."

Leilani slowly follows behind Koa, her eyes drifting back to the attic door as they head down the stairs. The sound of playful bickering and laughter floats down to her ears as they step off the last step together. Koa turns to see Leilani still clutching the toys to her chest and takes them out of her hands, tossing them in a trash bag. Kao grabs the bag and heads outside to toss it with the other trash. Leilani watches him by the front door, rubbing her arms as a sudden chill passes over her.

Chapter Four

Present Day

Leilani stares up at the ceiling as the soft sounds of crickets slip through her open bedroom window. She groans as she rolls over and stares out the window, watching the beautiful stars twinkle in the midnight sky. Leilani feels comfortable, but being in such a foreign house is keeping her awake. She is glad that she doesn't need to go to work the next day, but she also wishes she could fall asleep. She forces her eyes shut, but sleep only reaches the very tips of her mind, then let's go, pushing her back awake.

She rolls away from the window as a light breeze blows into the room. Sweet smells from the yellow Hibiscus plant and from the heavenly Plumeria trees in the yard rides through the open window on the night breeze to her nose. But there is another smell under these heavenly smells that she can't quite put her finger on. She wrinkles her nose as the other smell becomes more apparent and she nearly gags. Leilani pulls the covers over her head, stopping the sweet and putrid smell from invading her nose.

Hours later, the sun peeks through her open window and the birds sing to one another as they fly past. Leilani opens her eyes to the morning sounds, surprised at how quickly morning came. She knows she has to finish unpacking, but since she barely slept, she gets more sleep instead. She closes her eyes and thankfully the sandman listens this time. Soon sleep takes over and once again Leilani is slipping through the clouds into a dream.

Leilani stands in front of her house, enjoying the sight of the fresh coat of paint. The windows and front door are wide open, with music spilling out into the driveway. She can hear screaming, laughter, and a lot of chatter floating through the air, and it brings a smile to her face. She walks towards her house, hands in the pocket of her short jean shorts, whistling a little tune. But the more she walks towards the house, the house seems to be just a few feet away from her. She tries to run to the house, but she still can't get closer. She stops running and bends over, resting her hands against her thighs, and does her best to catch her breath.

A low rumbling draws her eyes away from the house and up to the blue sky. To her horror, the white fluffy clouds have turned dark and crash into one another until they cover the blue sky. Birds become silent as another rumble rolls across the sky and lightning races down to the ground. Leilani screams out in terror as lightning hits her house repeatedly. The joyous sounds of laughter melt into cries for help and the screams of bliss turn into screams of pain. The front door slams shut as the wind picks up and the windows slam, breaking the glass. Leilani yells, but the thunder and wind drown out her frightened yelling as more lightning slams onto the ground behind the house. Flames erupt in her backyard and on the roof where the out-of-control lightning has struck. She takes a step forward, but it feels like she is moving in slow motion.

Leilani falls to her knees as she watches the house crumble under the weight of the flames. The screams have died, and the heat reaches for Leilani hungrily, not yet satisfied from the blood it has already consumed. Tears stream down her cheeks as the wind tosses ashes up into the air, ashes from the burned house and from her friends. The ashes rain down on her as Leilani struggles to her feet so she can escape the fingers of the fire.

Dark laughter fills her ears as she stands shakily on her feet in front of the almost burned home. She takes several steps back as an evil presence seems to reach through the flames towards her. Leilani looks down when she feels a small hand take a hold of her left hand and a slightly bigger one grab her right. She sees a little girl about ten years old and a little boy about eight beside her. They look up at her with empty eye sockets and sad facial expressions.

Leilani screams but can't let either of their hands go, both clutching her tightly. The children turn back to face the house and lift their bloody palms to the house as the fire licks the lawn in front of them. Leilani squints her eyes and turns her head as the fires reach them. As soon as the fire is in reach, a scream emits from the ghostly children and the fire seems to flinch away from their extended hands. They let go of Leilani's hands, and she collapses to her knees, pressing her hands tightly over her ears to block out the horrible screams. She watches the two children move forward towards the fire while the fire bends back, moving away from them.

The deadly fire shrinks back into the vast pile of ashes that is all that is left of her beautiful home and her closest friends. Soon the fire has died out to nothing more than a light gray wisp of smoke. The dead children stop screaming as they take one another's hands, then turn to look over their shoulders at Leilani. Leilani panics and stumbles, her eyes spotting a blue car in the boy's free hand and a bunny in the girl's hand. Her mouth opens to scream again but nothing comes out, the wind picking up some ashes and throwing them into her face, causing her to choke. She crawls on her hands and knees backwards when her foot hits something and grabs it, dragging her off her hands and knees..

Before she hits the ground, she sits straight up in her bed, gasping for air as sweat pours down her forehead and down her back. Leilani throws off her covers and quickly gets out of bed, pacing back and forth, suddenly energized by the nightmare. Leilani sits on her bed for a moment, trying to rationalize the dream. She knows who the children are, but what about the strange lightning and fire? Was this the angry neighbor using his emotions to conjure up what she fears the most? Being struck by lightning or being eaten alive by fire?

Leileni shakes her head and stands up from her bed, walking over to her dresser. She pulls out some work clothes so she can finish unpacking, but before she dresses, she decides she needs a shower, regardless of whether she would need another one later. She watches the water as it hits the bottom of the tub then swirls down the drain before she shakes herself out of her trance and undresses. Stepping under the hot water and closing her eyes, Leilani lets the warmth wash away the sweat and lingering fear.

After several minutes, Leilani dries herself off and dresses quickly, suddenly feeling the urge to leave the house. Maybe a walk around the neighborhood would help clear her mind and chase away the last remaining images from the nightmare. Leilani finishes getting ready and hurries down the stairs while putting her hair in a ponytail. She grabs her keys before bolting out of the front door and away from the strange house. She gets down the driveway but stops, remembering that her phone is in the kitchen. Leilani throws her hands up in frustration as she slowly turns towards the house. The house stands before her ablaze and she can smell the burning wood like she had in her dream. She closes her eyes as the panic rises through every fiber of her being. And just as suddenly as it has appeared, the fire vanishes, taking the smell with it and leaving only sounds of happy birds chirping and the beautiful smells from the surrounding flowers.

It had been so real, *felt* so real. She knows she has to go back inside to grab her phone, but she can't move.

"Move, Leilani," she whispers to herself. "Go inside and get your phone." Leilani shakes herself free from the strange trance she is in and runs to the front door, her feet pounding on the wooden porch. She unlocks the door and races through the front entry to her right into the kitchen. Leilani scans the kitchen as she hurries to where her phone is, thankfully not seeing anything out of the ordinary. She stops in front of her phone, but her hand stops reaching for it when something catches her eyes. Sitting beside her cell phone is the ripped-eared bunny and blue car with the paint chipping that Koa had taken and thrown away yesterday.

With shaking hands, she pockets her phone, then picks up the toys, taking them outside to where her trash bins sit. Leilani clumsily opens one of the trash cans and throws the toys inside. She takes out her phone and snaps a few pictures of the toys inside the trash can so that she can have documented proof that she had thrown them out herself. Leilani saves the pictures on her phone, then sends them to her email. She walks away from the house, her eyes on the trashcan as if she is going to see the lid fly off and the toys float out of the trashcan by some unseen force. Not seeing anything, she heads down the driveway, determined to walk around the neighborhood before she tackles the rest of the house.

After her walk, she feels better, the last of the nightmare gone from her mind. Leilani convinces herself that her nightmare is from her stress of having bought a house and heads back inside, hoping unpacking more will relieve her sudden anxiety. She drops her items on the table by the front door. Leilani walks into the kitchen to get herself a glass of water before she heads into the office. Nalani had dropped a few boxes off yesterday, so she has less to pack up and bring with her at the beginning of the next month. Leilani opens the first box and turns on her small radio onto a station that plays soft jazz. Leilani opens the boxes to see what is inside then sets them closer to the bookshelf so Nalani can organize her books after she moves in.

After moving the boxes around to make it easier for Nalani to unpack, her phone rings in the other room, catching her off guard. She leaves the office and grabs her phone from the living room. She returns to the office and gets comfortable in the office chair. Leilani looks down to see who is calling her, but it just says unknown. Her curiosity gets the best of her, and she swipes the screen in order to answer the mysterious caller.

"Hello?" she says, unsure of who will be on the other side. No one answers, so she repeats herself, annoyance creeping noticeably into her voice. "Hello, is anyone there?"

The phone suddenly grows hot in her hand and a scratchy, evil laugh fills her ear. Leilani nearly drops her phone as she quickly switches hands and presses the warm phone back to her left ear. She can still hear the demonic laughter that causes the hairs on her arms and the back of her neck to stand straight up. "Who is this? What do you want? Koa, are you trying to scare me?" she shouts angrily into her phone as fear builds in her chest, causing her heart to speed up.

The laugh only continues, and the phone gradually becomes warmer in her hand. Now too much for her to manage, she yelps and drops the phone on the desktop, seeing what looks like wisps of smoke as it burns into the desk. The laughter grows, and she pushes the phone away from her, doing her best to ignore the burning sensation she feels when it touches her skin. Where the phone had sat is a large burned mark, which leaves her unsettled. She closes her eyes for a moment and takes in a deep breath, trying to calm her nerves. When she opens her eyes to look at the burn mark, but now it is nowhere to be seen. Feeling scared, she rushes out of the office.

Leilani runs out of the office, slamming the door behind her, and nearly falls on the stairs as her legs shakily give out on her. She strains to listen but the evil laughter has stopped. She sits on the stairs, trying to catch her breath and debates whether she should return to the office and retrieve her phone or if she should leave it and do another task on her list. Her mind reels with questions and she pushes herself off of the stairs and takes a few steps towards the office.

Growing frustrated, Leilani stomps back into the office, not wanting to let her fears get the best of her. She marches over to where her phone sits on the ground, having accidentally pushed it so hard it fell off the desk. The phone sits on the screen and Leilani can't see any more wisps of smoke anywhere near it. She kneels next to it and gingerly touches it, expecting to pull away quickly because of the heat. The side of the phone is cool to the touch, and she crawls her fingers around the phone and over its sides but still feels no heat.

She picks up her cell phone and flips it over to stare at the black screen. She presses the side and waits for a moment until a beautiful bright pink flower, a picture of her own, appears on the screen, welcoming her back to her phone. It then fades and her lock screen pops up, asking her to use her special code in order to unlock it. She skims her fingertip over the lock, then hits the button for the recent calls, but there is no number on the list marked unknown.

Leilani scrolls down the list, then back up again, but it only shows the names of her family and friends. Nothing stating someone from an unknown number had called not even ten minutes ago. She shakes her head and laughs at herself as she locks her phone again. She needs a nap! Simply put, she needs a nap because the lack of sleep is making her imagine things. Leilani heads up the stairs to her bedroom, sheds the clothes that she had worn while walking, and climbs into her comfortable soft night pants and her short, light blue nightshirt. She yawns as she crawls under the covers and once her head hits the pillow, she immediately slips into sleep.

Chapter Five

Twenty Years Ago

The old neighbor sits on his front porch, eyeing the neighbors around him. Ever since he lost her five years ago, he had stopped going out unless it was to get groceries.. Roy takes a swig of his beer as he stares across the street at her house, his eyes hooded. He had asked her to sign it over to him. She refused. And it wasn't as if he had the money to buy it right out. And now there was a family living there, a family who had purchased the house and were actually living within its walls. .

Roy takes another drink from his beer, wanting to drown the pain. She visited him every night, her eyes soulless, her skin sallow. Then she would morph, her face melting away to skin and bones, her hair falling out in clumps into his hands as he held her, her mouth opening and closing in gasps. "Roy. . . Roy." Her voice would come out strangled as her fingers clutched at him . . .

Every night this happened, so every night he struggled to stay awake. He hates the nightmares, and he hates the house. It's his burden and his curse.

Her family hated Roy, still hates him, and he knew they sold her house to spite him. She had put in her will that she only wanted people renting her house. She was insistent that if people bought and lived in it, they would make changes she didn't authorize, and it was *her* house. She wasn't leaving it by choice. In her deteriorating mind, she believed that renters, who would have to ask to make changes, were best. Then her house would stay in tact the way she wanted.

But then she went and insisted on signing the house over to *them*. Roy could see her smiling coyly at him. It was as if she knew she was making his job harder. He took a long drag of his beer, wiping his mouth on his sleeve. Shadows move deep within the house across the way, and lights, dimmed by closed curtains, switch off.

A few days after her funeral, he had walked out of his front door and nearly threw up when he saw a for sale sign, its post white and pristine, swinging in the gentle breeze in front of her house. The family hadn't followed her will. They were selling her house against her wishes and there was nothing he could do. He watched in horror as family after family trampled through her beautiful home. Then early one morning, the for sale sign was covered by the word he had dreaded the most–sold.

He tips the bottle of beer, swallowing the last dregs, and stares up at the night sky, smirking to himself. He knows what he has to do now. He has to get the family out of her house no matter what it takes. Roy turns his glare to the house, watching as more lights turn off one by one, the family retreating to bed for the night. Roy stands and hurls his bottle at their house.

The glass shatters at the end of his drive and the dogs of the neighborhood start to bark. He curses under his breath since he will have to clean up the glass before he can leave the next day to follow the family, but throwing the bottle felt good.

Roy rubs his hands on his dirty pants and saunters back inside his house, turning off his lights and locking the door. He will make the family move and he will take care of her nasty family who sold her house in the first place. Roy let himself fall asleep that night and when she appears, he promises her he will make everything right again.

Chapter Six

The last box sits outside, unfolded, and in the recycling can. The house is unpacked and put together how Annie likes except for the bedrooms, since she said that her kids can decorate them the way they want. The next day, after the strange encounter with the crazy driver, the family heads to the nearest paint store to pick out paints. The painting fest begins downstairs with beautiful beiges and creams, even with a splash of light oranges. The bathrooms upstairs and downstairs are different shades of blues and greens while the kids paint their rooms purple, pink, light blue, and navy blue. Wanting mealtimes to be simple, Annie decides cereal for breakfast, sandwiches, and chips for lunch, and takeout for dinner.

After the third day, the painting is finished, and all the tarps are back in the garage. The house feels fresh after they have hidden the stark white walls under beautiful paints. That morning, Annie wakes up early and quietly makes her way down the stairs. She starts the coffee maker, stifling a yawn, and makes their first cooked meal in the house. She sets everything out on the counter and sets the table. She can hear movement upstairs and glances at the clock to see it is about seven-thirty in the morning. Annie finishes cooking, the delicious smells from the food drifting into the air and dancing through the vents.

"Thomas, kids, it's time to get up and come have some breakfast before we go hiking," she yells up the stairs.

Minutes later she can hear her children hopping out of bed, getting dressed, and rushing for their doors. Thomas is already walking down the stairs as the bedroom doors fly open and eight legs carry their kids down the stairs quickly. Thomas leans up against the railing as the kids scream and hurtle past him, laughing. The family sits at the table and the four kids nearly inhale their food, barely chewing, as they rush hungrily through breakfast. Annie sips her coffee as she watches them, shaking her head as she looks at her husband, who is also watching the kids as he slowly chews on a piece of buttery and grape jammed toast. After breakfast, Thomas cleans up while Annie and the kids go back upstairs to get ready.

Annie locks the front door and laughs, turning when she hears her kids urging her to hurry and get in the car. It's a beautiful sunny day with a few puffy white clouds rolling across the sky and birds chirping gaily. Annie runs down the front porch stairs, her brown hiking boots clumping with each step, and she tosses the keys to Thomas, who stands beside the driver door. She makes her way around the car to the passenger door and opens it when she hears her kids urging her to hurry again.

"Hurry, Mom," the twins say in unison, their voices each cracking a bit with annoyance.

"Okay, okay, sheesh," she says before she slowly gets into the car.

"MOM!"

Annie quickly closes the door and holds her hands up in surrender as Thomas chortles and starts up the car. Annie buckles her seatbelt as Thomas backs the car out of their driveway, still laughing. The kids are all strapped in and eager to go hiking to see a waterfall, then head over to the Polynesian Cultural Center to walk around and partake in a real luau. The sun is shining, and the family is excited about their adventures for the day.

Trees cast shadows over the car as Thomas follows the windy road, drawing the family's attention to their breathtaking surroundings. Lindsey and Lucas pull out their cell phones and snap pictures while Tony and Tina stare out of the back windows, oohing and awing at the sights. Thomas continues down the road, following the directions given to him by Annie until he reaches the driveway that will take them to the hiking trail.

He pulls the van into an empty parking spot and turns off the car before he pushes the door open. "Okay, Thorntons! It's time for some fun. Get your cameras ready for some amazing picture taking and yes, some of those will be with the family." He turns in his seat and eyes everyone. "I need a new one for my profile picture." He laughs as he unbuckles his seat belt and jumps out of the car. As he gets out, he can hear groans coming from his teenagers, which makes him laugh harder.

The kids pile out of the car, happy to be doing something else other than unpacking. A cool breeze floats over the family as they join other tourists and locals at the front of the hiking trail, looking forward to heading to the waterfall. Annie and Thomas walk behind their children, hand in hand, and smile as they watch their kids take pictures of their surroundings, of themselves, and group pictures together. Thomas and Annie pose for their own pictures with and without their children.

Annie clicks another picture of a native bird on the tree limb overhead, enjoying the fresh smells surrounding them. She feels at ease on Oahu and knows that she will love living here with her family. The fear of nearly getting run off the road is still very fresh in her mind, but she keeps a cheerful face and does her best to not let her family know that it still bothers her. They reach the end of the hiking trail and, to their amazement, stare at a gorgeous waterfall cascading down the side of a cliff into a giant pool of water. They step up to the railing around the pool and take several pictures of the waterfall by itself, of a few selfies, and, of course, plenty of family pictures. After they have taken their pictures, the family watches in awe as two waterfall divers show off their skills.

Lucas snickers and says, "Maybe I should get a job doing this." He watches a few girls waving at the divers as they climb back up to the top of the waterfall in order to jump again.

Thomas looks down at Tony, who returns a 'yeah right' look. Thomas pats Lucas on the back. "Sure, son, you could do that."

Annie hugs Lucas by his shoulders. "I know you want to catch the attention of girls, hunny, but do something less dangerous." She pats his shoulder before she looks back at her family. "Okay kids, time to hike back to the car so that we can head to the cultural center. I can't wait to see what they have there for us tourists to explore and I really can't wait to see the luau." Her eyes sparkle with excitement as she heads back onto the trail.

Lucas and Lindsey walk side by side, comparing their pictures from their cellphones and their digital cameras. Tony and Tina walk behind the twins, holding hands and giggling as they skip along the trail. Annie and Thomas walk behind their children, unaware of someone trailing behind them, an ugly expression on his face as he watches the happy family.

The family drinks water and chats as they pile into the van while Roy shuffles to the parking lot behind them. He waits behind a tree, hissing at a couple who look at him as if he is crazy. The couple looks at him with surprise and rushes to their car, glancing nervously back at him. They climb into their car and quickly drive by the strange man hiding behind the tree.

As Thomas drives through the parking lot to exit, something catches his eye that makes him do a double take. An old beaten-up green truck, the same truck that had tried to run them off the road about a week ago, sits alone in the back. Thomas quickly averts his eyes, not wanting to draw his family's attention to it for fear of ruining their wonderful day. It may just be a coincidence or a different truck and he still wants to have a great rest of the day and not scare Annie. If Annie finds out about the truck, she'll make them leave.

Thomas does his best to not seem stressed or worried as he checks behind them to make sure the truck isn't following them. Thomas lets out a silent sigh as he returns his eyes to the windy road in front of them, keeping his attention on driving and continuing their day together. He talks to his wife, checking behind them from time to time, but not enough to draw suspicions about what he is doing.

A few cars back, the man grips the steering wheel until his hands hurt and his knuckles become chalky white. The man chews hard on the piece of gum as he does his best to keep his truck from being noticed by the Thornton family. He follows the van until it turns left into the parking lot of the Polynesian Culture Center. He passes the center after the Thorntons and a few other cars had gone into the giant parking lot and continues to drive until he can safely turn around. Roy pulls into the parking lot and drives slowly around until he sees the family's van, the family already at the entrance of the center and disappearing inside.

Roy parks toward the back of the parking lot so he can keep their car in sight of his truck. He climbs out of his truck, making a face as he looks up at the huge, beautiful entrance to the Polynesian Cultural Center. Roy hates this place, but he has to go inside to watch the horrible family who have moved into his girlfriend's house. He has made a promise to the one he loved, who was taken from him too soon and he will not break it.

He slouches as he walks up to the front to purchase a ticket to enter the center, to attend the luau, and attend the last show of the evening. After a half an hour of walking around, Roy finally catches sight of the family watching a local climbing a tree with nothing but his bare hands and feet in order to retrieve a coconut. People clap and laugh as the man wiggles back down the tree to the ground and takes the prize to another man, who is waiting for him on a small wooden stage. The grumpy-faced man never let his eyes wander away from the family, even with the laughter he hears around him. The father hugs his youngest son and then points up at the tree, then back to the two men on the stage.

The youngest daughter and oldest son lean close, looking at their camera. The youngest daughter then takes the camera, and the oldest son shows her how to take a picture of the man cutting into the coconut. She shows the picture that she has just taken to her other siblings and parents, who instantly praise her for a job well done. The man flinches and has to look away, disgusted at the affection he sees between the children and the parents. But once his stomach stops churning, he looks back just as the demonstration ends and the audience walks away.

Annie takes out her camera and looks at her family. "Okay, guys let's get a couple of pictures with these two here and then move onto the next village."

The two men standing on the stage welcome the Thorntons with open arms and take a few pictures with them. After the pictures, they say their goodbyes, and the family follows the path to where a large boat sits on top of a sturdy wooden platform. The boat, someone beautifully carved out of wood, sits high so that visitors may see it up close and be able to walk around it. The family walks around the boat, snapping pictures of it, next to it, and in front of it.

Standing not too far is the creepy neighbor, eyes studying each face before he walks past, not wanting them to become suspicious of him. Roy isn't sure how he is going to get them out of the house yet, but stalking them every day for the past few days has been helping him figure out a few ways to scare them out of the house. Roy finds a shady bench beside the flowing river that sits in the middle of the center and glares down at the water.

He could have dealt with them renting the place as the others have, but they have *bought* the house and are going to *live* there. The daily will ruin it! A flash of sunken eyes and rasping breath has Roy rubbing his temple. He promised to let no one buy the house and live in it themselves. RBut someone has, so he has to change it quickly. They can stay and live on Oahu, just not in his neighborhood or in *that* house.

Someone laughing pulls him back from his thoughts and he blinks until his eyes focus on the slowly rippling water's surface. Roy turns to see people passing by and he quickly stands, wondering how long he has been lost in his thoughts. He walks back to the boat but as he fears; they have moved on and he can no longer see them.

"Roy, is that you? I haven't seen you out of your house in ages," a familiar and irritating voice says.

Roy turns to see an old friend of his standing by the boat with his own family taking pictures. Roy waves his hand at the man quickly before he takes off down one trail to see if they are looking at something down there. But they aren't anywhere close by. He finally catches up to them in another village, talking to another family as they admire the surrounding village. The families exchange numbers then go together into the next village, cameras clicking until an announcement comes over the loudspeaker.

A cheery voice welcomes everyone, then announces that there is going to be a water parade on the river in the middle of the center and that everyone should make their way over there now if they wish to see it. The Thorntons and their new friends get some suitable spots for the floating parade, chatting excitedly and showing off the pictures that they have already taken throughout the center. Roy slinks to a tree and leans against it, not wanting to watch the parade. Too many painful memories of her . But since he doesn't want to lose sight of the family again, he growls under his breath and stays.

Enchanting music fills the afternoon air as the water parade begins. The first flat wooden boat decorated in pretty flowers floats its way out from under a bridge, with four men paddling and four women kneeling in the middle. Once clear of the bridge, the women stand and dance to music that is prominent in the village they represent. More boats float on the river with men and women wearing beautiful costumes from each village of Samoa, Aotearoa, Tonga, Fiji, Hawai'i, and Tahiti.

Cameras click repeatedly while others turn their video lenses towards each boat floating on the water, catching every dance from the different villages. The Thorntons and the other family sit close together, enjoying the parade and laugh together when the last boat passes, and the men dance so hard that those who are paddling the boat fall into the water. The ones paddling climb back on the boat and get it moving again, shaking their heads, and letting the water fly off from their hair. The Thorntons take their last few pictures and Thomas stops the video camera, the family still chuckling.

The two families walk together to the theater in order to see the movie that is playing, *Ocean Life*, and disappear inside. A few minutes later, the man slinks inside, not looking forward to sitting through the movie. He grabs a seat a few rows back from the family, his eyes narrowing as the lights slowly turn off, plunging everyone into complete darkness. Music fills the noisy theater room as the screen lightens to a soft blue. A voice fills the theater as a wave crashes onto the screen. Silence falls over the theater as the guests listen to the calming female voice talk about the ocean and the majestic creatures that live under the water. For nearly two hours, the screen shows the audience divers, fish, coral, and the bodiless voice talks about the different species and how humans have to take care of them and the ocean or the future generations will have nothing to see for themselves.

Roy yawns loudly while the voice and sound effects lull him back into his memories of when he had taken his girlfriend there several years ago. He crosses his arms over his chest and lowers his head until his chin rests on his chest. He rolls his eyes for the hundredth time until the lights finally slowly come back on, and everyone applauds and stretches. Conversations bang loudly into his ears as he stands and stretches himself, feeling his body come back awake. Roy shakes his head and runs his fingers through his almost greasy hair. He needs a drink!

Thomas leads his family out of the theater and into the bright sun, squinting against the sudden glare, and he quickly slips on his sunglasses. He checks the tickets for the time of the luau and gives Annie a look. They say goodbye to the other family, who are going to the luau at a different time and make their way to where they will wait for a few minutes until the doors open to let everyone inside a huge open theater. The younger kids laugh and play while the teenagers text their friends some pictures they have taken. Annie and Thomas watch their children as they chat and sit for a while. A few seconds later, everyone around them stands and moves towards the doors as they slowly creak open. The Thorntons stand and fall into the line, holding hands so that they don't get separated in the crowd.

Roy watches as Annie slips her arm around Thomas while Lindsey and Lucas step up on either side of their parents. The two little brats stand in front of them with huge grins on their faces as they face a camera.

Roy takes in a sharp breath as he feels pain in his heart, memories dragging him out of reality and into the past. He stubbornly pushes the memories to the side and focuses back on the family, his irritation growing. The family shout, "Aloha" and the cameraman snaps a picture of the Thorntons with a male and female in traditional Hawaiian garb, and as they move through the doors, Roy maneuvers himself a few people behind them. He knows both the small ones will recognize him if they see him, and he isn't ready to play his cards just yet.

At the door, two more beautiful Hawaiian women slip large flowered leis over each person's head as they are greeted. Roy shakes his head, letting the woman know that he doesn't want one, but either she didn't see the gesture or is ignoring him, a lei finds its way onto his shoulders. He chokes and gags on the strong floral scent and sneers at the woman before he turns away. He hisses under his breath as he glances around, having lost sight of the family again. Unable to handle the sweetness of the flowers, Roy angrily rips the lei off and tosses it ino the nearest trash can. He continues to look around, feeling his blood pressure rise with his anger. They have to be here, but where?

Roy clutches at his head as a headache that was a nuisance before, screams at him. The laughter and chatter around him rings in his ears, making the headache grow until he is almost blinded by the pain. Finally, he spies Tony and Tina skipping after their hostess to their seats at a long wooden table several yards away. The headache quiets down slightly, but not enough for him to not blame the Thorntons for causing it in the first place. After all, they are the reason he is here stalking them. He cracks his neck, enjoying the sounds of the popping, and resumes his watch.

Excitement fills the air as more and more people stream in and take their seats. The Thorntons continue to talk with their table companions, not knowing that Roy is sitting at the table directly behind them. A voice comes over the speakers welcoming everyone to the luau and that they will introduce the King and Queen of the luau shortly. Once the voice grows quiet, servers scatter around the tables taking drink orders and hurrying off in order to fill them before the luau begins.

Roy eats along with everyone but instead of watching the show, his eyes never leave the Thorntons. He has already lost sight of them twice today and it was getting on his last nerve. The luau came to an end after many beautiful dances and a few blessings from the King and Queen of the luau. Roy nearly jumps out of his seat in order to escape the crushing crowds. He wants to be ahead of the family this time.

Roy hangs around outside a gift shop while the Thorntons pick up a few new items inside. He watches as the family enter the amphitheater for the final show the Center has to offer. He hadn't known what time their show was or if they would even go, so he couldn't follow. Roy decides to sit in his truck and wait for the family to come out after the show, that way he can follow them back home. Roy shoves his hands into the pockets of his old jeans and heads to the parking lot. With his head down, he hurries to his truck so he can wait.

Roy drums his thumbs on the steering wheel, bored, as he watches people slowly trickle out of the cultural center's front doors. He rolls his eyes as more and more cars drive away, their headlights splashing the darkness with murky yellow lights. He groans and curses under his breath as he starts up his old truck and follows a small Audi out of the parking lot. He hadn't thought about how he wouldn't be able to keep an eye on the family in the parking lot. Too many cars leaving at one time has caused him to lose the family for a third time. Roy grips the steering wheel tightly as he drives back to his house, hoping the family is already there. He still doesn't know what he is going to do, but he has to think of something better than just following them around.

Chapter Seven

Present Day

    Leilani groggily wakes up, confused for a moment as she gazes tiredly around her room. She pushes the covers back and grabs her phone off the side table. Once her fingers feel the phone, she pulls it closer to her until she can wrap her hand around it and pick it up. She touches the screen, and it comes to life, it's softly glowing clock app showing she had been asleep for nearly four hours.

Her eyes widen and she stretches her arms up over her head before she pushes off the covers and sits up to see the sun has begun its journey over the middle of the afternoon sky. She stands and walks to the window while she checks a few text messages and voicemails she received while sleeping. The voicemails were from her mom and Larry from work, while the text messages were from Koa, Nalani, and someone she didn't know. Listening to the voice mails, she makes a mental note to call both Larry and her mom back in a bit as she sits back down on her bed.

She turns her attention to the text messages and quickly responds to both Nalani and Koa, answering their questions; Koa asking about work while Nalani asks about having dinner together tomorrow. Once she finishes texting them back, Leilani's finger hovers over the unknown text message, wondering if she should open it or immediately delete it. What if it is spam? Or what if it is a virus hidden inside the text message? But if she doesn't click on it and it's important, then the person will be mad at her.

Deciding to chance the virus and not the possibility of an angry co-worker or friend, she clicks on the text message and opens it. The screen turns black as she waits for the message to load up on her phone. Suddenly, photos of a horribly bloody crime scene appear. Her mouth drops open when she scrolls through the pictures, one gory picture after another flashing to life before her eyes. The longer she looks at them, the more the pictures seem to move, coming to life. One of the last pictures is of a woman lying on the floor in her bedroom in a pool of blood, staring unblinkingly at her with a pair of smashed glasses beside her, her mouth frozen open in a silent scream.

Leilani tries to look away, but she too is frozen, unable to touch her screen to delete the pictures. She gasps and nearly gags when she sees the very last picture of the little boy and girl from her dreams sitting trapped in two chairs with no eyes, just bloody holes. They were trying to hold hands. Sitting behind them were their favorite toys covered in their blood.

Finally, her teary eyes lift away from the gruesome pictures, and she drops her phone on her bed with a soft, anguished cry. Leilani sits on her bed, unmoving until the growl of her stomach and the churning inside reminds her she hasn't eaten all day. She knows she must, even as the gruesome photos float through her mind. Timidly, Leilani lifts her cell phone and flips it over to see the cold black screen waiting for her to turn it back on to show the beautiful flower once again. Taking in a shaky, scared breath, she turns on her phone, bracing herself as it springs back to life to her text messages. She closes her eyes once the screen pops up and takes in a few quick breaths as she slowly forces her eyes open.

"Come on, Leilani," she mutters to herself. "Stop being such a chicken and open your eyes." Her eyes fly open, and her breath catches in her throat when she sees the text message with the pictures is gone! But how can that be?

She scrolls through her messages, searching for what she has seen that's not there. She checks the deleted folder, but again, there is no scary unknown text message present. Her hands shake while she stares down unbelievingly at her phone. Nothing? It makes no sense! How could a text message she had just read completely disappear? She shakes her head, trying to wrap her mind around everything. She decides it is time to read more about the house and see if anyone else who had lived in the house has experienced anything like what she has been experiencing.

She rubs the rest of the sleep out of her eyes as she heads out of the bedroom and down the stairs. Ignoring her growling upset stomach, she enters the office and sits down behind her desk, turning on her desktop. She opens the Internet as soon as it warms up and types in her address to see what she can find. Article after article pops up about the horrible murder that had happened in that house twenty years ago. One website even promises to provide pictures from the crime scene, which piqued her curiosity. Without hesitation, she clicks on the link, but to her dismay, there are no pictures of the crime scene provided in the article. It was a cheap way to get people to click and read the article by the author. She shakes her head and reads through the article anyway, but finds nothing new. The author only spoke about rumors and didn't talk about the details of each murder or about the madman who had killed them and then accidentally killed himself.

The family moved in twenty years ago and were planning on living there, but after being tormented by a neighbor, they looked for a new home in a different neighborhood. The old grouchy neighbor from across the street used a key that he had made a copy of from the wife's keys and went into the house where he brutally murdered the family, then accidentally killed himself. After reading what she already knew about the case, she continues to search and read a few other websites until she stumbles upon an article that explains in more detail what had happened that night. She clicks on the link and to her surprise, the same pictures she had received in the text pop up at the beginning of the article. She slowly examines each gruesome picture, her memory replaying the pictures she had seen on her phone before and matching them to the pictures on the screen. These are the same pictures that were on her phone, but how did they get on her phone in the first place?

After she examines the pictures, she turns her attention to the article to read more about what happened twenty years ago. Her stomach growls angrily again at her. She groans, annoyed by the interruption, but she stands and heads for the kitchen in order to retrieve something to eat. She opens her refrigerator and peers inside, trying to figure out what she wants, even though her stomach still churns from the pictures. A few minutes later, she is back in front of the computer with a salad covered in ranch dressing, a few breadsticks, and a leftover pizza from last night.

Leilani places everything beside the computer and picks up a piece of pizza, taking a big bite, ignoring that it is still hot. Leilani puts it back down on the plate and looks for her drink, but remembers she left it in the kitchen. She hurries back into the kitchen to retrieve it, not noticing a shadow lurking close by as she walks back into the office. Leilani sips her Dr. Pepper, then takes a few deep breaths before she scrolls down past the last picture again to where the story begins, her eyes capturing every word.

Twenty Years Ago

Annie and Thomas sit in two beautifully carved rocking chairs on the front porch and sip at their glasses of red wine. The kids are inside the house finishing up their homework before bedtime. Annie reaches over and takes a hold of Thomas' hand as she gazes around the quiet neighborhood. She closes her eyes, squeezes his hand lovingly, and takes in a deep breath, smelling the rich hibiscus flowers that grow in their yard and throughout the neighborhood. The stars twinkle brightly overhead, and the hundreds of night creatures sing their songs happily around them.

It has been two months since they moved to Oahu, and everything has been going great with the kids and their schooling, and their jobs. The only issue that they have been having is the harassment they have been receiving from some stranger who seems to have an issue with them living in their house. It took them almost a week before their front window could be fixed from one attack and then after that, their cars were vandalized so they had to get those fixed. After the cars and window were fixed, threatening letters became constant in their everyday mail, forcing Thomas and Annie to collect the mail after work even though their kids love to get it after they get home from school.

Thomas has gone to the police several times, but they were no help. Even those on the base say they can't help but the higher-ups were told and are up in arms about the whole situation. So, the family now lives in constant fear and is looking for a new house. But their money is tight at the moment because they are just getting a foot in their new jobs and have to pay back the loan for the house and cars. Neither Thomas nor Annie feels safe in the house anymore and Thomas has taken it upon himself to sleep downstairs on the couch with his guns nearby.

Annie opens her eyes and looks at her exhausted husband. "I think you need a break tonight, Thomas. You are exhausted, so tonight you will sleep in bed with me, okay?"

Thomas is about to argue but stops himself short, knowing that arguing with Annie will get him nowhere, so he agrees with her instead. "All right, tonight I'll take a break from standing watch and sleep with my beautiful wife." He lifts her hand to his lips and kisses it. "We have heard nothing in a few days, so maybe the crazy person has grown bored with us and is going to leave us alone." There is hope in his voice as he stands, pulling Annie to her feet. "Let's go check on the kids and get to bed. I am ready to collapse."

Annie stands and slips her arm around his waist, the couple heading inside, their glasses in hand. The door closes and locks behind them, the front lights turning off for the night.

As soon as the lights go off, a figure appears at the end of the driveway, a toolbox in one hand and an ax in the other. The figure walks closer and swings the ax with each slow step, the light from inside the house casting strange shadows over the man's stubbly face. Angry eyes glare at the house as he makes his way slowly up the driveway, taking his time and sticking close to the shadows. He wants to give the family time to go to bed and fall asleep before he enters the house. He stops in the shadows and watches as one by one the downstairs lights turn off, then the ones over the stairs, the shadows disappearing from the man's face. He continues to swing his ax, growing bored and angrier each moment he has to wait for them to go to sleep.

Inside the house, the family gets ready for bed, the kids already upstairs. Annie and Thomas go through the downstairs and make sure that they lock the windows and doors for the night before they begin their rounds of turning off the downstairs lights. They trudge up the stairs after having set their glasses on the kitchen sink and talk excitedly about their plans for tomorrow. They go to each of their kid's rooms, lock their windows, and say their good nights. Annie and Thomas retreat to their bedroom, change clothes, wash up, and turn off their own bedroom light before getting into bed. Darkness washes over the entire house, and those inside snuggle under their warm blankets, ready for a good night's sleep.

Roy slithers out of the shadows and creeps closer to the side of the house, still swinging his ax as he gives the family more time to fall asleep. He stops in front of the house, puts down the ax, and pulls out the key that he had copied after he had slipped the keys from Annie's purse while they were out two weeks ago. His letters hadn't scared the family away, nor did any of his other tricks, so it was time to step up the game. He will invade their home and kill them. It's that simple! That way, they will have to leave, even if it is in body bags, and then he will have kept his promise to Tracy. He will keep that promise no matter what the consequences.

He noiselessly picks up the ax and makes his way to the side door in the backyard and sets his things down while he slips the key into the lock, having to fumble for a minute since there are no lights on. Roy finally gets it in the lock and turns the key until he hears a click, letting him know the door is now unlocked. He pockets the key and retrieves his ax and toolbox before he pushes the door open. He steps inside with a bright smile on his face and closes the door behind him, locking it again.

Upstairs, Thomas rolls over in his sleep with Annie snuggling up close to him passed out while the man downstairs moves from room to room. It tempted him to break a few items now, but he knew it would wake up the family before he could kill them, so he just quietly walks to the front entryway to get to the stairs. He steps on the stairs but freezes when the house creaks as it settles around him, startling him for a moment. He chuckles as he walks up the stairs again; the house growing silent once more.

He stands at the top of the stairs and glances at the closed doors. He knows he has to subdue the family before he can start his t, so he sets down the axe and toolbox on the top step and snaps open the toolbox. He rummages through the toolbox for a moment until he finds what he is looking for and pulls a rag free, duct tape, and a bottle of chloroform. He leaves his items behind on the stairs as he quietly stalks into the parents' bedroom, grinning as he stares at the two sleeping peacefully in bed.

After nearly two hours, the family is sitting in the dining room chairs with their legs duct taped together and their arms duct taped to the arms of the chairs, facing one another and still unconscious. Thomas wakes up to the sounds of metal hitting wood, the sound hurting his head. He groans slightly as he forces his eyes to open, even though he still feels groggy and wants to sleep longer. His eyes close again and darkness overtakes him until he hears a soft voice calling to him, but it sounds so far away that he isn't sure if it's a dream or not. He forces his eyes open again when the voice creeps through the fog in his head and he can hear fear. He blinks a few times until his vision clears and he sees Annie staring at him, her eyes full of horror and unable to move.

Thomas looks down to see his legs duct taped together and his arms duct taped to the arms of one of the dining room chairs. He tries to speak but can't, his mouth hurting every time he tries to talk or pulls his mouth open. He feels something wet slip down his chin, but he can't tell what it is since he cannot wipe it off. He looks around to see his family also stuck to the chairs by a mess of duct tape. His children all have their heads down with their chins resting on their chests, unmoving. He looks back at Annie and his eyes open wide when he sees Annie couldn't have said his name out loud because someone had sewn her mouth shut, blood dripping down her chin.

Annie's glasses are on but lopsided and tears are sliding down her cheeks, mixing with the blood on her chin. He turns to look at his children, wondering if their lips have been sewn together too or if whoever has done this to his family had simply duct taped their mouths closed in order to keep them quiet. To his horror, Lucas and Lindsey both raise their heads, and both have their mouths sewn shut. He cries out even though it hurts when Tony and Tina lift their heads next, both having lips sewn shut and caked blood on their chins, which tells him they were the first to have the deed done. He will make whoever did this pay!

Loud clanking noises draws his attention away from his frightened family and he sees the dining room table is up against the wall while the chairs are sitting in a circle in the middle of the room, facing each other. He looks at the table where the clanking noises are coming from and sees a tall man with thinning hair in the back standing in front of the table taking things out of an old rusted red toolbox. Thomas watches as the man pulls out a pair of pliers and sets them on the table beside what looks like an ice pick. Thomas silently demands for the man to turn around in his head so he can see the man's face.

"I asked you all nicely to move, but you didn't listen or wouldn't listen, and that was a big mistake," the man's gravelly voice says as he continues to unpack the toolbox. "I made a promise to the woman who used to live here before... before the cancer claimed her life ten years ago. I promised her, Tracy was her name, that her family would only ever rent this house. And that is how it went for years until now!" The man's voice nearly shouts the last statement before he grows silent as he takes out the last item from the toolbox, a hammer. He looks at it for a minute in his hand before he sets it down roughly on the table. "I have lived across the street for years monitoring the house." He slowly turns around, slipping on rubber gloves and putting safety goggles down over his eyes. He is already wearing a zipped up throw away suit over his clothes so that once he has finished the deed, all he has to do is step out of it and burn them in his fireplace at home. "I loved her, you know, so I will do **anything** in order to keep my promise to her. I already took care of her horrible family."

A chill runs down Thomas' spine when he hears that this man has already killed Tracy's family because of this house. This crazy neighbor is going to kill them just because they bought the house and are living there. He knew he had to escape in order to save his family from this lunatic before he kills them. Thomas lifts his hands to see if he can find a side from the tape that he can pull free, but his skin on the under part of his hand seems to be stuck. He pulls up harder on his left hand and he screams as much as sewn lips will allow, as the flesh from his hand rips away from his bones, muscles, and tendons.

Roy looks over at Thomas with a cruel smile and holds up a container of gorilla wood glue. "You can't escape from me. I've made sure of that. You didn't want to leave the house and after tonight, you never will."

All eyes are on the crazed neighbor as he eyes each family member, then his instruments as if he is quietly planning each member's demise. His eyes settle on Lindsey while his hands roam the table for a weapon to use. He glances back at the table and picks up the hammer.

Roy lifts it up and looks back at Lindsey, "I am sure that having a teen girl can be quite the headache." He steps up slowly beside her, "Always texting... never listening because she is always on her cell phone." He walks around her until he is standing directly in front of Lindsey, bringing down the hammer, and smashes each of her fingers again and again.

Lindsey screams behind her sewn lips, the threads ripping a little because of the force of her mouth trying to open, causing fresh blood to drip down her chin. He lifts the hammer but stops as everyone shouts at once, their muffled cries pleading with him to stop the pain he is causing Lindsey. He turns to look around the circle, Roy's eyes meeting each member as he spins the hammer in his hand a bit before he whirls around and slams the claw part into the left side of Lindsey's neck, blood spurting out from the sides of the claw and running down the handle of the hammer. Lindsey's eyes bulge and her breathing comes out fast as her body shakes from the sheer shock of what has just happened to her. Roy stares down into her eyes as he rips the claw free, pulling skin, blood, and muscle out of her neck. He turns on his heel with the hammer tightly held in his hand and sprays the family with bits of Lindsey.

Annie and Thomas watch in horror as their eldest beautiful daughter takes her last breath, her chest heaving a few times before it is as still as her heart. She stares at them, not seeing them as her life ends abruptly and terrifyingly. Tina and Tony sob as they close their eyes and lower their heads, wanting to block out what they have just witnessed. Lucas quietly stares over at his dead twin, his chest heaving as he struggles with the sight and thought of never seeing or talking to her again.

The family grows quiet when they watch Roy move back to the table for a new weapon. Roy drops the hammer on the table and picks up a box cutter, the sound of him sliding it open echoing in their ears. He points the blade of the box cutter at each of the family members as he plays with the switch that pushes the blade up and down, his hungry gaze falling on Lucas. He smiles widely, showing a few missing teeth, and he steps up behind the teen boy.

Lucas struggles to look behind him at Roy but can't, his body stiffening when he feels something cold against the back of his neck. Lucas turns his scared gaze to his dead twin, knowing that soon he will join her on the other side. He then looks over at Tony and Tina, doing his best to look at them with no fear. He can see dirty tear streaks on their pale cheeks glistening as fresh tears appear.

Roy reaches around Lucas and runs the blade down Lucas' left arm, leaving a trail of blood. Lucas clenches his jaw as Roy continues to leave bloody trails all over his back, legs, arms, chest, and even his face. Roy walks around the boy, giggling crazily as he slashes at the terrified teen with the box cutter. Lucas closes his eyes any time he sees the blade come near his face, not wanting to lose an eye even though he knew if the man wanted to slice his eye, he would have done it by now. Again and again, the blade slices through his skin, cutting veins and muscle, causing the blood to pool around his feet. The pain finally numbs enough to where all he can feel is his skin slicing open and the blood seeping out of the hundreds of little wounds. He feels himself growing tired from the constant shock to his body, and from the blood loss. His eyes slowly close as he allows sleep to take over, no longer feeling anything, and the cries from his parents and siblings become quieter.

"Well, it looks as if he has grown tired from the fun we are having," Roy says, laughing as he watches Lucas fall unconscious. He moves towards the table to put down the bloody blade, but Roy stumbles a bit on the leg of the boy's chair and the box cutter slides under Annie's chair. Roy looks for it but can't find it since Annie quickly hides it under her bare feet and shrugs, making a mental note to find it after he finishes the family off. Roy turns back to the table to look at what he has left to use, and his spidery fingers reach down to grab something that the family can't see, since his body is in the way. He holds fast to the tool and spins, charging at Lucas, slamming a screwdriver into Lucas' right temple.

Lucas' body convulses as the screwdriver pushes through his temple, cracking through his skull, and pierces his brain. His eyes fly open and if Roy hadn't sewn his mouth shut, his jaw would have dropped wide open. His eyes roll upwards as the man twists the screwdriver around in his temple, snickering at the sounds that it made while it spun with a bit of effort in his skull. The man breaks the screwdriver free of Lucas' temple and then drives it straight down through the top of his skull, finishing the job.

Chapter Eight

Twenty Years Ago

Annie and Thomas stare at their lifeless twins as their hearts pound against their chests. They feel that they have failed to keep their children safe from this harm. They only have Tina and Tony left, but how can they save their youngest children and themselves? Annie glances downwards to see the box cutter still under her foot and she moves her feet again in order to hide it, flinching as the blade slices her foot. She raises her eyes to the man who just stands there staring down at Lucas, unmoving and unblinking, not caring about what he has done. Annie glances at Thomas, who looks broken, as he struggles against the restraints that hold him in place.

Roy leaves the screwdriver in the teen boy's head and steps back to the table, pulling off a rusty-looking wrench from the table next. His eyes are now staring into the eyes of Tina as he walks closer to her. He nearly trips again, cursing under his breath as he kicks Lucas' chair, causing his dead body to jostle around, Lucas' head rolling from side to side. Annie shakes her head, uncontrollably sobbing, and her fingers reaching for her poor scared daughter. She has to hurry with the box cutter and free herself to stop him from killing Tina. Tina cannot look away from the irrational man's eyes. Her lips are sore, she has puked twice now in her mouth, and the acid in her stomach is hurting her a lot since she had to swallow her puke. She just wants to go back to bed, but their scary neighbor is in their house, and he has killed her older sister and brother violently.

Tony squeezes his eyes shut when he sees Roy staring at his only sibling left and knows that Tina is going to be next. He wishes he had his favorite blue race car with him to help him be brave, but he didn't know where it was at that moment. He hears a mumbling voice trying to say his name, and he opens his eyes to see Tina painfully reaching her hand out towards him, her eyes no longer glued to the man that hovers over her. He knew he had to be strong at that moment for her and the rest of his family so he reaches for her hand too even though he can feel the glue ripping his skin off his hand and arm. Tina moves her gaze from Roy when she feels movement from her brother. She looks over at him and their eyes lock, the siblings not looking away from one another.

Annie quickly works the box cutter with her feet again until she can grasp it with her toes. Quietly and quickly, she wiggles her legs until one of her legs moves up in the duct tape, nearly pulling it free. She lets the box cutter drop from her toes and covers it with her feet once again when she sees Roy turn to look over at her. She begs through the smeared glasses and sewn lips for him to let the rest of her family go. Roy only laughs at her pleading and bends down to look into Tina's tear-streaked face and red-rimmed eyes.

"You saw me first on the very first day that you all had moved into this house. You smiled a pretty little smile at me and waved your precious little hand," he hisses at Tina. "I turned my back on you, and you should have told your mommy and daddy about what had happened. Especially when you and your brother here had seen me at the restaurant that night. Maybe then you all would have left this house and none of this would have happened. Your big sister and your big brother would be alive right now and you all would be safe." Roy laughs in her face, his breath pushing her bedhead curly hair back, and the stench from his breath causes the poor girl to gag. He continues to laugh in her face as he places the mouth of the wrench around one of Tina's fingers.

Tina's eyes turn away from Tony's as she feels the wrench close tightly around her pointy finger. She looks sharply up at the man as he twists the wrench ever so slowly to one side.

"Well, that caught your attention now, hasn't it?" he growls cruelly at her as he twists the wrench back the other way, twisting her finger again.

Suddenly, pain shoots up into her hand when he jerks his hand and the wrench twists so hard that it breaks her finger, leaving it at a weird angle. Tina's eyes widen as he loosens the wrench and then tightens it around the next finger, again slowly twisting it from side to side. She shakes her head, causing her curls to bounce wildly around her head as he nods his head, twisting the wrench more. Roy jerks his hand and breaks her finger, again leaving it at a weird angle before he continues to do it to all of her fingers on her right hand.

While Roy is breaking Tina's fingers, Annie moves her legs more. She frees one of her legs, grabs the box cutter with her toes again, and lifts her leg until she can grab the handle with her left hand, making sure to not draw any attention to herself. Thomas sees what Annie is doing and nods his head, urging her to keep going. Annie slides the blade closer with her fingers until the tip cuts the layers of duct tape.

"No more waving for you, young lady. Didn't your parents tell you it's not safe to say hi to strangers?" he says as he stands up, leaving the little girl crying again with her fingers bent in inhuman ways. The man glances over at Tony, cocking his head to the side and scratches the side of his head with the wrench. "Now for you, I think I will use my handy-dandy pliers."

Annie stops cutting through her restraints and hides the box cutter under her arm, letting it slice the glue off the chair. She felt the blade also slice off some of her skin, but she didn't care, numb to any pain. Roy looks at Thomas and Annie. He cocks his head to the side when he notices blood dripping down the sides of the chair from her arm. Assuming that she has been trying to pull her arm free, he shrugs his shoulders and walks over to the table to retrieve the pliers. Finally finding them, he towers over Tony and looks down at the little boy, a glint in his eye.

Tony curls his fingers into his palms to protect them from the man, even though he knows that the action is futile. Roy watches the boy's attempt to save his fingers from him and applauds for the attempt, hitting his open hand with the pliers. He kneels in front of Tony and gently taps the back of the boy's hands with the pliers to get him to open his hands.

"Now, now little one, the sooner you give me your little fingers, the sooner this will be all over with for you," he says as he smacks the back of Tony's hands again, this time harder.

Tony shakes his head as he tries to move his hand away from Roy and the pliers. Roy slams the pliers against the back of Tony's hands again, bruises appearing once the pliers hit the knuckles and veins. Roy continues to hit the pliers against the boy's hands until the skin breaks and he bleeds, causing Tony to cry. Unable to take the pain any longer, Tony releases his fingers, and they dangle tiredly in front of the man's eager eyes. Roy roughly takes a hold of one of Tony's hands, ignoring the hoarse cries of the young boy.

"Hm... this little piggy went to the market." Roy chuckles as he says the old nursery rhyme and grabs the boy's thumb. He opens the pliers and slips the bottom half under the nail, closing it so that they secured the nail in between the two parts. Tony continues to shake his head, no longer able to scream, cry, or fight against the lunatic. Roy pulls the pliers upwards, ripping the nail free from Tony's finger. Roy continues to say the rhyme as he rips off each nail, letting the nails fall into a bloody mess on the floor just in front of Tony's bare feet.

Annie cuts her arm free, slicing the glue and skin off before she works on the duct tape. Once her arm comes free, she quickly slices the blade under her other arm that is still trapped by the glue. She is about to free her other arm when the man finishes with her poor son's fingernails, and she has to hide the box cutter again. She has to time her attack just right. She watches him return yet again to the table, placing the bloody pliers down and this time retrieving the ice pick. She knows she has to attack now, or she will lose her last babies. Roy stands in front of Tina and lifts her head with one hand while he lifts the ice pick over his head with the other.

"Time to say goodbye," he whispers roughly at Tina. "Can you wave bye-bye for me?" He laughs at his own sick joke as he stares down into Tina's pale face.

Annie cuts the last of the duct tape off of her arm, and then the tape that still binds her legs together. She stares up at the back of Roy's head, takes in a deep breath, and nods. It's now or never! She lunges forward out of the chair with the box cutter in front of her and she slams the blade into his side, catching him fully off guard. She forces the blade up deeper under his ribs by pushing up on the lever. Roy screams in shock and pain, dropping the ice pick to the ground with a loud clunk and letting Tina's face go. Annie pulls the blade free and stabs Roy again, this time deep into his back. He cries out again as he swings around and backhands Annie hard across the face, causing her to rip the box cutter free from his back and stumble backwards.

Annie hits the ground hard, but she hangs onto the box cutter for dear life. As soon as her vision clears, she can see Roy withering in pain in front of her daughter. She takes this opportunity to run, and she rushes out of the room just as he grabs for the axe that is propped up against the table leg. She glances once at her still trapped family before she rushes out of the dining room and up the stairs. She would have gone out of the front door, but he is at her heel, so the only escape now is up the stairs. She rushes into her and her husband's room, slams the door behind her, locking it, and runs over to the window.

She puts the box cutter down on the dresser before she tries her hardest to get the window unlocked and opened so she can climb out of it. But the lock won't budge! Thomas hasn't fixed it yet!

She jumps and spins around as the ax blade slices through the wooden door and splinters it; the splinters raining onto the floor on both sides of the door. In a few quick, hard strokes, Roy is through the door and searches the room for her. He spies the box cutter on the dresser, so he knows she is unarmed, and stalks over to the closet. He shoves back the door and peers into the darkness of the walk-in closet, pushing around the hanging clothes with the ax to see if she is hiding inside. Not finding her in the closet, Roy heads over to the bathroom and pushes the door open to look inside. He sneaks in and looks behind the door, but she's not there. Roy stumbles over to the shower where the curtain is closed and pushes it aside, but the shower stands empty.

Annie quietly pulls herself out from under the bed and glances back to see that the man is still in the bathroom looking for her. She looks forward again and pushes her cracked glasses back on her nose before she crawls towards the broken door. She does her best to keep her scared breathing quiet for fear that the man will hear her and rush out of the bathroom. She glances back in time to see Roy leaning against the bathroom door, watching her, and looking quite amused.

"And where do you think you're going?" Roy asks as he stumbles towards her, his wounds making it hard for him to walk.

Annie tries to get to her feet, but she isn't fast enough. Roy grabs Annie by her hair and tugs her head back sharply so that she is looking up at him. He laughs in her face as he places the axe blade to her throat, cocking his own head to the side as he watches her heaving chest. Annie breathes hard through her nose as her heart hammers against her chest, threatening to explode. He moves the blade, letting it only bite her skin a little before he takes it away, watching as blood forms little droplets around her neck.

"What a pretty necklace you have on," he jokes badly as Roy shoves her to the ground with one foot, letting her hair go.

Annie grunts when she falls to her face and quickly crawls towards the dresser. Roy stands still, leaning against the ax's handle as he allows her to get to the dresser and grab the box cutter. Annie spins around and throws herself towards him, Roy not moving out of the way or swinging his ax at her. She knocks Roy down to the ground, using her full weight while she swings the box cutter in front of her.

Roy grabs her wrists to hold them just above his skin. Roy hits the ground hard, but not hard enough to knock the breath from his lungs. He lets her get a couple of strokes against his skin with the box cutter so that she thinks she has the upper hand, but the pain annoys him. He catches her hand and twists it painfully one way, then the other, in order to cause her to drop the box cutter. Annie cries out and drops the box cutter uselessly onto his chest. Roy risks letting go of one of Annie's hands and scoops up the box cutter, having dropped the ax. Annie tries to claw at his eyes once he lets go of her hand, but he is quicker than she is and holds up the box cutter in the way. Annie's hand comes down onto the box cutter, the blade sinking straight through her palm until it is sticking out the other side and severing her tendons. She tries to gasp, but the efforts only make her lips ache from trying to pull against the thread. He smirks as he yanks the box cutter out of her hand, but instead of just pulling it back down out of her palm, he slices it through her hand; the blade slicing out from between her ring and middle finger.

Annie falls backward off of him, holding her bloody hand up, and yelling into her closed lips. Her glasses fall from her face, and she tries to move away from him on her knees. A bloody trail smears into the carpet behind her as she continues her agonizing escape, her blood sinking into the carpet and staining her knees. Roy only laughs behind her while he kneels down to retrieve the ax handle, dropping the bloody box cutter onto the floor. Annie looks over her shoulder and screams, the thread breaking apart and drawing more blood along her lips.

The ax comes down hard and fast into Annie's left shoulder, splitting her shoulder open. Roy pulls the ax free and slams it back down, breaking through her bones and causing the sharp ax blade to slice down further until the blade stops halfway through her ribs. Roy adjusts his stance so he can pull the ax free, stepping and shattering Annie's fallen glasses. Since the ax seems to be wedged inside of her body pretty tight, he has to wiggle it from side to side, causing her ribs to break and more blood to spill free. He grunts as he attempts to free the ax that is stuck in her ribs. Annie's mouth now hangs wide open, ripped and mangled as the last of the sewing thread tear away. Her eyes cloud over as she coughs; blood slipping out of the corners of her mouth. Her body slumps forward, the ax wiggling loose.

The ax jerks free and the pool of blood becomes a small ocean that covers the bedroom floor as Annie lays in the middle of it, and her body twitches in death. Roy lifts the bloody ax and places it over his shoulder as he walks out of the bedroom, still grasping onto the box cutter. He eyes the blood that is splattered all over his throw-away suit once he reaches the stairs. He shrugs a bit as he whistles and heads down the stairs, stomping his feet along the way in order to let the rest of the family know that he is coming back down.

Tina, Tony, and Thomas sit in anticipation as they listen to the man whistle and stomp his way down the stairs. Thomas continues to wiggle his legs until they came undone. But now that his legs are free, he didn't know how else to get free since Annie had taken the box cutter with her when she had escaped. He tries to pull his arms free from the glue, but his skin sticks fast. He clenches his jaw tight and pulls up harder, grunting as he feels his skin pulling away from his bones. Both Tina and Tony sit silently across from him because of the pain that has flooded their little bodies. Their smudged faces now show nothing but sadness and exhaustion from the entire ordeal.

The stomping ends and Roy steps inside the dining room, looking over at the kids, seeing Tina and Tony's heads falling forward so that their chins rest against their chests as they slowly slip unconscious. He shakes his head and makes a clicking sound with his tongue to catch their attention as he drops the axe loudly onto the ground. He watches as the children flinch at the sound and drops the bloody box cutter on top of the table. He turns to look at Tina and Tony again, who are now looking at him with half-opened eyes.

Roy directs his attention to Thomas with a sick smile on his face. "I am sorry, but your wife has joined your older children. Or am I sorry?" The small sick smile turns into a cruel grin as he laughs at Thomas, spit flying out of his mouth.

Thomas shakes his head, not wanting to believe that his wife is gone too. He should have never gone upstairs and slept in their bed. He should have stayed on the couch with his guns, only sleeping here and there. Thomas would have been able to prevent this with just a few shots from his gun. He should have listened to his gut and head, not his heart and exhaustion. Now his family is being killed by this maniac one by one in the most horrific ways. He continues to beat himself up inside his head as he watches Roy pick up the ice pick and step up to Tina.

Tina looks up as Roy stands in front of her, her fight gone, and sees him lifting the ice pick over her face. Thomas cries out at Roy, trying to catch his attention away from his little girl, but it didn't work.

Roy let go of Tina's head and instantly Tina's head slumps forward. Tony can feel the acid churning in his stomach and the vomit threatening to rise, even though all he can do is swallow it back down into his stomach. Tony turns his face away from Tina, gagging and coughing behind his sewn lips, the pain in his stomach growing. He wishes he could cut his mouth open and throw up already. Thomas can't cry any more tears as he stares at his young daughter, feeling numb and helpless. His tired, red-rimmed eyes burn as they turn to Tony just as the man lifts Tony's head and stares down into the little boy's scared eyes. Tony looks from the man to his dad to his dead family and then back up at the man. Tony knew that this was going to be his last night on Earth.

Thomas tries to cry, scream, and yell, but his throat only closes, making it hard for him to breathe. The man hears Thomas struggling with his breathing and he turns to face Thomas to see what is happening. He stares at Thomas for a few minutes, enjoying the suffering. But he still wants to have some fun with the man too, so he spins on his heel to face Tony and finishes the job. Tony's frail body shakes from the trauma before the little boy takes his last quivering breath, becoming still.

Thomas continues to struggle to breathe, coughing hard, and tries to regulate his breathing through his nose. But the task is overwhelming because of the disgusting stenches invading his nose. His efforts only cause him to choke more, this time making him choke more on his spit. His chest heaves painfully as he looks at his four dead children. His eyes lift to the ceiling, and he stares as if he could see through the floor to where his wife l dead on their bedroom floor. His chest rattles and fills with excruciating pain as his heart pounds harder and harder against his rib cage. He keeps his eyes on the ceiling; only half hearing the man as he walks back to the table and loudly opens the toolbox.

Roy lifts the top organizer from the toolbox and sets it down on the table before he picks up a cordless nail gun he had purchased a few years back but never used until now. He loads the nail gun with long nails and turns to face Thomas, the last living person who invaded his Tracy's house. Roy aims the nail gun at Thomas and moves closer to him, closing one eye in order to get a better aim with the odd tool. He stops walking and shoots Thomas again and again with the longest nails that he could find at the store that would fit his nail gun. Thomas coughs, gasps with closed lips, and flinches every time a nail enters his body. Roy shoots his captive first in the legs, then moves up to the arms, thighs, and chest before he moves up to the neck and face last. Roy runs out of the long nails after about thirty minutes and moves on to the medium-sized nails, laughing coldly with each shot.

After about an hour, the sounds of morning birds chirping pierce through the veil of bitter laughter and extremely low grunts. The sun slowly rises, signaling that Roy has stayed too long and soon the darkness wouldn't shelter him from prying eyes. He curses under his breath since he knew he had played too long with the family. Scolding himself as he stops shooting Thomas' body with nails and squeals in delight because the man that sits in the chair is no longer recognizable. Not wanting to waste any more time, Roy quickly packs up his toolbox. Because his back is turned, he doesn't see the slight movement coming from Lucas, who's will has pushed him to still live even after his injuries.

Lucas opens his eyes to see that everyone has passed and that the man is packing up, getting ready to flee the scene of the crime. With the last bit of rational thought and strength, he shuffles his feet forward, hoping that the man will trip over him and fall to the ground, knocking himself out long enough for the police to catch him. Unable to do anything more, Lucas closes his eyes and becomes still as he waits for the man to make his move. The man locks the toolbox and leaves it on the table as he looks around to see if he has left anything behind. He reaches down and grabs the handle of the bloody axe that still lies beside the table. As he turns to face the bodies, he sees a lone nail that had somehow escaped him sitting in the middle of the room, just past Lindsey and Lucas. He strides towards it, swinging his axe, and doesn't see that Lucas now has his feet pushed forward.

Roy reaches down for the nail while he walks, and grunts in surprise when he stumbles on the boy's feet. Lucas takes his last breath once he feels the man trip over his feet, allowing death to take him. Roy puts his hands out to catch himself and sees that his actions would harm him more than help him as the axe blade comes into view directly underneath him. He tries to not land on the blade of the axe but fails. The blade cuts through his body with ease, giving the man only time to cry out in pain and anger for a split second.

He coughs a bit as he falls to his side with the axe still sticking out of him and blood flowing freely from the open wound. His eyes stare down at the axe before he looks up at the surrounding bodies. His anger grows, numbing the pain he feels, gasping out crossly, "This... wasn't supposed... to happen. I... was supposed to... live." His eyes roll up into his head and he dies a few agonizing minutes later.

Chapter Nine

Present Day

Leilani stares at the screen for a few minutes before she hits the print button on her desktop so she can have the pictures and the story for later. Her eyes stare at the name of Roy Taylor, the name burning into her mind after she finishes reading about how he killed the Thornton family and then how he himself is killed by accident. He was a cruel neighbor who murdered the family and apparently others in another family because they had sold the house. Leilani shakes her head when she closes the article and turns to face the printer as it spits out the article.

Roy Taylor scowls out of the picture at the bottom of the article beside Tracy, who owned the house and died from cancer. Her family, who Roy had found and murdered three weeks before he murdered the Thornton family, all smile up at Leilani as well. Roy had been in and out of jail before this situation, according to another article that she had found that was solely about the man behind the murders. His family was thoughtful and helped in the community, but they didn't know where they had gone wrong in raising Roy or why he was so hateful towards others.

Roy started at a young age by assaulting others, but it never went beyond just a harsh beating. Roy ended up going to a psychologist to see if they could help him figure out why he felt like he had to attack others. It seemed to everyone that knew him that if he liked a girl, he would become overprotective of her and that's usually when the assaults occurred. Whether he assaulted the girl herself or anyone who was rude toward her or who dated her or even against those who voiced that they liked her. His parents even sent him to an institute, but they released him on account that they deemed him cured after three years.

Roy then apparently moved to Oahu once he was free, and no incidents ever occurred until the murders. His parents and other family members never talked to him after the institute released him and he never contacted them either. They were still alive when he died, but no family or friends attended his funeral.

Leilani closes the articles and shuts off her computer, staring down at the pictures again. She shuffles through the papers, trying to put them in some sort of order. She stares at the picture of Tony and Tina, the memory of her nightmare and the kids who had helped her escape from the hungry flames vividly appear in her mind. She knows then that the kids in her dream with the bloody empty eye sockets have to be Tony and Tina protecting her, while the hungry flames must have been Roy Taylor. But how could that be? Are they real or are they just a figment of her imagination? Could they be ghosts?

She has to find someone who can help her figure out if her house is haunted or if her dreams are just that, dreams. She looks around the office and feels like it is closing in on her. She leans down and grabs a bag from under the desk, deciding to escape the claustrophobic feelings of her new home. Leilani packs her laptop, along with the articles she printed, and heads out of the house. She packs her car up and drives to her favorite coffee shop in North Shore. She decides she will search for a paranormal investigative group that live on the island she can reach out to for help on this matter. She reaches the coffee shop and gives an enormous sigh of relief, feeling better. After she orders a coffee and scone, she claims a table and sets up her laptop. The article slips out of her bag and floats to another table, tapping the leg of one of the four patrons sitting at the table, who is sipping on their coffee.

Shaggy raven black hair falls across curious emerald green eyes and a tanned forehead as the young man bends down to see what has hit him in the leg. The two other guys who sit with him continue to talk while the one female in the group bites into her delicious BLT, a bit of mayonnaise dripping from the sandwich onto her deep purple lips. She laughs behind her closed mouth as she grabs a napkin with her stylish, manicured black fingers from the middle of the table and wipes the mayo before it hits her chin. The man picks up the papers and looks them over for a moment, his eyes scanning over the horrifying pictures and the sad story. His eyebrows knit together as he flips through the pages, making a slight sound in the back of his throat that catches the others' attention.

"Teddy, what is that?" the young woman asks before she takes a sip from her Pepsi.

Teddy turns the first page so that she and the other two can see the gruesome pictures. They all stop eating or drinking and set their items down when they see the pictures. They know instantly what they were, their own faces looking at the article curiously.

"Is that really what I think it is?" she asks as she takes the pages from Teddy, flipping through them, her eyes skimming the words.

"It is, Aaliyah. It's about the Thornton murders," he says and takes the papers back when she finishes with them. Teddy turns his attention to those sitting around him, wondering who is looking into the gruesome murders. His eyes linger on one pretty young woman sitting at the table behind them as she quickly taps away on her laptop, her eyebrows scrunched together in bewilderment and unease.

The guy to his right watches Teddy's eyes and turns his own electric blue eyes to the woman on the laptop. He then looks back at Teddy with a questioning look, wondering if maybe she is the one who has lost the article. A pair of dark brown eyes from the last man who sits by Aaliyah looks at the other woman as well, noting by the look on her face and the speed of her fingers on the keyboard that she is searching for something.

Without hesitation, Teddy stands, grabs the article, and heads over to Leilani's table. He smiles down at her. "Excuse me, I'm not sure if this is yours or not, but I wanted to ask you, anyway. Do these papers belong to you?"

Leilani looks up from her laptop screen to meet the tall man's kind eyes as he stands beside her. She looks at the papers in his hands, then bends down and searches her bag for a moment. "Yes, those are mine. They must have fallen out when I was taking out my laptop," she says as she looks back up, settling back into her chair. "Thank you for returning them to me. I really appreciate it." She smiles at him as she takes the articles from him. Her fingers close around the papers and she looks into his eyes for any signs of laughter or any signs that he has read them and now thinks that she is some nutcase for having such a horrible article in her possession.

The man nods and says, "Not a problem. Um... I hate to pry, but I saw the names Roy Taylor and Thornton on the papers and was wondering..."

Leilani places the article in front of her and strokes her hands over the papers, smoothing out the few crinkles. She keeps eye contact with the stranger in front of her, ready to defend herself if need be. "You read correctly. I am doing a bit of research on the murders."

"That is pretty funny because my buddies and I are researching the same case," he exclaims as he points to the table behind him with his black thumb. His friends wave at her before the other man turns to look back at her with a lopsided grin on his face. "You see... we are paranormal investigators, and we would love to go inside that house to see if it's really haunted or if the stories are just stories."

Leilani stares at him for a minute before she laughs, waving for him and his friends to join her just as her latte and scone are brought to her table. She thanks the waitress as the others join her. As soon as the waitress leaves, she takes a bite from her scone and turns her laptop around so that the small group can see what she has been looking up. They see she has been searching for paranormal investigators. They look at her curiously over the screen as she turns the computer back around, taking another bite from her scone and a sip from her salted caramel latte.

She sets her cup back down and takes in a deep breath before she gazes at each person sitting around her. "My name is Leilani Kahanaui, and I am the new owner of the Thornton murder house." Her voice grows quieter as she looks around then makes eye contact with Teddy. "Maybe today is your lucky day and mine too."

"Wow, what a coincidence," Teddy says with amazement. "My name is Ted Russo, Teddy, and these are my friends and team, Stan Gow, Glen Morgan, and Aaliyah Morgan." He points to his friends as he introduces them to Leilani. "And we are known as The Hunting Paranormal Four."

"It's very nice to meet all of you," Leilani says with a sigh of relief, shaking each member's hand.

Aaliyah cocks her head to the side, "Why were you looking for a group of paranormal investigators, Leilani?"

Leilani sighs heavily, afraid to explain about the nightmares and visions that she has been having to these strangers. But she knows she has to trust someone and tell them before she goes insane with dealing with everything in the house alone. Before she can speak, Stan stands and walks around behind her, reaching around her to type with quick dark brown fingers on her laptop. Her screen changes as a ghost appears along with their faces and names.

"Before you tell us, read our website so you can get to know us and what we do a little better," Stan tells her as he returns to his chair. "I know you don't trust us yet. I mean, we are complete strangers, so hopefully reading our website will make you more comfortable with us. Then if you feel you can trust us, you can tell us what is going on."

Leilani goes to the bio page to read more on the four, starting with Teddy, since he seems in charge of the group. She reads that not only is he a paranormal investigator, but he is also an author with five books already published and one being published in two months. It also says he is a tour guide for the Pearl Harbor Monument. He has lived on Oahu for most of his teen years, having graduated from both high school and college on the island with his bachelor's in science and his master's being in paranormal studies. It talks about his first experiences as a kid in one of his old houses where he had seen his deceased grandmother. Seeing her ghost intrigued his curiosity at a young age, and he began going to haunted locations to catch more ghosts on film and on his tape recorder. Leilani reads about how he nearly died in an accident where he fell through the floor at an old abandoned house, but he continued to push forward and for the longest time did investigations against his parents' wishes while he was in school.

She clicks on Glenn and Aaliyah's picture next to read about them, reading first that they have been married for eleven years and that they had met in college while working on their bachelors and masters in parapsychology and psychology.

Their same interests drew them together, and they dated through college in Pennsylvania. They had moved to Oahu eight years ago after having gone there for their honeymoon and having fallen in love with the island life. Now Glenn works as an investigator and a surf instructor at a very well-known and well-loved surf shop down in Waikiki. Aaliyah is an investigator and works as a nature tour guide and conservative educator with one of the more popular hotels in Waikiki.

Last, she clicks on Stan's picture to read that he also graduated from college and had lived most of his life in Arizona. He moved to Oahu on a whim, having grown tired of Arizona and wanting a more tropical feeling, a warm but not too hot island feeling. So, he did his research and fell in love with the ghost stories of the islands. He wanted to learn more about these stories and other legends firsthand, so he knew Oahu would be the best place to move to, even though his parents were against it at first. Stan had met Glenn at the popular surfing club when he was looking for a job, and they both became surf instructors and friends.

She reads how Teddy used to be a one-man show, but that had changed when he met Glenn and Stan during a surfing lesson. They talked after the lesson about their paranormal experiences, and the three became friends. Teddy then met Glenn's wife, Aaliyah, and he told them about his one-man group, asking if they would be interested in joining him in not only starting a better paranormal investigating group but also helping to debunk hauntings and help others with real hauntings. They have been a group together for nearly six years and have investigated several places over the years. The group has helped several skeptics become believers and has helped several people experiencing strange things in their homes either debunk them or validate their claims. She then skims the page that is dedicated to those with stories about what they had felt or seen and how the group had helped them either debunk the claims or validate with evidence. She happily reads that they don't just help those living on Oahu, but are also sought after on the other islands.

She could sit there and read all day, but she knows the others are waiting for her to finish and hopefully tell them what has been going on in her new house.

She closes her laptop and picks up her cell phone that is sitting beside it and pulls up the pictures, searching for the toys that she had found in the house. They haven't returned, but she knows that Teddy and the others would be interested in knowing that bit of information, along with the nightmares and visions. She sets the phone down in the middle of the table along with the picture of Tony and Tina dead in the chairs with their blood covered toys sitting on the ground by their feet. Aaliyah takes the phone and the picture, raising an eyebrow when she sees the toys in the picture covered in blood, then when she looks at the picture on Leilani's phone showing the toys sitting in the trash can.

"Their toys?" she asks as she passes the phone to Glenn so that he can see.

Leilani chews on her bottom lip before she nods and glances around at them. "When I first went on a tour of the house, the bunny showed up in the closet in what used to be the little girl's room. Nalani contacted the owners to see if it belonged to them, but they said that it didn't. They then told us it possibly belonged to Tina, but I thought nothing about it at first. Nalani, she is my friend and realtor, threw it away. Or I had thought that she had thrown it away, but then it showed up while we were moving my stuff in. But this time, it was the bunny and the little boy's racecar. I had found them up in the attic while putting some boxes away, but they hadn't been there until after I was ready to leave."

Leilani wrings her hands tightly in front of her, growing nervous. But she keeps telling herself they don't think she's crazy and they will believe her, so she continues speaking. "My friend, Koa, I work with him, took the toys and threw them into a large trash bag so he could dispose of them for me with the other trash. I thought on trash day the next day they took away the toys with the trash. After the toys had been thrown away, everything was fine, no toys, nothing. My first night in the house, I couldn't sleep at all, but when I finally did, I had a horrible nightmare where I was having a party with my friends. They were in the backyard swimming, having a BBQ, laughing, and having fun while I was standing in the front of the house just listening to it all. I then decided to join them and... and... that's when..." She takes in a shaky breath as the nightmare pounds on her temples as she tells them about it, but she didn't really want to remember it again.

Teddy sees the pain in her eyes as she is about to tell them about the nightmare. He moves his chair closer to her and takes a hold of her hand, squeezing it lightly to let her know she is among friends. Stan takes the phone and paper from Glenn, eyeing both pictures before he places them in the middle of the table and returns his attention back to Leilani.

She takes in another deep breath before she continues staring down at the computer in front of her. "I tried to get closer to the house, but it seemed as if the house didn't want me to get closer. Then there was lightning! No storm, just lightning and it hit the ground in front of the house, behind the house, and even hit the house itself repeatedly." Her voice cracks when she talks about the lightning. "It just kept hitting and hitting until the house turned into an enormous ball of fire, and my friends... they..." She shakes her head and does her best to not cry.

"The fire then tried to kill me, reaching out fiery fingers towards me. But Tina and Tony appeared and somehow, they deflected the flames and saved me. They walked back into the house after the fire was completely out, holding hands and holding the toys. The next day I went for a walk, but I had forgotten my cell phone, so I turned to go back but the fire was there again while I was wide awake. I closed my eyes, and it went away. When I went back inside to get my phone, the toys were there on the counter next to it. I threw them away and took that picture you saw on my phone so that I can prove to myself that if they came back, I wasn't going crazy and that I had thrown them away. I even watched them empty the trash can, too."

Stan and Glenn exchange excited yet worried looks with one another while Teddy continues to stare at Leilani, his eyes growing dark with a bit of anger, since he hates when people are nearly harmed by evil spirits. He knows they will have to go into the house and find the source of the evil, get rid of it, and help Leilani claim her house back. A thought struck him, and he became curious, his eyes falling to her laptop as other questions flow into his mind. Have other owners experienced the same thing?

Leilani sees Teddy eyeing her laptop, and she slides it over to him as if she could read his mind. "I've just started researching the house after the family's murder. I don't know if anyone else has been experiencing what I have been. The owners that I had bought the house from won't talk to me about it. Once the sale was completed, they stopped talking to Nalani, and she just contacted them to say thank you again."

"Well, you are further than we are in the research. We just caught wind of the place maybe two... three years ago, but with other houses and haunted places we had lined up, we could never really start looking into this house and the hauntings surrounding it. Now we have some free time, we are ready to jump into the research. Maybe if it is okay with you, we can do an investigation at your house," Teddy says.

Leilani nods her head and says, "I will definitely allow you guys into the house to do an investigation. I go back to work in three days and my friend, Nalani, is moving in soon. We decided we want to look for roommates, but this whole ghost thing would put a damper on things." She chuckles as she grabs her phone, opening her calendar app. "When do you want to come to the house?"

Teddy raises his eyebrows, shocked that she said yes. "Wow, thank you, Leilani, but well, we don't want to run into this completely blind, so we can't do it right away. But I'll give you my number and we'll keep in touch to schedule everything as well as to update you with any information that we may find in our research." He smiles at her as he reaches for her phone.

Leilani lets him take her phone, watching as he punches in his name and number into her contacts. She takes a sip of her iced latte and pulls her laptop back in front of her, scrolling through her emails. She felt out of place, awkward suddenly, just sitting with the group and not knowing what to talk about. She is usually very talkative with others, including complete strangers, since her job calls for it, but this situation has taken away her confidence to make light conversation. Teddy hands her back her cell phone and looks around the suddenly silent table.

"We'll finish lunch and then head over to the library to do some research. Maybe the librarian can point us in the right direction regarding the other owners of the house. Maybe your friend can help us out too."

Aaliyah shakes her head as she puts down the last bite of her sandwich on her plate, digging into her purse. She retrieves a small green spiral notebook and pen, flipping it to a blank sheet of paper. She passes it to Leilani, who jots down Nalani's number, information for the owners that she had bought the house from, and the number of the realtor the homeowner had used to sell their house through. Leilani hands the pen and notebook back to Aaliyah.

"We will call the realtors first," Aaliyah says, accepting her items back. "I'm done eating. Will you come with us to the library, Leilani?"

Leilani sits up straighter as she eyes her schedule to see if she has time and nods, "I have to work on a project at home for my job, but I can join you for at least an hour or two at the library." She turns off her laptop and packs up her bag. She stands and stretches before she takes the last sip of her latte, eager to get to the library. She shoulders her bag and follows Glenn and Aaliyah out of the coffee shop, with Stan and Teddy at her heel. She walks out into the bright sun, slipping her sunglasses back over her eyes from their perch on top of her head. Stan stops by a black excursion and calls the realtor who sold Leilani the house. Everyone stands around while Stan introduces himself and asks questions. Leilani watches as Stan's face grows dark, frustrated already with how the conversation is going.

Leilani rolls her eyes and holds out her hand for Stan's phone, which he hands over without hesitation. She puts it up to her ear to hear the man threatening Stan, but she clears her throat, stopping the man mid-sentence, "Hello, to whom am I speaking?" She listens for a moment. "Oh, why hello again, Mr. Addams. This is Leilani. My friend Stan has called because I have asked him to. I have been experiencing some unusual and quite frightening things the past few days while living in the house and all they want to know is if the previous owners have gone through what I am going through now."

She grows silent as she listens to the man on the other end sigh heavily and then talk in a low cracking voice. She nods her head as she listens. A smile spreads across her face as she raises her eyes to look at Stan. "Yes, thank you very much, Mr. Addams. I would appreciate you emailing me the stories." She says goodbye before she hangs up and hands the cell phone back to Stan, looking quite smug. "Tonight, he'll email me all the stories he and his wife have heard from the previous owners. But he has asked us to not call any of the other owners and bother them. These stories are for our eyes only, agreed?"

The four agree with her and promise not to show the stories to anyone else, though Teddy looks disappointed. He was hoping to write a new book surrounding this case and the new stories, but now he will have to look elsewhere for stories he will write in his book. He knows he can find plenty of other stories, but he felt these new ones would be gold.

"Well now, that we have that settled," Leilani says as she crosses her arms over her chest. "Are we ready to head over to the library?" She points to her car over her shoulder. "Anyone want to ride with me?" She smiles at them as she walks backwards slowly. "Anyone?"

The others laugh as she continues to walk slowly backwards towards her car. Teddy shoves his hands into his pockets and walks up next to Leilani, keeping pace with her, "I'll go with you, Leilani." He has a sheepish boy grin on his face when he looks back at his friends, knowing that once they get in the car, they will crack jokes about him and his eagerness to go with the pretty girl. "We'll see you guys there then?"

"Sounds good! Closest library?" Glenn says as he unlocks the car doors for Aaliyah and Stan.

"Yep, the closest library is about ten miles away from here, so we will see you there," Leilani confirms. She spins on her heel and she and Teddy head for her car. She unlocks her car, and they hop in, waving again as Glenn drives past.

Leilani turns on the radio and some popular pop music croons out of the speakers at them while she pulls out of the parking lot. They make small talk during the drive, talking about music, their favorite beaches on Oahu and the other islands, their favorite places to eat, favorite books, about living on Oahu, and about their jobs. Leilani pulls into the parking lot of the library, spying Glenn, Stan, and Aaliyah waiting for them by the front door. She parks and she and Teddy join them. They talk for a few minutes before they split up into groups so that they can work faster on the research.

Teddy and Leilani take the old newspapers in the back of the library while Stan talks to the librarian about anyone she knows who might know about paranormal incidents in the house. Glenn and Aaliyah look at articles on the computers, scanning headlines and articles to find out anything more about the murders. They all work diligently, but before they know it, an hour and a half has gone by, and it is time for Leilani to head home. They meet in the library's front to say their goodbyes before Leilani heads out with a few books checked out about the paranormal in hand, including one written by Teddy, and heads for her car.

Before she had left, Teddy looks at her worriedly. "Are you sure you'll be okay going back to the house by yourself?"

Leilani smiles at him and places a reassuring hand on his shoulder. "Don't worry about me, Teddy. I promise that I'll be fine going back home alone. And I also promise that if anything happens that I will call you immediately." She writes her cell phone number and home line on a piece of paper, handing it to Teddy.

He waves as she drives past him, then heads back inside to get back to work. He passes Stan, who is standing just outside the front door on his cell phone. The librarian had given Stan a few numbers from those she knew who had a few ghost stories.

Teddy drops back into his seat and pulls the newspaper that is dated from twenty years ago closer to him, skimming the titles. They had looked for any incidents before the murders, but the one article that they had found about the man who had first built the house years ago for his wife was an honest and gentle man. He and his wife had died in the house in their sleep and neither had any enemies. After that article, there is no news about the house, those who lived there, or any paranormal activity. This ruled out their theory that the house itself was evil and had taken over Roy Taylor's soul, who then murdered the family.

Teddy flips the pages one after another until he stops on the third to the last page to see the story about the murders. He reads the story intently, taking some notes on a few things they didn't know, like the police officers' names and the neighbors who had called the police when they had suspected that something was wrong two days after the murder took place. The principal from both kids' schools also called the police, having grown worried when none of the children had shown up. The Veterinarian hospital called as well, this making the police act. Even the military sent someone out to the house two days after the murders, having grown worried about the Thornton family. They arrived at the house at the same time as the police.

Teddy sets the paper off to the side once he finishes reading it and pulls a paper that is only a few months after the murders from the pile in order to see if he can find out what had happened to the house afterwards. He finds a brief article stating that because the rest of Tracy's family had been murdered, there was no living relative to take ownership of the house. This meant that the local bank took ownership. Teddy writes the date, the name of the bank, and that Roy Taylor had murdered the rest of Tracy's family. He skims the newspapers for other stories to see if they kept record of when the house was first sold to new owners, but there is nothing.

He shuffles through the newspapers but he found no more articles about the house until five years later after the murders. Teddy reads about how a maid that the family had hired had gone missing. The police searched the house but found nothing. They had looked for the maid for nearly a year, but there were no traces of her, so the family sold the house and moved back to the mainland. Teddy writes the date, names, and what had happened, writing in as much detail as he can. He folds the paper and places it on the 'already read' stack of newspapers. He continues to scan the newspapers for more stories on the house but there was nothing. Teddy sighs heavily as the stack to read slowly dwindles.

Finally, something catches his eye that had happened about fourteen years after the murders. The family claims that things were being moved or have gone missing in the home. They said the window in the front shattered for no reason right in front of their eyes. They also found what looked like bloodstains on the floors in the master bedroom and the downstairs dining room.

They said that they saw blood trailing from the dining room up to the bedroom and then back down again, but the police wrote it all off as a hoax or kids playing a joke on the family.

Teddy finishes with the newspapers, only finding a few stories about people complaining about strange noises, missing items, missing people, the front window breaking for no reason, and blood being seen on the floors. But the stories are sparse, with only seven stories reported in the newspapers over the past twenty years. Teddy sits back in his chair and taps his pen against the notebook as he re-reads everything that he has written. Seven strange stories surrounding the house, but there must be more. What about the three-missing people? Where are they? Are they dead?

Teddy gets up and returns the newspapers to the back of the library. He collects his things as he glances around to see if he can find his friends. He hopes they are finding more useful information than he has so far. He walks around the library before he finds Glenn and Aaliyah still hard at work on the computers, a few articles already printed out and stacked on the desk next to Aaliyah. He gently touches her shoulder in order to let her know who it was, so she didn't yell at him for taking the articles. Teddy sits down at the table directly behind Glenn and Aaliyah's computers, and reads what they have found.

While the group is still investigating in the library, Leilani has made it home and has begun her own work for her job. She emails the hotel manager along with Koa and their team to let them know they will receive another email from her with the project so they can review it, make corrections, and send it back to her to fix if necessary. Leilani leans back in her chair, rubbing her eyes as she fights exhaustion before opening the program she needs on her desktop. She clicks on the file she needs and dives into the work. Leilani stops in the middle of typing something and wonders if Glenn or one of the others have contacted Nalani yet. She chews on her lower lip as her eyes drift away from the computer screen to where her cell phone sits on the desk and wonders if she should call Nalani.

Unable to fight the urge any longer, Leilani grabs her phone and dials Nalani's number, hoping that she will answer right away. Nalani finally answers after the fourth ring and from the tone in her voice; Leilani could tell that Nalani was having a long day.

"Hey Nalani, it's me. Are you busy right now? I wanted to ask you something real fast." Leilani says, feeling anxious. "If not, then we can talk tomorrow at our lunch date."

"No... no, we can talk right now. What's up, Leilani?" Nalani says quickly as she sits back in her chair, glad for the distraction.

"I was wondering if you have received a phone call recently. And if you have received a phone call, what did you two talk about?" Leilani asks as she balances her cell phone in between her ear and shoulder. She eyes her computer screen for a minute before she makes a few changes, finishes the last part of the ideas for the project, and saves it. She then sends it to everyone who needs it so they can review it and give her feedback.

Nalani laughs and says, "I was wondering if you were going to call to see about that." Nalani taps her finger on the desk for a moment, her eyes on her screen where she has the website for The Hunting Paranormal Four open. "Glenn was very professional when we talked on the phone, and it quite surprised me when he told me who he was and why he was calling me." She turns in her chair so that she is staring at the wall where she has a beautiful castle from Ireland hanging up and sighs heavily into the phone. "Leilei... why didn't you tell me about this? You could have told me you were experiencing strange things in the house."

"I don't know... maybe because they just happened and I just by chance ran into this paranormal group. And I guess maybe because I was afraid that you would laugh at me," Leilani says, spinning in her chair. "And why didn't you tell me about the strange things that were happening to those who lived in this house?"

Nalani sighs heavily. "Because you know I don't believe in ghosts or any of that paranormal stuff. I thought they were just stories. I never thought they would be *real*." She turns back to face her desk and looks down at a picture that sits at the right of the computer; the picture of herself and Leilani smiling together on the beach close to Diamond Head. "You need to get out of that house, Leilani, just until we can figure out what to do next. You can stay with me until we get a plan started. Maybe we can get a priest?"

Leilani shakes her head even though Nalani can't see her. "I already know what I'm going to do next and it's not getting a priest. I'm going to have the team stay here a few nights and see if they can finally put an end to whatever is going on in this house. This is my house now... our house... and I want to live here until I'm old." She glances back at her computer when she hears a low ding that tells her she has a new email. She quickly clicks on it to see that Larry is the first one to respond with a few changes and suggestions. "Look, I know that this is probably making you nervous and all that, so if you don't want to move in yet, that is totally cool with me. I am going to stay here and figure out how to help put these spirits to rest."

Nalani smiles and says affectionately, "Brave little Leilei." She sighs and runs her hand over her face, trying to wipe away her exhaustion. "You do what you have to do, but please be careful. And you're right about all of this having made me nervous, so I was going to call you later today after work. I was going to tell you I'm going to go stay with my mom until either you move out of the house, and we can get a new house together or you rid that house of the spirits and we can move in to live in that house." She chews on her lower lip. "I will do what I can to help you, but I know you talked to the other realtor. He called and told me he is sending you stories, but that you are not to bother any of the previous owners. The only list I can give you is the list of how many other owners there were and a list of the neighbors that live in the neighborhood now."

Leilani smiles at her computer and says, "Thanks Nala, I really appreciate all the help you're giving me... us." She checks the time, sighing at the hour. "Listen, I have to get going because I've promised to get this project done for work today." She cocks her head to the side as she stares blankly at her computer screen. "I might do some extra research and see if the hotel where I work is haunted. Do you think the hotel could be haunted?"

Nalani laughs at her friend and says goodbye before she hangs up and returns to reading the website. After she finishes reading, she returns a call from another one of her clients. Meanwhile, Leilani sits chewing on the end of one of her red pens. She has printed out her ideas for work and stares at it as she thinks of ways to make it better. She does what she can to it, makes the corrections online, and then resubmits it for everyone to look over again. While she waits for their feedback, she does some research on the hotel where she works, her discussion with Nalani having piqued her interest in seeing if it is haunted. Leilani might ask Teddy if she can join them on one of their investigations after they take care of her house. Disappointed, she finds nothing about the hotel, but it sparks more interest in the paranormal, and she researches other haunted areas around Oahu.

Leilani opens one of her desk drawers and pulls out an empty notebook, fishing around another drawer for a working pen. She titles the notebook Haunted Locations with a thick blue sharpie pen and flips the notebook open to the first blank page. She writes the places she finds online along with their addresses so she can look more into them and talk to Teddy about them to see if they have ever done an overnight investigation at any of the locations she found. After a few minutes of working, Leilani hears something moving behind her, but she ignores it, clicking on the next button in order to pull up the next page of haunted locations, already on page 4.

The hairs on the back of her neck and arms stand straight up while a shiver runs down her spine. Refusing to acknowledge the noise, Leilani swallows the lump in her throat as she continues to write. As she does so, whatever is behind her stealthily moves towards where she sits. It's nothing she can pinpoint. There's no sound, and with her head turned away, there's nothing to see, but instinctually, she knows she's not alone. Fear courses through her.

Leilani doesn't stop her writing, but her hand shakes, and the words she writes come out wonky. She keeps waiting for a skeletal hand to tap her on the shoulder or for a loud bang to completely unnerve her. Instead, Leilani hears what sounds like whispering from behind her, creeping closer and closer. Her eyes dart from paper to screen and back to paper, but they never stray to look behind her. Not now. It's too late. Whatever it is is too close. Leilani's breathing comes out in quick breaths as she slowly lifts her hand to the mouse and clicks it on the next button, moving to page 5.

As she moves her hand away from the mouse and plants the tip of the pen back onto the paper, her hand freezes. The fear within her veins has turned to ice, and she can't move anymore. Trying to turn her head, Leilani's neck twitches slightly but no more. The whispering is now almost directly behind her. She tries to move again, but her neck muscles refuse to move. Soon the whispering ceases and Leilani feels a breath on the back of her neck.

It's as if the breath releases a spell. Forcing herself to move, Leilani drops the pen on her desk and spins around to see who is behind her. The room is empty. Clutching tightly to the back of the chair, Leilani searches the room frantically, looking for anything that might be out of place. No one stands behind her in the office, but she can still feel the prickling breath on the back of her neck, so she knows it has happened.

Afraid to have her back to the open room, she slowly twists back around in her chair to face her desk, gasping when she sees her word processor is open and the sentence 'We are here' has been typed in big bold letters repeatedly. She shakes her head. It's impossible. Leilani had heard nothing, let alone the subtle clicking of the keys on her keyboard as if someone were using it. There had been no sounds, and yet here is a message from whoever is in her house with her.

Leilani picks up her cell phone with a shaking hand and takes a few pictures of her screen before she saves the document, closes the word processor, and leans back in her chair to look at the pictures. She opens her text screen and attaches the pictures to a new text. After she has made sure that the pictures are really there, she quickly types in the time, what exactly has happened leading up to the pictures, what she had been doing before the pictures, and then what she was doing during the note being typed onto the screen. Last, she adds Teddy's cell phone number to the sender spot. She hits the send button and waits for a few minutes until her phone tells her it has been sent to the number provided. Leilani goes to set down her cell phone on her desk, but she drops her phone onto the ground and pushes the rolling office chair back away from her desk as a terrified scream escapes her lips.

Chapter Ten

Teddy taps his pen against his paper as he reviews everything they have collected so far at his house. They are still waiting for an email from Nalani, Leilani's friend, as well as from the bank that she bought the house from to see if they know any other stories. He has also contacted other local realtors for more stories, hoping they will send him replies soon. His teammates have gone home after several hours of talking about the case. They didn't want to make plans with Leilani just yet until they had more information and stories. Tomorrow, they will make more phone calls and venture into her neighborhood to talk to the neighbors.

Teddy pulls a journal close and writes more information that he may use in his new book. As he writes, his mind shifts to Leilani, wondering if she is okay and if she has experienced anything else since she had gone home. Teddy glances at the clock on the wall of his office to see that it has been a few hours since their last talk. He jumps a bit when his phone vibrates with a new text message, and Teddy grabs it from his desk next to him.

"Leilani?" Teddy sees her name flash on the screen, his eyebrows knitting together in confusion.

Pictures pop up on his screen, and the first thing he notices is a dark figure standing beside the front door, staring straight at the phone. The next pictures are from Leilani's computer screen that has bold letters repeating the same thing to the bottom of the screen. He reads the long text about the computer screen, then returns his attention back to the shadow person she has sent him. He quickly uploads the picture to his computer and messes with it until he can see that it is Roy Taylor glaring menacingly, not at the phone but at Leilani!

Teddy nearly chokes when he sees an evil man glaring at Leilani, not caring to hide himself from Leilani. He quickly goes into his contacts, slides his fingers quickly until he finds Leilani's number, and touches it to call her. He places the phone to his ear and listens to it ring a few times, growing more anxious with each ring.

Finally, after the fifth ring, a scared, hushed voice says his name. "Teddy?"

"Hey Leilani, yea, it's me. Listen, I saw the pictures you sent me. I'm about fifteen to twenty minutes away," he says as he turns off his laptop and scrambles for the front door. "I'm coming over to your house right now." He grabs his keys and shoves his wallet into his back pocket, running out of the door in an instant. "Where are you right now, Leilani?" Teddy jumps into his car, starts it up, and quickly pulls out of his driveway seconds later.

Leilani takes in a shaky breath. "I'm hiding in the master bedroom closet." Her voice is low but still cracks slightly as she speaks. "I think he's gone, but I don't want to go to make sure. I'm too scared he's still there in the office waiting for me."

"That's okay, Leilani. I want you to stay where you are. Don't come out until I get to your house, okay?" Teddy says as he makes a left on the highway. He keeps his eyes on the road and his hands clutching the steering wheel tightly, his phone sliding around on the passenger seat with each turn. He doesn't speed, but he still drives as quickly as he can so he can get to Leilani's house. "Stay on the phone with me too and I'll let you know once I'm in your driveway."

Teddy can hear her shift from the slight rustling sounds behind her as she tries to get more comfortable inside the closet. "Okay, but please hurry, Teddy. I'm terrified."

Teddy squeezes the steering wheel, feeling helpless as he takes the exit that will take him to her neighborhood. At a stoplight, he quickly switches to text without hanging up on her and texts his friends the pictures and what he is doing. "Just stay on the phone and talk to me while you wait. What were you doing before this all happened?"

She laughs quietly at the question. "Well, I had finished my work and kept thinking about what you guys do, so I looked up online about the hotel where I work at, seeing if it is haunted. But it turns out that nothing vaguely interesting, paranormal or not, has happened at the hotel. Maybe a few celebrities staying there and a couple of fights that were so bad they called the cops. But there weren't any tragic murders that have left behind a paranormal footprint. All of this happened before I worked there, too. I was quite disappointed to find this out." Teddy hears her shift again and the slight squeak of the closet door. "Then I looked at other places that are haunted and have been making a list so that I could show you to see if you've gone there to investigate. I also wanted to ask if I could go with you and the others on an investigation after all of this is over with."

Teddy chuckles, "I don't know, Leilani. It all depends on how this one turns out first. You may not want to go with us after all of this mess with your house." He listens to her laugh, doing her best to keep her voice quiet before becoming still. "Leilani? Are you okay?" His body grows tense as he pulls his car down her street. "Get to your front door now and let me in." He pulls into her driveway. "Leilani... Leilani? Are you still there?"

Teddy parks and grabs his phone from the seat beside him before he hops out of the car and scans the house for any movement. He presses his ear to the phone and listens for a minute before he hears the distinct sounds of a door creaking open and heavy breathing. Teddy runs to the front door. Through the phone, he listens to Leilani breathing hard as she pounds down the stairs. The door yanks open and a frazzled Leilani appears in front of him.

"Leilani!" Teddy pulls her into an embrace, relief washing over him.

She hangs up her phone as she hugs him tightly, her body shaking from the fear. She sighs in relief and looks up at Teddy after breaking the hug. "It felt like you would never get here," she says in a shaky voice. She pushes Teddy backwards out of the front door and off the porch, shutting the door behind her.

Teddy allows her to drag him away from the house and to his car, where they climb inside and sit for a moment in silence. Teddy's eyes the house as he absentmindedly scrolls through his text messages. His eyes drift down to his screen, and he stops his scrolling when he finds their group text. He texts his friends the address and to bring their sleeping things along with investigation items. He asks Stan to stop by his place and grab the equipment he has stored in his place, along with some clothes. He looks at Leilani, whose eyes never leave the house, and gently takes a hold of her hand.

"The team is going to come over and we are going to stay until we figure this out, okay?" he says. Teddy smiles at her and gently squeezes her hand reassuringly when she looks at him.

Her eyes look away from his face back to the house, her face pale. "Thank you, Teddy, I really appreciate the help." Leilani takes in a deep, shaky breath before she unfolds herself from the passenger seat and slowly climbs out of the car, letting his hand go.

Teddy quickly jumps out of his car, closing the door behind him, and stands beside her, resting a hand on her shoulder. He stares up at the house, watching each window for a moment to see if he can see anything moving. Nothing! Two cars drive up behind them an hour later and the doors open. Teddy turns to see Aaliyah, Glenn, and Stan staring at the house with eyes wide and jaws slightly dropped open in awe.

Teddy leads her over to the back of Glenn's van, pulling open the back door to show Leilani all their equipment that they will be using. "We need to get set up and begin talking to the neighbors. I want to get all the information that we can to help us possibly understand Roy better."

His team agrees with him and quickly unloads the van, placing the big boxes on the ground and piling up the smaller ones on top. After Glenn looks around to make sure Roy isn't lurking somewhere inside, Leilani and Aaliyah grab a few of the smaller boxes and place them inside. The men set up the cameras around the house while the girls finish bringing in the equipment and stashing them in the office. They set up their home base in the upstairs room where Stan will stay during their investigation. He will also monitor the screens throughout the night and after he sleeps, he will review the footage.

Teddy shows Leilani how to work each of the handheld devices since she will join the investigation with them the following night. They agree not to do an investigation that night since they aren't fully prepared.

After they set everything up, Leilani makes them a late dinner, the clock over the stove reading 8 o'clock. Leilani stirs the homemade soup she has quickly thrown together, but her thoughts turn to the investigation ahead. She doesn't know what to expect, but she knows she has to stay strong. Just being in the kitchen alone makes her nervous. The hair on the back of her neck stands on end, and she glances over her shoulder from time to time, thinking she can hear Roy breathing in the corner, shivering at the thought of him watching her at this very minute, unseen by her. But it is only her imagination–hopefully.

Leilani is about to call Aaliyah to join her so she's no longer alone when the laughter from the living room stops and she turns to see four people walking into the kitchen with their heads tilted back and their noses in the air. She lets out a quiet sigh of relief when she sees them and smiles. She waves for them to sit down at the table in the dining room as she cuts the hot garlic bread on the pan. Leilani grabs plates and bowls, sets the table, and carries the bowls over to the stove. She dishes up the soup into the five bowls, handing them one by one to Teddy. After the soup is on the table, Leilani places the garlic bread into a bigger bowl and heads over to the table, setting it down in the middle. They each thank her before silence falls over the table as the group eats their food. Leilani glances around the table at the others and then around the dining room as a feeling of peace seems to fall over the house for the first time since she had moved in.

"This soup is amazing, Leilani," Aaliyah says. "I would love to get the recipe from you and then *maybe* my husband will eat what I cook." She glares at Glenn, who looks back at her with a startled look on his face.

"I like your food, hunny," Glenn says, stumbling a bit over his words. "I do. I swear."

"Uh huh!" Aaliyah laughs and shakes her head. She bites into her bread, giving Glenn a look that makes him give her a fake horrified look.

Stan and Teddy laugh at what is going on while Glenn holds up his hands as if asking what he had done to deserve this. Leilani's smile widens as she watches the four friends joke around, making her miss her own friends. Dinner ends and she serves them some pineapple-coconut sweet rolls for dessert she had made the other day. She also makes a fresh pot of coffee that fills the air with delicious aromas of chocolate caramel and macadamia nuts. Leilani sets out smaller spoons, sugar, and cream so that her guests can make their coffee how they enjoy it best.

As they sit, enjoying their coffee and dessert, Teddy turns his attention to Leilani again. "Leilani, you were telling me before that you have been looking at haunted places around Oahu. Can we see some places you found? Maybe we can go there and investigate together. Or if we have already been, we can take you back and see what you experience."

Leilani grows excited and quickly heads out of the dining room in order to retrieve her notes from the office. She reaches the closed door and freezes with her hand on the doorknob, afraid to go inside because she doesn't know whether she will run into Roy again. Leilani remembers they have their eyes on her since Glenn has connected their equipment to his phone and he has it in plain sight. Feeling safer knowing they are watching her every move, she shoves the door open, flips on the lights, and rushes over to the desk. She hastily collects her notebook and the papers she printed out earlier from her paranormal research and rushes out again without looking back. She leaves the door wide open and the lights on as she crosses back to the dining room to join the others. Leilani takes her seat and places the stack of printed papers in the middle of the table and opens her notebook to the first page.

Stan pulls the notebook close. "Oh, I love looking at paranormal places." He reads a bit of the first place out loud to the group while the others listen intently.

Teddy, Glenn, and Aliyah pick up the papers and shuffle through them while they continue to listen to Stan read from the notebook. They talk about the other haunted places for another hour, but the long day finally catches up to them. Leilani returns the information back to the office after she cleans up the kitchen, and the group tiredly make their way to their rooms for the night. At the top of the stairs, they say their goodnights and head inside their rooms, closing the doors behind them. Teddy sits down on the bed and looks around, knowing the room he is staying in used to belong to Lindsey. Stan took Tina's old room, while Glenn and Aaliyah will sleep in Lucas' old bedroom. Teddy kicks off his shoes and falls backwards onto the bed Leilani had purchased for whoever rents the room, letting out a low groan as he stares up at the ceiling.

Stan plops down on a small portable chair in front of the computer screens and watches the house for a few moments while everyone else gets ready for bed. He turns the screens off that show inside the bedrooms in order to give everyone their privacy and he stands. He stretches before he moves over to his bag on the foot of the bed. He fishes out his dark green pajama bottoms and changes his clothes before he heads to the bathroom. He washes up as quickly as he can so he can return to the bedroom to get back to the computers.

As he walks out of the bathroom towards the room, his eyes scan the dark stairs to see if he can spot anything unusual. But nothing on the dark stairs moves. He has a powerful urge to walk over and peer over the railing into the darkness below. Stan leans against the railing and stares down into the black abyss, his eyes adjusting slowly to the lack of light. But nothing moves down below him. He shakes his head and is about to return to his room when he hears a low voice cursing from somewhere downstairs. Stan freezes and his eyes widen as he hears the voice move from the kitchen to the office, still cursing.

Just behind him, a bedroom door opens, and Teddy appears in his old ghost hunting shirt and blue-checkered pajama bottoms. He raises an eyebrow when he sees Stan leaning over the railing. Teddy creeps up beside him and is about to talk, but Stan holds up a finger to his lips. He then touches his ear to signal for Teddy to listen closely, pointing downstairs. Teddy watches Stan's signals, then looks downwards, listening but not hearing anything at first. He nearly jumps when the cursing finally reaches his ears. He straightens up as he listens to the gruff voice as it moves into the office; the door slamming closed and nearly shaking the entire house. The two return to Stan's room and scan the screens to see if the downstairs cameras are catching anything. The night vision cameras they have set up in the office show nothing at first, but after a few minutes, the papers that they had been looking at earlier fly off the desk. They can distinctly hear a gruff male voice talking and cursing.

"Roy is going on a rampage it sounds like," Teddy says uneasily, as he watches the last paper flutter to the ground. "There is no telling what he might do tonight." He glances nervously over at Stan, watching his friend's expression grow more concerned as the room grows quiet.

Stan nods and says, "I'll stay awake and keep watch, but I think someone needs to stay in Leilani's room for tonight. Might not do much, but I think it might help a little."

Teddy nods and looks back at the screen to see that the papers are no longer moving and he can't hear the voice anymore. Stan writes the time, which camera they were watching, and what they have heard and seen in a notebook he has sitting next to the computers. Teddy pats his shoulder before he leaves the room and goes to talk to Glenn and Aaliyah. Stan watches for several seconds as they talk, then sees Teddy motioning for them to follow him back to Stan's room.

Teddy points to the office that is still quiet. "Stan and I just witnessed some major activity in the office a few minutes ago. The cameras recorded visuals and sound."

Stan nods his head, his mouth in a tight smile as he says, "Yea, Roy just threw a tantrum over something. I heard him walk from the kitchen to the office, cursing up a storm. Then, once Teddy joined me, we heard the office door slam shut. We came in here to see if we could see anything on the cameras and that's when we saw papers fly off the desk."

Glenn chuckles at the thought of Roy throwing the papers around the room. "A ghost threw a tantrum like a little kid. How ironic."

Aaliyah looks at the screen that is linked to the camera in Leilani's room, spotting the young woman standing in front of her bedroom window, pushing the curtain back. The guys also look over to watch Leilani stare outside for a moment, then lock her window for the night. She retreats to her bed, stifling a yawn with the back of her hand, not knowing what is going on downstairs or that she is being watched.

"Who will stay with Leilani?" Teddy asks as soon as the bedroom lights turn off and they can see Leilani crawling into bed.

Aaliyah looks at the men and shakes her head. "No way am I going to let one of you two single boys stay in there with her."

Stan and Teddy look surprised while Glenn gives his wife a pouty face as Aaliyah quickly hugs and kisses him before she says good night. She leaves the room, shutting the door silently behind her, and walks over to Leilani's bedroom door. Her eyes scan the dark stairs beside her and the empty hallways behind her, feeling apprehensive. She reaches the door and lightly taps on it to catch Leilani's attention before she falls asleep. She listens as she hears sheets being pushed back and light footsteps as Leilani crosses the room to the door. A few seconds later, the door opens, and Leilani squints out at her, looking quite confused.

"Aaliyah? Is everything okay?" Leilani opens the door further and glances behind the woman down the hallway, not sure what she is expecting to see.

"Everything is fine, Leilani. We just had a little experience downstairs that we caught on our cameras, and we thought it would be best if I slept with you." Aaliyah smiles as she tries to keep the fear and unease out of her voice.

Leilani rubs her eye as she steps back from the door and allows Aaliyah to enter her room. Aaliyah walks past Leilani and squeezes her arm gently. Leilani closes the door and locks it behind her before the two retreat to the bed. The girls crawl into the bed and even though they are exhausted, they lay awake, staring at the ceiling while the boys sit in the other room, debating their next step.

"I know I said I wanted to wait, but I think Glenn and I should go downstairs and try to communicate with Roy tonight. Maybe even try to talk to Tina and Tony," Teddy says as he turns away from the screens.

Glenn nods his head in agreement. "Yea, I actually agree with you on this one. Maybe we can get this Roy guy to move on and leave Leilani alone tonight." Glenn leaves the bedroom for a few moments, returning with his navy-blue bag that holds his equipment. "I'm ready, Teddy. Let's do this."

Teddy nods and follows Glenn out of the room, quietly closing the door behind them. Teddy turns off the hallway lights, plunging them into complete darkness before they start down the stairs. Stan turns off the lights in his own room and hunkers down for the night in front of the computer screens. He makes sure his walkie-talkie is on the right channel by calling Glenn and waiting for an answer, then sets it down beside the computer. With a sharpie, he quickly jots down the case number, the address of the house, and what they are investigating on the front of the notebook. He opens the notebook to an empty page and grabs a pen.

Stan clicks the pen and writes the date, time, and all the details of what he had experienced out in the hallway. Then he writes the details of what he and Teddy had seen on the screen. As he writes, his eyes are on the screens so he doesn't miss anything. Once he has finished writing the details, he writes the date, time, the room that Teddy and Glenn are in, and what they are about to do on a blank page. Stan places the pen down on top of the notebook and grabs his headphones out of one of his bags.

He plops back down in the chair and plugs them into the computer, setting them on his head. Stan takes off one side of the headphones so he can listen for the girls or for any other noises while still being able to hear Glenn and Teddy down in the office. Stan notes in the notebook that Glenn and Teddy have cleaned up the mess Roy made and states what equipment went where in the room. His pen point rests on the paper as he scans the other screens again before he returns his attention back to Teddy and Glenn.

Teddy double checks the equipment he and Glenn have set up, then sits down cross-legged on the floor. He points to Glenn, who turns on their equipment to record what happens, and sits down across from Teddy.

Teddy turns on the tape recorder, speaking only loud enough to make sure the tape recorder picks up his words. "We are currently in the house that was involved in the Roy Taylor murders twenty years ago. It is a little past 11 o'clock at night and Glenn and I are doing our first EVP session in the downstairs office." He clears his throat and takes in a few deep breaths.

Glenn moves a bit to get comfortable and looks around the dark room as he plucks up a smaller hand-held camera with night vision. He scans the room with it, peering through the small lens. He trains the camera on Teddy for a moment, then lowers the camera down to show the tape recorder that sits beside Teddy's knee. Teddy pulls the EMF meter out from behind him and holds it out to show the camera that they will monitor the lights. Glenn picks up the laser temperature gun and hands it to Teddy so that Teddy can show the camera the temperature of the room while they talk to whatever spirits may lurk close by. Teddy checks the temperature a few times and lets Glenn capture it on the camera before Glenn moves the camera up to record Teddy.

"Ready to start?" Glenn asks as he scans the room with the camera one more time before turning it back to Teddy.

Teddy nods and readjusts his legs. "My name is Teddy, and I am with Glenn. We wanted to talk to the spirit or spirits that are in this house. We do not mean any harm but we hope we can talk to you." He points to the device in his hand and says, "This device will only check the temperature of the room. This other device that I am talking into will record your voice. And this last device that is closer to Glenn will let us know you are in the same room by just waving or touching it and it'll cause the lights to go on. Is there anyone with us right now?" Teddy grows silent as he gives any spirits time to answer the first question. "If you are here, can you tell us your name?" Again, he grows silent for a few seconds, his eyes constantly roaming around the room. "Can you make a noise for us so that we know you are here or somewhere nearby? Maybe knock on the wall or the door or even a quick knock on the desk there beside us?"

A light knock on the door interrupts Teddy. He and Glenn quickly look over at the door, taking in sharp breaths. Glenn had closed it once they were inside to help muffle their voices, so their talking didn't wake the girls up. Teddy picks up the walkie-talkie as he glances over at Glenn, then back to the door. "Stan?"

"Yea, I heard it too, and no one is standing on the other side of the door," Stan says as he eyes the camera that shows the opposite side of the office door. He jots down the information in his notebook as he watches the two men turn to face the door.

Glenn quietly stands up and walks towards the door, the camera trained on it as he quiets his breathing. He is about to place his hand on the handle when the knock comes again, a small gentle knock that is low on the door. Glenn glances back at Teddy and instead of grabbing the door handle, he moves his hand to the height of where he believes the knocking is, showing the usual height for a small child. Teddy raises an eyebrow and motions for Glenn to return to his seat in front of him so that they can play this out to see what happens.

Teddy clears his throat before he faces the door again. "You have our permission to enter, little one." His body tenses as the office door opens, stays open for several minutes, and then closes behind whoever has entered the room. "Tina? Tony? Is that you? Are you the ones joining us right now?"

Silence falls over the room, then the EMF meter lights flicker on, a low buzzing confirming that it is indeed the childrens' spirits that have walked into the office. The sound and lights stop as Glenn trains the camera on the EMF reader so they can catch the phenomenon on video. Teddy uses the laser temperature gun and notes that there is a sudden drop in temperature in front of the two devices. Glenn records the changes with his camera and then returns the camera to the EMF meter.

Teddy thrusts his hand into the cold spot, then withdraws it, feeling the change instantly from warm to cold and then back to warm. He shivers and feels the hairs on the back of his neck and on his arms stand up. He takes in a bit of a shaky breath as he does his best to calm his pounding heart and he puts his hand back into the cold spot. Suddenly, it feels as if a little hand gently grabs his wrist. Teddy's voice catches in his throat as he feels the tiny fingers squeeze gently around his wrist then let go, leaving only the coldness of the touch behind. Glenn notices Teddy's sudden reaction and that he is no longer asking questions, and his eyebrows knit in confusion at his friend.

"Teddy, are you okay, man?" Glenn asks.

Teddy nods his head slowly as he catches his breath. "Yea, I was just touched." Teddy looks over at Glenn, but before Glenn can talk again, Teddy jumps back into questioning the two spirits. "Tony, did you just touch my arm?" He stares at the EMT meter, but all the lights stay dark. "Tina?" Before he could finish the question, the lights jump on quickly, flickering briskly as Tina answers him. "Wow, Tina, thank you for letting me know and for touching me. Is there something that you wish to tell us?"

The lights blink to life, grow dark, then blink more urgently as Tina manipulates them. Glenn swallows hard as he watches the lights turn themselves on and off with awe. No matter how many times he witnesses the EMF meter being manipulated by a spirit, it always catches him off guard. He keeps the cameras trained on the device, but he feels his hand shake from holding his arm up as still as he can.

"Tina, if you need to tell us something then please talk into the other device." Teddy picks up the voice recorder and holds it up so Tina can speak directly into it.

Time seems to stand still while Teddy and Glen sit quietly, both of their arms holding their equipment up shake. Stan watches the screen as he sits on the edge of his seat, almost holding his breath as he waits for the session to be over. His eagerness is getting the best of him since he wants to get his hands on the tapes. Finally, after a long pause, he hears Teddy ask more questions to Tony and Tina. He quickly jots down each question into his notebook so he can write out the answers after listening to the tapes. He writes the time and what else is happening or not happening elsewhere in the house before he continues to write the yes and no questions.

Stan drops the pen and stretches, his body growing stiff from sitting for so long. He stands up and places the headphones on the table before he walks around the room. He turns his back to the screens as he continues to stretch, bending down, and sighs when his back pops. While Stan is busy stretching, Teddy and Glenn have stopped asking questions so Tony could talk into the recorder. On the screen that shows the outside of the office, Roy appears. Roy glares at the door for a moment, then stalks away, heading towards the stairs. Stan turns back around to face the screens just as Roy disappears down the hall, where he walks into Stan's room. Stan sits back down in his chair and places the headphones back over one ear, scanning the screens. Roy stands directly behind Stan, his eyes narrowing down at the man in front of him.

Stan keeps his eyes on the screen, hearing Teddy say goodbye to Tony and Tina and ending their EVP session, not realizing there is an evil spirit standing behind him. Stan looks at the time and grunts, surprised it has already been nearly two hours since they started. He watches as Teddy and Glenn clean up the office and pack up the equipment into Glenn's bag except for the voice recorder. He wipes his face as he prepares himself for a long night of reviewing the material.

Teddy turns off the recorder, places a blank tape in it, and pockets the other tape they have filled during the session. He turns the recorder back on and sets it on top of the desk. "If anyone else wishes to talk, I will leave the recorder here on the desk for the night." He looks around the room one last time before he heads to the door behind Glenn.

Glenn opens the office door and makes his way to the stairs with Teddy on his heel and the bag over his shoulder. Teddy closes the office door before he quietly heads up the stairs after his friend, yawning and looking forward to some much-needed sleep. He stops at the top of the stairs and nods to Glenn as Glenn waves and heads for his room. Teddy walks over to Stan's room and lightly knocks on the door. There's no answer. He knocks again, hesitant to just enter because the last time he did so, he had walked in on Stan changing. But he's worried. There's no response to his knock and no sound coming from the room at all—not that he can hear anyway.

Teddy's eyebrows wrinkle together. He knew Stan was tired and was hoping to get a good night's sleep before unexpectedly coming to Leilani's, so it was possible he was sleeping. Wake him up or let him sleep? He rests his hand on the doorknob, twisting it to open the door and enter when he hears a noise to his left.

He turns to see Glenn peeking out of his room. "Hey, Glenn, can you check to see if Stan is in the bathroom before you get to bed? He's not answering the door and I've knocked three times already. He could just be sleeping. You know how tired he was. If he's up, though, I want to check in with him."

135

"Yea sure, Teddy, you've got it," Glenn exclaims as he walks over to the closed restroom door. He raps on the door lightly, then louder a few seconds later. "You in there, Stan?" He leans his head close to the door, straining to hear any movement inside. He grabs a hold of the door handle, and it turns easily in his hand, letting him know it isn't locked. He pushes the door open to reveal a dark empty bathroom and no signs that Stan had been there recently. He looks back over at Teddy as he closes the door again. "Sorry Teddy, but he isn't in there."

Teddy faces the bedroom door again, but he finally decides to let his friend sleep. They got a lot of footage, and Stan could go through it later. Teddy has a feeling this isn't going to be an ordinary paranormal investigation, so sleep will be essential for them all. Taking one last look at the door, Teddy turns away. He'd see Stan tomorrow.

Chapter Eleven

Aaliyah rolls over in her sleep beside Leilani. Leilani glances back over her shoulder at her sleeping friend before she turns back to face the window. She sighs as she stares at the clear night sky, watching the stars wink down at her. She has tried to sleep for the past two hours, but knowing that there is something happening in the house is making it exceedingly difficult. What happened downstairs that has made everyone jumpy? She rolls slowly onto her back and closes her eyes again, sighing heavily as she tries to fall asleep. She hears some thumps and bangs coming from what sounds like Stan's room and smiles, thinking to herself that she isn't the only one having a hard time falling asleep. It's possible one of them may be restless and is up to get a light snack or a glass of warm milk to help them fall asleep. She wonders if maybe she should join them for a glass of warm milk as her eyes spring back open. She carefully sits up and slips out of bed so that she doesn't wake up Aaliyah.

Leilani walks into the restroom and closes the door before she flips on the light. She stands in front of the mirror, staring into the glass and her exhausted eyes. She moves away, uses the toilet, and after flushing, returns to the sink to wash her hands. She let her hands sit in the warm water after she washed the soap off and then splashes the water on her face. She turns off the water and wipes her hands and face off on a gray towel. She sighs heavily as she turns the lights off and heads back into the silent bedroom. She stands just outside of the bathroom door, listening to the light breathing of Aaliyah.

The thumping in the other room has stopped, so she assumes they have finally fallen asleep. She tiptoes across the floor back to the bed but doesn't crawl under the covers just yet. Instead, Leilani walks over to the window and opens it a crack so that a cool breeze filters into the stuffy room. She bends down to the crack and breathes in the sweet night air. She smells the air again and catches a strange odor that is hidden under the sweet hibiscus flower, the same smell from when she moved in. Leilani takes another few sniffs, and gags when it builds stronger. She stands back up and shakes her head as she turns away, heading back to bed.

Standing in the shadows, Roy scowls at the two women, wanting to kill them as they lay in bed. He watches as the owner of the house returns to the bed and slips quietly under the covers. He is about to step out of the shadows when Tony and Tina quickly walk into the room, holding hands. They cross the room quickly and stand in front of the bed on Leilani's side as she gets comfortable. Tony and Tina clutch each other's hands tightly as they turn to face Roy, their own eyes narrowed as they protect the sleeping women. Roy glares at the two before he turns on his heel and stalks back into the closet, vanishing.

Tony and Tina walk over to the closet and peer inside to make sure Roy is gone. They quietly return to the bed and watch Leilani until she falls into a deep sleep. The children walk around to the other side of the bed and watch Aaliyah for a moment as she stirs, but she grows still again. They head for the door, but before they can pass through it, they hear Glenn and Teddy walking up the stairs. Tony and Tina listen to the two men trudge up the stairs and stop outside the bedroom door. The kids hear one of them tapping gently on one of the other doors. Tina whimpers as the knocking becomes a bit more urgent. They hear knocking on the bathroom door a few minutes later. Tony looks at his sister and places a finger to his lips to shush her. Tina nods and the two continue to listen as Teddy and Glenn speak quietly about Stan not answering the door.

"We didn't save him," Tina whimpers.

"I know, but we were downstairs talking to Teddy and Glenn," Tony says sadly. "We couldn't tell he was attacking their friend until it was too late." Tony gently tugs on Tina's hand. "Come on, sis. Let's go."

Tina nods and reaches down into the dark corner beside the door, picking up her favorite bunny and Tony's favorite toy car that she hands to him. They retreat to the bathroom and vanish from sight. Outside the room, Glenn and Teddy continue to whisper about how Stan isn't answering the door. Leilani moans in her sleep as she subconsciously hears the whispering outside of her door, but sleep has finally won the battle and won't let her leave the realm of dreams. Meanwhile,

Teddy and Glenn stand in front of the door, and just as Teddy turns to walk away and let Stan sleep, Glenn holds up his hand.

You're just going to let him sleep then? I know he was tired, but there's a lot of footage there we should go through. If we got it all, this could be huge." Glenn chews on his lower lip. "Anyway, no matter how tired he is, it's not like him to fall asleep after something this big."

Teddy nods in agreement, but he feels bad. Turning back to the door, he grips the door knob "You're right. We just have to go inside to see what is going on. He could be passed out in front of the screens again with the headphones on or something." He twists the handle and pushes the door wide open.

They step into the dark room, covering their mouths when they see what has happened inside the room. The only light came from the barely functioning computer screen while the other spat out electricity from its smashed screen. Glenn gags when he sees Stan's head smashed into the screen, a puddle of blood underneath his neck. His arms are bent until they are torn from his shoulders and tied up with computer cables. Stan still sits in the chair, but his legs are broken and bent upwards in front of his body, white bloody bones protruding from the shredded skin.

Teddy steps up beside Stan's body, unable to tear his gaze from the bloody mess that used to be their friend. Teddy stares in shock, unable to move. He hadn't heard a thing. Shouldn't he have heard something?

Glenn grabs a hold of Teddy's shoulder, staring into the farthest darkest corner of the room, nodding towards it. Teddy looks over just as the flash from the computer screen shows them a dark mass staring at them. Teddy squints his eyes so that he can see who is hiding in the shadows. His eyes widen in fear when he sees Roy Taylor standing in the corner, a smirk of pure evil spreading across his distorted face.

Glenn grabs Teddy's arm again, this time dragging his friend out of the room, and slams the door shut behind them. The stench of spilled blood fills their noses as they walk backwards, their backs hitting the stair's railing. They both jump and spin around, expecting to be facing Roy again. Their hands clutch the railing so they don't spill over the side and fall.

"What are we going to do?" Glenn asks as the two stare down into the empty inky black below them. "We've never dealt with a ghost that can kill before. A shove here, a touch there, but full-on death by their hands?" He is breathing hard when he turns to face Teddy, his face pale. "We need to leave now, Teddy. Tell Leilani that she needs to get her money back, sell it, burn it, whatever she needs to do and get the hell out of here, but this time, bro, we can't help her."

Teddy shakes his head, catching his own scared, shaky breath. "We have to help her because he has the strength to kill. Leilani could get hurt or worse."

"*We* can get hurt or killed; no, wait, Stan is already dead! You saw what Roy can do, and he had the look that told me he wasn't done messing with us. I won't put Aaliyah in danger, Teddy. I can't. I won't." Glenn turns away from Teddy, heading for Leilani's room, scared something has happened to his wife and Leilani.

Teddy takes a firm hold of Glenn's arm to stop him. Glenn reluctantly turns to face Teddy. "Glenn, please stay and help me with this problem. Leilani needs us even more than ever right now. I need your help, Glenn, please?" Although he pleads for Glenn to stay, he can tell by the look in Glenn's eyes that he won't be getting any help from his friend.

"No!" Glenn hisses at Teddy, pulling his arm free.

Teddy glances back to the door that now leads to Stan's death chamber before forcing himself to look away, feeling his stomach churn as the gruesome images revive themselves in his mind. He pulls out the tape that he had slipped inside of his front pocket after the EVP session. Deciding to try again with Glenn, he holds up the tape from the voice recorder and gives it a little shake.

"Stan wouldn't let us leave an investigation no matter what, Glenn," Teddy says. "We need to continue this investigation to avenge Stan and to keep Leilani, Nalani, and whoever else wishes to live here safe. Tina and Tony talked to us downstairs and we need to listen to it before we even think about leaving this house."

Glenn clenches his teeth then nods. "Fine, let's hear what the kids have to say to us." He goes to his room and grabs his tape recorder so they can play the tape. Glenn returns and pops the tape into the recorder and hands it to Teddy.

Teddy and Glenn lean in close so they can hear what is on it. Teddy hits the rewind button, hits play, and all they hear at first is silence. Next, they hear Teddy talking, introducing himself and Glenn to the spirits of the house, and knocking at Teddy's request. They continue to listen, hearing the office door open and close. After a few moments, they can hear a low whispering voice that belongs to a little girl. Teddy stops the recorder quickly as he looks at Glenn, who lifts his gaze and stares back at Teddy in amazement.

"Tina," they whisper in unison.

Teddy quickly presses play and Tina's soft voice comes through again, the two holding their breath as they listen to her intently. She tells them the story of her and her family's horrific deaths. It is long and winded, but she can tell them the whole story, only having to stop to rest and gain strength a few times. Finally, she grows silent and there is nothing more from the young girl. A few minutes later, Teddy speaks again, this time asking for Tony to talk. Silence follows and then a small, scared boy's voice comes through the light, shifting noises.

"Roy evil... we protect the house... he hates us, but he won't come near us because he can't." Tony stops speaking after the strange message for several moments, leaving Teddy and Glenn thoroughly confused.

They stand in the hallways in silence as they impatiently wait and hope that Tony explains what his cryptic message means about why Roy won't go near the kids or why he can't go near them. Maybe Tony knows how to stop Roy before the evil spirit kills again or even just a hint on how to stop Roy.

After what seems like an eternity, Tony's small voice breaks through the quiet room. "Roy fears us... our parent's love and fear of us getting hurt... still stays with us... Roy can't touch or hurt us, but we can touch and hurt him."

Tina's voice pipes in with her brother. "Helps us... protect the lady who bought the house... please."

"Roy can't touch us," Tony says again and then there is nothing but silence again.

The whirring of the machine continues until Teddy says goodbye and thanks Tony and Tina for taking the time to talk to them. Teddy hits stop, staring down at the device in his hands, his mouth moving, but no words coming out. Glenn leans back against the wall behind, pressing his forehead against his hands and closing his eyes as he tries to understand what they heard.

Glenn suddenly laughs lightly as he opens his eyes and looks over at Teddy. "Wow! Did we just really hear all of that?"

This comment breaks Teddy's trance, and he looks at his friend. Glenn and Teddy laugh fear-stricken laughs as their thoughts race about the danger they are in against Roy. Teddy still clutches onto the tape recorder as he uses his other hand to wipe away the tears from his eyes from laughing so hard.

"Yea, I think we actually did," Teddy says as he nods to the tape recorder. "One of our best EVP sessions yet."

Glenn nods and says, "I have to agree with you on that one, but what do we do now?" His laughter has died down and his face becomes serious as he stares at Teddy.

Teddy shakes his head, his own smile no longer on his face. "I don't know... there has to be more to the story, maybe even more to the murders. Something that maybe the kids didn't tell us or that hadn't been reported. I don't really get what Tony was telling us about how Roy can't touch them because of fear and love from the parents. It's not making sense."

Glenn chews on the inside of his cheek as he thinks for a moment. "Man, I wish I hadn't quit smoking. I could really use a cigarette right about now, or maybe two or three."

Teddy chuckles and says, "You and me both, brother, you and me both."

"Rewind the tape, and go back to Tina's story about their murder, but only to where she talks about hers and Tony's death. Maybe there are some clues there." Glenn sits down on the ground so he is more comfortable.

Teddy rewinds the tape as Glenn has instructed and clicks play as he sits down next to his friend. Tina's voice comes through once again, describing how Roy had tied them up to the chairs in the dining room with an evil smirk on his face. Teddy and Glenn continue to listen as Tina continues to tell them again about the deaths of their older brother and sister. Teddy swallows hard as he listens to the poor girl's sad voice describe the gruesome deaths in short breathy sentences. Glenn concentrates on the story more than he had before and visualizes every horrific detail.

He grabs Teddy's hand once Tina choppily talks about her and Tony's deaths. "Hang on! Let's hear that part again."

Teddy rewinds the tape, and they listen again to the sickening, torturous death of Tina and Tony. They hear Tina talk about how Roy had some difficulty in killing them at first, not able to harm them as badly as he had harmed the others. Teddy ponders on the information for a minute, then nods, as he understands what the little girl is saying.

"Their mom was killed before them, so her fear and her love must have somehow made a barrier around Tina and Tony to make it harder for Roy to kill them." Teddy turns the recorder off and sets it down on the ground. "Tony and Tina may be the key in saving us and getting rid of Roy. Their mother and father's love must still surround them."

Glenn stares down at the ground, still contemplating getting his wife and leaving. But Teddy needs his help, and he knows he needs to avenge Stan's untimely death. He also knows Stan would want him to help Teddy and Leilani. He takes a heavy breath, already regretting what he is about to do. "All right then, what do we do now with that information?" Glenn asks as he looks at Teddy. "Should we wake up the girls? Let them know what is going on now?"

Teddy nods and says, "Yea, I think we need to get this over with now instead of waiting another day. We need to jump in headfirst and get the kids to help us stop Roy." He stands up and walks towards Leilan's door, but pauses. A shiver races down his spine. Teddy glances down at his arms and sees his hair standing up before he turns to look at Glenn to ask if he had felt the change in the temperature.

"Yea, it feels a little cooler, but it could be just the night air." He hangs his head before rubbing his hands over his face and patting his cheeks. "Man! It's all catching up to me. It's like, all of a sudden, I could sleep for a week. And there's so much left to do. Come on, let's go wake the girls," Glenn says, nodding towards the door.

Teddy nods, his own eyes fluttering open and closed. He shivers as he feels a shift in the temperature, and it makes him think about the blankets he could be crawling under, a soft pillow, blessed sleep.

Images of Stan come unbidden to his mind, and his eyes open wide. He and Glenn stand in front of the closed bedroom door, but neither make a move to knock. Glenn leans his head against the door, his eyes closed, and Teddy rests his on the wall behind him.

"We need to get some shuteye before we tackle this ghost problem, or we'll have issues. But we need to call the cops and report Stan's murder too," Glenn says, exhaustion clear in his voice as well.

Teddy nods his head in agreement, his eyes once again closed. "Yea, let's make a call to the police and then maybe sleep for a couple of hours before we wake the girls up." He stifles a yawn as he fumbles for his phone in his back pocket.

Glenn fumbles for his phone too, but it drops with a low plunk on the floor next to his feet. He laughs a little, then leans down to retrieve it, letting his tired body sit down. Once he is sitting, he leans back against the wall beside the door. He feels a chill and pulls his knees up to his chest, resting his head on them. *Just for a moment*, he thinks.

Teddy sits down as well after he pulls his phone free from his pocket but cannot seem to see the numbers as he tries to punch in 9-1-1. The numbers and the screen swim before his eyes as he tries again and again to press the numbers into the phone to make the call, but soon the phone slips out of his hand and lays uselessly on the floor. He can hear soft snores coming from Glenn, the noise soothing. It's the last thing he hears before he too slips into a deep sleep.

A dark mist appears in front of them and dissipates until Roy is standing there, watching the two sleeping men. He snarls at them and bends down, reaching his hands towards Glenn and Teddy's throats. He curls his fingers on like claws since he is thinking about ripping their throats out. His fingers come inches from the unsuspecting men when he stops and glances up. He turns his head to look down the hallway and sees Tina and Tony staring at him. They hold hands as usual, taking comfort in one another, their eyes never leaving Roy's face. They shake their heads at what he is about to do, taking a tentative step forward. Roy's hands snapback and instantly he covers his ears as giggling and whispering bombard his mind. Still covering one ear, he swats his other hand at the kids as he staggers away from them and the two sleeping men. They walk towards him, forcing him to back up against the wall near the top of the stairs. Roy shakes his head, wanting to stop the whispering and giggling, but it doesn't help, and grows louder. He glances at the stairs, then back at the children before he quickly leaps down them and vanishes from sight.

Tina and Tony sit down in front of the sleeping men, keeping watch over them so they can rest in peace. Roy may have manipulated them into falling asleep so he could kill them, but they did need to sleep. All of them did. And the fact that they were all in the same area made it easier on the young spirits, so because they could stop Roy, they let Teddy and Glenn sleep, even if it was on the floor.

Chapter Twelve

Birds twitter in the trees outside as the sun sits a few inches above the horizon, clouds slowly rolling across a beautiful sunrise. Leilani slowly rolls from her back to her right side, sighing as she fights herself from waking up. She can feel movement beside her as Aaliyah also fights the urge to wake up, hearing her lightly moaning in her sleep. Unable to resist any longer, Leilani opens her eyes to see sunlight peeking in through the curtains. Leilani groans as she slowly sits up, her hair falling tangled over her face as she uses her arms to push herself up. She lifts her head slowly and, with one of her arms, she shoves her hair from in front of her face. She slips out of bed and quietly makes her way to the restroom so she can take a quick shower and get dressed before Aaliyah wakes up.

A half an hour later, she stands in front of the fogged-up mirror, dressed and brushing out her wet hair. Her eyes stare blankly back at her from the depth of the glass as she lays her brush down on the counter. Her thoughts about the investigation to come pushes all other happier thoughts from her mind. Is she ever going to be able to enjoy the house of her dreams or is this nightmare going to destroy her first?

Leilani heads into her bedroom to find Aaliyah now sitting up in bed, yawning and looking around with the bedhead. Aaliyah smiles at her as she stretches her arms up towards the ceiling, her shoulders and back popping lightly.

Aaliyah rubs her left eye and looks over at Leilani. "Good morning, Leilani," Aaliyah says after a yawn. "This bed is amazing! You'll have to tell me where you got the mattress from so Glenn and I can get one and sleep like babies."

Leilani laughs as she walks to the bed and sits down in front of Aaliyah. "I bought the mattress a few years ago at the Sleep on a Cloud store."

"Oh, I know that one," Aaliyah says. "I guess I know where we will shop in a couple of months once we have enough money saved up."

The girls laugh for a moment, Aaliyah feeling much better since she had slept in Leilani's bed after having heard about Roy trashing the office last night. She licks her lips as they suddenly feel dry at the thought of Roy, and she nods towards the restroom. "Can I take a quick shower?"

"Of course you can, Aaliyah. Let me grab you a towel and you can take as long as you want. The boys don't need to have any hot water for their showers." She winks at Aaliyah before she stands up and heads for the bedroom door so she can get a towel from the hallway linen closet. She opens the door and jumps backwards when she spots Glenn and Teddy sleeping up against the wall on either side of the door.

Aaliyah watches as Leilani jumps a bit and hurries over to see what is wrong. She sees Teddy and Glenn as well and laughs when she sees the two passed out on the floor. "It looks like they did their night investigation, but instead of making it back to their rooms, they made it this far and just passed out. It has happened before, so nothing to worry about." She kneels and gently shakes her husband's shoulder to wake him up. "Hey sleepy head, it's time to wake up."

Glenn stirs when he hears his wife's voice and feels her hand on his shoulder. He crawls out of the groggy sleep and forces his eyes open to see Aaliyah kneeling in front of him. He then spots Leilani standing behind his wife, staring down at him curiously. Glenn sits up from the wall and looks around, confused, not remembering having fallen asleep in the hallway last night. He turns his head to see Teddy asleep across from him and their phones on the floor in between them, both completely dark. He reaches out and gently smacks Teddy on the shoulder to wake him up. Teddy shakes himself awake, looking around just as confused, not sure why he is in the hallway. Teddy's eyes fall on the dark phones too and he scrambles to grab up his phone, pressing the power button, but the screen remains off.

"The battery must be dead," Teddy says as he pushes himself up, groaning as his body protests. Finally, on his feet, he looks at Leilani and Aaliyah as he straightens his wrinkled shirt. "Did you two sleep okay? I mean, nothing weird happened last night or anything?"

The girls look at each other before they look back at Teddy and shake their heads, letting him know nothing had happened as they slept.

"We slept just fine," Aaliyah says, still watching Teddy with a strange look on her face, her mind reeling with questions.

"Yea, nothing strange happened last night," Leilani confirms as Teddy stares at her with fear in his eyes.

Once he hears they slept peacefully, he sighs in relief and smiles. "Okay, good! We did our EVP session last night and just wanted to make sure that nothing strange occurred to you two because of it."

Aaliyah shakes her head with a small frown on her face, her eyebrows knitted together. "No, nothing out of the ordinary for us. We slept through most of the night. And I have to say that I slept like a baby on that bed so Glenn we will have to go get the same mattress."

Glenn slowly stands up beside Teddy with Aaliyah's help, trying to get his own phone to turn on, but it refuses. "I fully charged this thing last night. Why is it dead now?" He shakes the phone as if that will force it to turn on, but the phone stays dead. "The spirits must have needed to use the battery energy."

Leilani crosses her arms over her chest as she listens quietly in the doorway of her bedroom. She clears her throat and tells them, "I was just about to get a towel for Aaliyah so she can take a shower. I will get you all a towel as well if you would like to take a shower too."

Glenn shakes his head, as if his mind suddenly clears, his memory returning about what had happened last night. "We need to call the police. We found Stan murdered early this morning. He... he..." Glenn couldn't finish talking, his eyes lowering to stare down at the ground at his feet.

Aaliyah shakes her head, not believing what her husband is saying about their friend being murdered. She quickly brushes past Teddy and Glenn, quickly heading to the room that Stan is staying in while at the house. Glenn tries to stop her from going to the room but isn't fast enough to catch her by her arm as she rushes past. Teddy catches Leilani though and holds her back while Glenn chases after his wife as she enters the room. Aaliyah shoves the bedroom door open, not knowing what to expect inside, but she sees nothing out of the ordinary and crosses her arms over her chest, waiting for Glenn to join her.

"Baby, don't go in there, please," Glenn's voice trails off when he jumps into the room and grabs her arm gently by the elbow, ready to pull her backwards out of the room. But his hand slides off of her elbow when he looks around at an empty, blood-free room. Stan's body isn't sitting in front of the broken computer screens, hanging by bloody cords with a silent scream frozen on his face. Stan is just... gone!

Aaliyah looks back at Glenn with her eyebrows raised and a face that tells him she is not amused by the little joke or what she thinks is a joke being played on her. "He's probably downstairs getting coffee started or went out to grab us all some breakfast. Though I definitely find it funny that he didn't wake you two up when he saw you sleeping on the floor." She shakes her head and drops her hands. She pushes past him and walks out of the bedroom.

Teddy watches as Aaliyah walks out alone, Glenn still standing inside the room. He looks at her face but only reads annoyance, not a sign of fear, disgust, or distress, which is what he is expecting after having seen the horrors in the bedroom. She looks at Teddy with the same unimpressed gaze that she had given her husband before she walks back to Leilani's room to take her shower. Leilani frees herself from Teddy, shaking her head as she heads to the linen closet and grabs four of her guest towels. She walks down the hallway and drops three of the towels into Teddy's hands without saying a word and walks back into her room, shutting the door behind her. The door opens a second later and Aaliyah quickly walks out and heads into the other bedroom she and Glenn are sharing. A couple minutes later, she emerges with clean clothes and a small sundry bag in her arms. Teddy walks to Stan's room, entering the room where Glenn still stands dumbfounded. The towels drop from Teddy's hands onto the floor with a soft thud as Teddy scans the pristine room before he looks questioningly over at a silent Glenn.

"Glenn, where is Stan?"

Glenn shrugs his shoulders, finally able to tear his gaze from the room to look at Teddy. "I don't know." He swallows the lump that has formed in his throat from the sudden mix of strange emotions. "He was here... right here last night."

Teddy walks over to the bed and lifts the pillows, looking for any signs of blood, shaking his head. Glenn finds his ability to move again and heads over to the side where the equipment sat the day before, but the spot is completely clean. The only sign that there have been cases is the light imprints they have left behind on the carpet. Even Stan's small bag of clothes is missing from the end of the bed, confusing Glen even more.

"All of his things are gone, too," Glenn says in a strained voice as he looks at Teddy. "What is going on?" He stares down at the empty spot where the tables and computers had sat, then raised his eyebrows. "We need to get downstairs. Maybe Aaliyah is right, and he's out getting coffee and breakfast for us." Glenn rushes out of the room and heads down the stairs, nearly tripping, but catches himself before he falls down the last few steps.

Teddy tosses the pillows back onto the bed and hurries after Glenn, also hoping Aaliyah is correct, and Stan is downstairs. He steps off the last stair and looks around anxiously, but nothing has changed since last night. Glenn heads over to the front door, unlocking and opening it to take a peek out in the driveway. The sun glares down on them as Teddy joins Glenn and they peer out to see that Stan's car was parked in the driveway. Glenn closes the door, and he turns to face Teddy with a puzzled expression on his face. Teddy mirrors his look, but the sounds of someone on the stairs cause them to turn to see Leilani heading down towards them.

"Have you found Stan yet?" she asks when she reaches the bottom step. She leans against the banister, raising her eyebrows as she looks from Teddy to Glenn and back again.

Before they can answer her, Stan walks out of the office and gives them a crooked smile, "Find Stan? Is Stan missing again?"

Teddy and Glenn stare at Stan with their mouths gaping open. Leilani smiles and says good morning to him as she pushes off the banister and heads off to the kitchen.

"Stan?" Teddy asks, not believing his eyes at that moment.

Stan looks at Teddy and nods. "Yea, the last time I checked I was Stan."

Glenn sighs in relief. "We thought Roy had gotten you and that you were dead. Your room... you... I..."

"Glenn, calm down, okay? I'm right here," Stan assures his distraught friend. "Where's Aaliyah?"

Teddy recovers from his loss of words and blinks a few times before he says, "Oh yeah, um, she's upstairs taking a shower. Uh Stan, where is the equipment?"

Stan sighs heavily and says, "I packed it into the car. There was some weird electric surge a few hours ago so you'll have to grab extra gear from Glenn's place while I take this stuff back to my place and try to salvage what I can." He shrugs a bit as if it isn't a big deal before he turns towards the stairs again. "Morning Aaliyah."

Aaliyah walks down the stairs, her hair still wet from her shower, and she smiles at Stan, "Good morning, Stan. Did my idiot husband tell you he and Teddy thought you were dead?"

Stan nods his head and chuckles slightly, but says nothing on the subject as Leilani returns from the kitchen. Stan opens his mouth to answer Aaliyah but sees Leilani return and shuts his mouth, raising his eyebrows. Teddy, Aaliyah, and Glenn all turn to face Leilani as she stops in front of them with a questioning look.

"So, would you all like me to make some breakfast, or would you rather I go pick us up some food? Or maybe we go out for breakfast on this beautiful morning?" she asks.

"I wouldn't mind going out and taking a break from this place," Teddy says, Glenn nodding his head in agreement.

"I need to get started on salvaging the film, so maybe bring me back a bagel and cream cheese or something," Stan chimes in as he points back to the office.

Glenn laughs and says, "That's our Stan ready to work and will eat only if people bring him food."

Stan grins sheepishly at Glenn and shrugs. "Yea, yea, yea." He turns on his heel and heads back into the office, talking over his shoulder, "I'm going to leave in a bit, but I'll be back by the time you all do if not a bit after, but I will be back. And hopefully I'll be back with good news, not bad news." He waves to them before the doors close.

Aaliyah looks at Teddy and Glenn over critically, wrinkling her nose a little. "I think you two should shower and change before we go out." She waves her hand at them to get them moving back to the stairs. "You both look all wrinkled and disheveled."

Teddy and Glenn head back up the stairs and retrieve the towels and their clean clothes before they take turns in the guest bathroom for their showers. Teddy stands in Stan's room as he waits for Glenn to finish. He strolls around the room, scrutinizing the entire room again in order to see if he can see even the smallest traces of blood that would prove the Stan downstairs is not the real Stan. He looks closely at the bed again, but there are still no traces of what he and Glenn had seen. But he did just see Stan downstairs with his own eyes, so why is he looking in the room again? Did Roy make them just think that he had killed Stan just to unnerve them and get them to leave? Teddy shakes his head, feeling very unnerved by it all, and heads out of the room to see if Glenn is done taking a shower. He stops in the doorway and turns around to look at the room one last time, still feeling uneasy but not able to place a finger on what is causing the feeling. Still seeing nothing out of the ordinary, he turns away and heads for the closed bathroom door, not hearing the water running any longer.

Teddy raps a knuckle on the closed door, saying through the door, "Hey Glenn, are you done in there yet? The girls are getting impatient downstairs."

Glenn opens the door and steps out, looking like his old happier self. "That shower definitely helped a lot." He leaves the door open and heads back to the bedroom to put away his clothes.

Teddy steps into the bathroom and closes the door behind him, dropping his clean clothes, the towel, and his sundry bag on the counter before he stares blankly into the mirror. Dark circles have already formed under his eyes, making him look older and more tired than he truly felt. He feels awake, maybe groggy, but that is slowly fading the more he moves around. He turns away from the mirror, undresses, and turns on the water, looking forward to a hot shower. Once he sees steam, he steps in and closes the shower curtain, letting the warm water rain down over his sore body.

He is still racking his brain about how he and Glenn had fallen asleep in front of the door and why their phones were now dead when both had been fully charged. Shaking his head, he hurries and washes his hair, knowing the others are still waiting downstairs for him to finish up. Teddy turns off the water and stands still, watching the rest of the bubbly water disappear down the drain, keeping him mesmerized. He shakes himself from his trance and dries himself before stepping out of the tub. Teddy looks at his clothes, confused because they are on the floor now, as if someone has pushed them off the counter in a huff. He wipes his dripping face with the towel as he continues to stare down at his clothes, still quite confused because he had heard nothing, nor had he felt anything while he was taking a shower. Teddy eyes look over at the door, half expecting for the door to swing open as he gets dressed.

Once dressed, Teddy rushes out of the eerie bathroom and spins around as he walks backwards until he bumps into the stairs railing. Nothing moves inside the bathroom that he can see, so he turns and heads for the top of the stairs, his hand sliding across the wooden banister. Behind him, the bathroom door slowly swings closed, not making a sound as it clicks shut.

Teddy rejoins the small group as they wait in front of the door, chatting about what they want to eat and where they should go for breakfast. He steps up behind Leilani and smiles at them. "So, have we decided on where we will go to get breakfast?"

Glenn nods, "Yea, I have an idea where we can go." He opens the front door and allows Aaliyah and Leilani to walk out into the sunny day. He follows them out and yells over his shoulder, "Good luck, Stan! We will see you soon, buddy."

Teddy steps out last and grabs a hold of the door handle to shut it behind him, but he stops and looks towards the closed office doors. He can't hear Stan moving around inside, but he knows that his best friend is busy working on trying to find the lost data as much as he can while at Leilani's house before he goes home to figure out if he can salvage anymore. "See you later, Stan!" Teddy hears a muffled response from inside, closes the door and heads off to the car.

They all pile into Glenn's gray jeep and buckle themselves in as Glenn maneuvers the car out of the driveway. Aaliyah flips on the radio from her seat in front and slightly bobs to the music. Teddy and Leilani chatter about the team's other cases in the back seat. Glenn joins in the chatter while Aaliyah rolls down her window and enjoys the breeze as it pushes past her face. She closes her eyes and breathes in deep, letting the pungent smells of gas from the other cars and the sweet island smells mix in her nose. The news that someone had brutally murdered Stan and then seeing him appear downstairs quite alive has really shaken her.

After about a thirty-five-minute drive on the highway, Glenn gently turns his wheel and takes the off ramp to their right, stopping at a red light. A few streetlights later, Glenn takes a left turn and enters a parking lot that is slowly filling up with the breakfast crowd, parking in the first empty spot he comes across. The friends pile out of the car and follow behind an older couple to the front door. The couple ahead of them opens the door and the sounds of chatter, laughter, and clinking from people's plates and cups flows out over them, calming their rattled nerves.

The group is soon sitting in a booth towards the back of the restaurant where it is quieter. They glance over their menus and as soon as their waiter appears, they order their drinks and food. They want to be left alone as much as possible so they can speak freely. Their waiter returns with their drinks then heads off to his other tables.

Leilani stirs sugar, squeezes the lemons into her tea, and stirs again to mix it all up. She takes a sip and smiles, "Mm perfect." She looks over at Glenn and then at Teddy. "Did you guys learn anything last night during your EVP session?"

Glenn and Teddy turn to look at one another while Aaliyah looks on, interested to learn the information too as she stirs sugar and creamer into her hot coffee. She takes a sip, looks thoughtful for a moment, and then pours in another creamer, stirring it again. Leilani takes another sip as she looks from Teddy back to Glenn, noting their sudden look of discomfort. Teddy and Glenn each quickly take a drink from their cold drinks in order to prolong themselves from having to answer Leilani's question, even though they knew that they would have to answer, eventually.

Teddy swallows his coke before he looks over at Leilani, taking in a deep breath to calm his nerves. "Actually, yes, we learned something. We contacted Tina and Tony when we were in the office last night." Teddy leans in closer and lowers his voice as he re-encounters what had happened last night in the office while they wait for their food. He doesn't tell them about Roy murdering Stan since they had seen their friend alive earlier–something he's still trying to understand.

He quiets down once their waiter returns to the table with another waitress at his heel, carrying their steaming plates of food. He hands out the plates to each person, refills drinks, and leaves so the group can enjoy their meal in peace. Silence once again falls over the table while everyone enjoys their breakfast, taking a break from ghost talk while they concentrate on their food. Teddy thinks about the conversation they had with the ghost children, chewing on a piece of toast.

Leilani watches as she eats, noticing that he has grown quite sullen as he stares blankly down at his plate of food, hardly touching it suddenly. He seems to eat on slow autopilot, only coming out of the trance to blink or drink is his coke occasionally. She looks over at Glenn, who seems to be in the same sullen thoughtful trance as he eats, yet Glenn enjoys his food at a normal pace. She looks at Aaliyah, who is staring at her husband, her eyebrows scrunched together worriedly. There is something bothering the two men, but they aren't telling them what it is about. Is it about the conversation with Tina and Tony? She has to say that the conversation is strange and alarming, but she doesn't think that it is the only thing that is bothering the two.

Leilani goes back to eating her food as an awkward silence falls over the table. Only a few thank you's are said whenever their waiter returns to refill their drinks. When he returns to ask if they would like anything else to eat as he removes some of the empty plates, the group thanks him again but declines.

The four return to the car in silence and pile in, Aaliyah carrying a to-go bag with food in it she had ordered on the way out of the restaurant, almost having forgotten to buy something for Stan. They quietly buckle themselves into their seats, ready to get back to the house to see if Stan has saved anything. There were too many questions and not enough answers, so they agreed to do another EVP session. They will do it in the dining room where the most harm had been done to the family in order to see if they could get a stronger connection with Tony and Tina.

Aaliyah sets the bag on her lap and watches the world pass outside her window as her one fear continues to plague her mind. "How will we protect ourselves against Roy?"

Glenn looks over at her for a split second, then looks back at the road, not knowing how to answer her truthfully. Teddy plays with his shirt while staring hard at it, as if the answer will magically appear on the material. Aaliyah looks at the others, waiting for someone to answer. But she receives nothing but deafening silence mixed with the sounds of passing cars.

Leilani pulls out her cell phone from her purse and dials, hoping that Nalani will have some suggestions. She waits impatiently as the phone rings and rings again. Finally, a voice on the other end says hello. She sighs in relief. "Nalani, I'm glad you answered. Can I ask you a question? Maybe your grandma will have an answer for us." She listens for a moment as Nalani answers "Okay, great. Look, don't freak out or anything, but I need to know what we can use in order to protect ourselves from an evil spirit."

Glenn glances in the rear-view mirror at Leilani for a moment, looking hopeful that Nalani or Nalani's grandmother can tell them what they will need for protection. Aaliyah turns in her seat so she can see Leilani. She takes in a sharp breath and her hands clench together as if she is praying, taking in a sharp breath.

Leilani continues to listen to her phone, hearing Nalani talking to her grandma in the background, glad she has caught her best friend visiting her grandparents. She perks up as she makes eye contact with Teddy when she hears Nalani bring the phone back to her lips to speak with her. A smile crosses her face when she hears what Nalani has to say. "Thanks Nala, you and your grandma are the best. Tell her I'll come and visit her soon." She ends the conversation and slips her cell phone back into her purse before looking outside to figure out where they were. "Okay Glenn, do you know where the closest nursery is from where we are now? They said that we would need ti leaves. I need to pick some up so I can plant them in the four corners of the property. Nalani's grandma also recommends that we wear ti leaves leis as well in a horseshoe around our necks."

Aaliyah grabs her cell phone that sits in the cup holder and searches for the nearest plant nursery or flower plant shop that sells ti leaf leis and plants. She scrolls a bit, then finding what she is looking for, taps on the direction button, and places it where Glenn can see and hear the directions. Glenn follows the directions and soon parks outside a nice nursery that looks promising. It is clean, well-kept, and full of colorful flowers, lush plants, and bushes that would make any garden the envy of the neighborhood.

Not even bothering to look around, Leilani hurries off to the nearest employee while the others fan out and begin their search for the plant Nalani's grandma has recommended. "Aloha, excuse me." She waits for the petite, short-haired woman to put down a small pot of yellow flowers..

The woman returns Leilani's smile and stands up straighter. "Aloha, how can I help you today?"

"I want to give a few ti plants and ti leaf leis to a few of my friends since they have just bought a new house. Could you point me in the right direction, please?"

The woman clasps her hands together, saying, "Oh, aren't they beautiful plants?" She leans in conspiratorially. "Supposedly, they protect against evil spirits when they're placed in the four corners, if you believe in that kind of thing, but who knows? And a little protection never hurts!

"We have quite a few of the leis inside where you check out, but the plants are right over here." She waves for Leilani to follow her and leads the way towards the front of the nursery. The woman stops in front of a section that holds healthy green, yellow, red, and orange plants. "Here we are! This section is full of ti leaf plants. If you find ones you'd like to purchase, just take them inside. There you can check out, and by the checkouts are the leis in a special refrigerator."

Leilani thanks the woman and bends down to inspect the plants as the woman heads back to where she is working. Leilani pulls out her phone and sends a group text message to the others so they can find her in the nursery, and soon they are each carrying two ti plants each, the plants snuggled tightly in their arms as they head for the registers.

It doesn't take long before Glenn spots a couple of stand-up refrigerators against the wall next to the registers. Inside are full of colorful leis and other stunning Hawaiian bouquets in tall and short vases. Leilani pulls out six cool containers from the refrigerator. She thinks for a minute, then grabs a seventh just in case they need an extra for any reason. Teddy wheels over a cart he's found, and they all place the plants they're holding as well as the leis onto it before making their way to the checkout line.After paying, the group makes their way to the car. Leilani and Aaliyah get in, resting the lei containers on their laps, while Teddy and Glenn place the plants in the trunk. After a short drive, they park in front of Leilani's property, their eyes fixed on the looming house, but no one makes a move to exit the car, afraid that something will jump out at them and do them harm.

Finally, Aaliyah breaks the silence when her foot brushes up against the bag containing Stan's still warm breakfast. "We better get this inside to Stan so he can eat. We don't want a hungry, or a *hangry*, Stan."

Teddy glances over to the cars on the street. "It looks like Stan's car isn't here, so we'll have to put it in the refrigerator for him until he gets back." He opens his door and steps out, freezing when he hears a soft, hollow whisper. His head snaps around to see where the whispering is coming from, fear in his eyes. The sound comes again: a wind chime hanging from a porch on a house across the street. He sighs in relief, relaxing as the whispering chimes continue before walking to the trunk and popping it open so that they can unpack the plants.

Aaliyah holds up the food bag and says, "I'll go inside and put this in the fridge then." She hops out of the car and heads for the front door, her eyes scanning the windows as she moves closer.

Leilani collects four of the leis containers and follows Aaliyah to the front door. "I'll go with you so I can put these in the fridge too. Don't want them getting too hot before we have the chance to wear them during the investigation." She carefully maneuvers the containers to one hand and pulls her keys free from her pocket. "Plus, I have the keys." She chuckles as she unlocks the door and steps aside as she balances the containers so that they don't fall.

Aaliyah grabs a container from the top and pushes open the front door, entering the quiet house with Leilani at her heels. Attempting normalcy, they talk about how they will need to go back to the nursery once things have calmed down and take their time to study the flowers and other plants to add to their own gardens. Glenn and Teddy follow a few moments later carrying the ti plants and set them down on the porch so they can plant them in the yard in a little while. The boys can hear the girls putting away the leis in the kitchen. They eye the closed office door, not hearing any movement inside. Their eyes roam up the stairs to the closed doors, the entire house quiet. Glenn still feels uneasy being in the house and still wishes he had left last night with his wife, but now he has to stay since he promised he would help.

Teddy turns when he hears Aaliyah and Leilani walk out of the kitchen to join them in the foyer. He raises his eyebrows as he sees the two girls grinning and shifts his weight from one leg to the other to face them. "Okay, what are you two up to?"

Leilani stops in front of them. "I know we need to get some sleep so we can be ready for tonight, but Aaliyah and I started talking about movies, and, well..." She smiles at Glenn and Teddy innocently. "Maybe we could watch a few movies before we have to take our naps?" She asks with her hands clasped in front of her chest, as if she is begging the boys to say yes.

Chapter Thirteen

A dragon soars through the sky above a small town, its shadow causing the villagers to run, screaming, and staring up at the dark belly of the beast. Fire erupts out of the dragon's opened mouth and rains down onto the houses and ground below. The fire hungrily eats at the carts and houses it touches while the humans continue to run away. Some stumble over themselves, nearly being eaten by the flames. A man rides in on a black steed, sword drawn, and yells as he rushes in to save the little town from the fierce dragon.

Leilani pulls a few pieces of popcorn from the bowl and pops them in her mouth. It is their second movie and third bowl of popcorn while the afternoon slowly fades outside. Teddy sits on the couch to her left while Glenn and Aaliyah cuddle on her right on the matching sea-foam green loveseat. She smiles as she watches Glenn and Aaliyah giggle and chat about the movie, making fun of some characters. She smiles lightly, and she turns her attention to Teddy, watching him as he munches on some popcorn while watching the man on the horse run his sword through the dragon's foot to cause it to become maimed. She continues to watch him for a bit before she turns her attention back to the movie, seeing the maiden kiss the young hero. She remembers how she used to love these magical fantasies as a little girl because she always dreamed of herself as the maiden being rescued by some handsome knight in shining armor.

In her dreams, the knight sweeps her off her feet and takes her off to some far-off exotic land where they get married and live in a beautiful cottage. But she grew up and her dreams never came true, so she went to school, dated a few great, as well as a few not-so-great, guys, and continued to drive herself forward in life. Just because she hasn't found her prince or her knight in shining armor yet doesn't mean she wouldn't. Blinking a few times, her eyes refocus on the screen to see the maiden talking to the King about the bravery of the man and telling her secret that she is the missing princess who had run away because the King had been trying to force her to marry a man she hated.

The movie goes on for another twenty minutes as the King and Queen celebrate the return of their daughter and the marriage of their daughter to the knight. Leilani smiles a small sad smile before she switches off the movie and checks her watch. She stifles a yawn before standing up to stretch, her guests following suit. They clean up their mess, take the bowls with them into the kitchen and wash them.

"Leilani, do you have a book I can borrow so I can read before bed?" Aaliyah asks as she puts the last bowl away.

Leilani nods, "Oh yea, sure, I have quite a few in the office that you can borrow." She motions for the three to follow her before she looks back at them, confused. "Has Stan returned yet? It has been a few hours since we have seen him." She pushes the door open and flips on the light, leading them inside. She looks around but her office looks untouched, even though she knows Stan had been working in there earlier. Aaliyah, Glenn, and Teddy each check their cell phones to see if they have any texts or calls from Stan since they had put their phones on silent for the movies. None of the phones show Stan has tried to call or left a text message.

"He probably fell asleep while he was working at home. I doubt he slept a lot last night after all the excitement," Teddy says, doing his best to sound confident in what he is saying, even though he has a sinking feeling. "I think I'll text him and find out where he is now. I won't call him just in case he is asleep. I don't want to disturb him." Teddy opens his messages on his phone, picks Stan's number, and quickly types his friend a message. He hits send and joins the others by the bookshelves.

Aaliyah is perusing the titles while Glenn and Leilani talk about a book Glenn has picked out to read. Teddy smiles at Glenn and Leilani before he walks over to the shelves to grab himself a book. Aaliyah snags one and tells Glenn she'll see him in their room, already eager to read the book. She waves before she leaves the office to head upstairs to the bedroom. Glenn looks at Leilani before he excuses himself and heads out of the office after his wife, not wanting her to be alone for even a second.

Teddy finds a horror paranormal book written by a newer author and turns to face Leilani. "Okay, I've found my book. Should we head upstairs?"

Leilani smiles and walks over to him. "Sounds good to me. Which book did you pick out to read?"

Teddy holds it up so she can read the title, *Backlash*. "I've read a few of her other books and really enjoyed them. I'm glad to see you have one I haven't read yet. And I'm glad to see that you have all her books so far in your library. I may have to borrow a few another time."

"Oh, I think you'll like that one. She apparently dreamed up some of it and turned it into a book," Leilani tells him as they head up stairs. "I've read an article about her, and she says that her dreams are where she gets most of her story ideas from and even has several dream journals."

They reach the top of the stairs and stand at the top awkwardly for a moment, Leilani moving her foot back and forth as if she is squishing an invisible bug. She then points over her shoulder towards her closed bedroom door. "Well, I better get into bed so I can rest up before our long night tonight. I can't even remember the last time I had to stay up all night long and could function the next day. I am glad I don't have to work tomorrow, or I'd be a walking zombie." She laughs as she takes a few steps towards her bedroom.

Teddy laughs at the joke. He lightly taps a finger on the book. "I'll come and get you when it's time to do the investigation tonight. We'll show you how to set up the equipment. That way, for the next investigation you go on with us, you'll know what to do."

Leilani's eyes open wide at the prospect of helping Teddy tonight with setting up the equipment and going on future investigations with her new friends. But a part of her silences that excitement when she thinks about having to come face to face with other ghosts like Roy. Leilani's mother always taught her she shouldn't be afraid of fear and to embrace it while facing it with the help of her ancestors. At that moment, she remembers the plants are still sitting on her porch, forgotten. "That sounds great! I just need to take care of one thing and then I'll either read until I nap or just go straight into napping." She turns and heads back down the stairs. She glances back at Teddy, before she continues down the stairs, not wanting to bother him with asking for help.

Teddy watches her retreat downstairs and heads to his room. He sets the book down on the bed before he walks back to the stairs and heads down to help Leilani with whatever task she has forgotten to do. He opens the front door to see she has taken two of the plants and is already off somewhere in the yard planting them. He grabs a couple of the plants and heads off into the yard to plant them. Several minutes later, all the plants are securely in the ground and have been watered. Teddy and Leilani head back indoors, hot, tired, and covered in dirt.

"I think I'm going to take a quick shower before I even think of dropping onto my bed and closing my eyes. I feel sticky and gross from all that work, but I'm sure I'll be napping instead of reading now," Leilani says with a little laugh.

Teddy says, "A quick shower and a nap for me too." They reach the top of the stairs and head off in opposite directions.

Teddy goes into the room, grabs some clean clothes to change into after a nice, hot shower, and is about to walk out of the room, when he pauses. His eyes fall on the book he picked out from Leilani's library and places the clothes down on the end of the bed before picking up the book and sitting . He flips the book open to the first page, eager to read what the author wrote.

Leilani takes a quick shower, happy to be rid of the sweat and grime. She walks out of the bathroom, dressed in her softest pajamas and her hair wrapped in a towel. She collapses on the edge of the bed and towel dries her hair as she stares at the wall. Once her hair is somewhat dry, she drops the wet towel onto the floor and falls backwards onto her comfortable bed with a sigh. She focuses on the ceiling, wondering how the investigation will go tonight. She wonders if they will learn anything from the children, or if Roy will attack instead.

She shudders and imagines the four of them, or five if Stan joins them, sitting in the dining room, talking to Tina and Tony through the equipment. She looks at Teddy, Stan, Glenn, and Aaliyah, feeling anxious as they set everything up, the dining room looking quite different with all the equipment around the room where usually there would be food and drink. Leilani rings her hands together as she watches the group finish putting up the cameras and place the other instruments on the table.

"Well, we're ready to start," Stan says as he turns on the last camera to record the entryway of the kitchen. He takes a seat next to Leilani while Teddy sits at the head of the table and Glenn and Aaliyah sit across from her. Teddy smiles reassuringly at her as he turns on the EVP recorder and the voice recorder for the session.

Glenn asks questions, pausing after each one for a minute to two before he continues to give the spirits enough time to answer before he asks the next question. Aaliyah uses a device to check any changes in the air temperature while Teddy uses a heat sensing camera, which will show him if another person were to enter the room. Stan quickly gets up to check the cameras to make sure they are all working properly and don't need fresh batteries.

Leilani hears what sounds like a whisper from behind her, causing her to turn in her chair. Glenn's voice becomes a low buzz, mixing with the sounds of beeping from another piece of equipment from across the room. She looks around behind her. No one is there, but the whispering continues in her ear. She laughs, chiding herself that she is being silly and that the ghosts won't try to hurt them. Maybe Roy, but she is confident Tony and Tina wouldn't hurt her or her friends. She shakes her head and turns back to face the others, the whispering now gone, the beeping and Glenn asking questions having gone quiet, too.

She shivers a bit, and rubs her bare arms as she turns to face Teddy to ask him what is going on, but her voice catches in her throat when she sees Teddy hunched over the table with blood spilling out of a large wound on his head. She covers her mouth as she stares into Teddy's dead gaze. The equipment he was using is now laying on the ground useless. Her breathing comes out quicker as she turns to see Roy pulling an ax free from Aaliyah's neck, already having butchered Stan and Glenn. Their blood is pooling under their bodies and dripping off the table to the floor. The sounds of the dripping blood become deafening as Roy slowly turns to face her. His eyes glint evilly in the room's lighting and he clutches the ax, ready to swing at her exposed neck.

Roy's laugh mixes with the sounds of dripping blood, making her dizzy, and the strong iron smell of fresh blood makes her feel nauseous. She throws her hands up as the ax makes an arch straight for her neck and face. A blood-curdling scream escapes her terrified lips and past the lump that has formed in her throat, nearly choking her. Roy's face melts away along with the room as Leilani pulls herself up into a sitting position on her bed in her darkened room.

Leilani blinks several times as the last of the nightmare fades from her mind, and she wakes herself up more. She looks around quickly to make sure she is alone. She catches her breath as beads of sweat roll down her forehead, making her uncomfortable. Carefully wiping the sweat away so it doesn't get into her eyes, she stands up on a pair of wobbly legs. She walks over to her bedroom window, pushes back to the curtains, and heaves it open, not caring that the evening breeze is still warm. It still brushes away the fear that she feels from the nightmare and warms her from the chill brought on by the nightmare. Leilani takes in several breaths as she watches the last of the sunset dip down behind the horizon, ending the day.

She turns around and stands completely still as she listens to the house, but there is only silence. Leilani heads into the bathroom, uses it, and stares once again into the mirror as she washes her hands longer than usual, the water gradually growing hotter. She yelps and pulls her hands out from under once the water becomes scalding hot. Leilani shakes her red hands and turns off the faucet.

As Leilani leaves the bathroom, she hears the faint sounds of an alarm coming from one of the other rooms. She walks out of her room after she dresses in other clothes and heads down the dark stairs. Leilani stifles a yawn as she heads into the kitchen and makes a pot of fresh coffee.

Leilani leans against the counter as she listens to her coffee maker heat the delicious hot liquid as it splashes down into the glass coffee pot below. Behind her, she can hear movement from the others upstairs and in her office. Her office? She spins around and hurries out just as Stan seems to phase through the office doors right in front of her.

"Stan! Oh my gosh, you scared the life out of me," Leilani exclaims with one hand on her chest and after she has fought down a scream.

Stan smiles at her. "Oh geez, I'm sorry about that, Leilani. I was just coming to see who was walking around down here." He shoves his hands into his jean pockets. "So, what's the plan?"

Leilani heads back into the kitchen, Stan stumbling a bit after her. "I'm making coffee right now and something to eat." She stands in front of the coffee maker to see the coffee is done. She moves to her left, grabbing coffee mugs and placing them on the counter.

"Oh, none for me, thanks," Stan says as he holds up a hand. "I've already reached my limit, and if I drink anymore, I will explode."

Leilani laughs as she puts away the fifth coffee mug. "Well, we definitely can't have any of that happen." She points to the refrigerator. "Oh, did you, by any chance, see the food in there that we brought back for you?"

Stan looks sheepish. "Oh yeah! I came in and got hungry, so I poked around in the fridge and found the food. I didn't want to bother anyone since I had a feeling you all were napping to get ready for tonight." He shifts his weight from foot to foot and shrugs a bit. "So? Investigation will be tonight then?"

Leilani nods and heads over to the fridge, peeking inside in order to find something quick and easy to make for dinner. She grabs the strawberry jam, deciding to make peanut butter and jelly sandwiches, carrots, and potato chips. She prepares the sandwiches, making several and places them on the island on a paper plate before she pours herself a cup of coffee and takes a sip, looking up at Stan. She puts down the mug and says, "Are you ready for another long night? Did you get any rest today?"

Stan clears his throat and says, "Yea, I um, got some work done because I kind of fell asleep at my desk while cruising the tapes. I'll try to work on the footage again later after I get some sleep after this investigation, I promise." He chuckles and turns when the upstairs doors open, and they can hear Glenn and Aaliyah. He pokes his head out of the kitchen and laughs as he moves back into the kitchen.

Leilani places two big bags of potato chips and a big bag of baby carrots on the countertop next to the sandwiches. She looks up at Stan as he laughs and heads into the dining room so he can get started on setting up. Leilani raises an eyebrow as she watches Stan retreat to the other room. "Stan, what did you do?"

"Only gave me and Aaliyah a heart attack," Glenn says as he and his wife enter the kitchen. "We were just talking about

Stan and then suddenly his head pops out from behind the wall."

"I think my heart literally stopped when I saw him grinning at us like the devil," Aaliyah chimes in as she gently pats her chest. "I hate when Stan does that!"

Leilani laughs and points to the dining room entrance behind her. "He ran in there if you want to kill him, Aaliyah."

Aaliyah rushes to the dining room, sticking her head inside. "Stan!" She leans back out and looks at Leilani, her nose wrinkled. "Yea, I can't kill him right now. He's already setting up the equipment." She grabs a cup and fills it with coffee before she sits down at the counter. "I'll kill him once he's done doing all the work," she says as she winks at Leilani and takes a sip of her coffee while her husband pours himself a cup.

A few moments later, another door opens from upstairs, and they can hear Teddy walk across to the bathroom, close the door, and turn on the water for a quick shower. Aaliyah raises her eyes up towards the ceiling as she listens to the water, then looks back at the other two. She takes another sip of her coffee and enjoys the hot liquid as it enters her veins and wakes her up more.

"He must have fallen asleep before he could take a shower," Leilani says as she takes half a sandwich and bites into it. She chews, then swallows before she talks again. "Teddy helped me plant the ti plants in the four corners of the yard, so we were both pretty hot and sticky when we finished. He said he would take a shower then nap. I guess the nap was too strong to resist." She takes another bite and chews thoughtfully for a moment. "Does it seem different to you? Like, does it feel different to you guys here at the house?"

Glenn walks up behind Aaliyah, taking a sip from his steaming mug and shakes his head. "No, not that I can tell." He takes another swig from his coffee, grabbing some chips and shoving them into his mouth.

Aaliyah reflects on what Leilani has asked for a moment before she nods her head. "Maybe it takes a bit for the plants to work on getting rid of the evil in a house?" She picks up a paper plate and places a few carrots, some chips, and a half of a sandwich on it. "Is there some sort of prayer or chant that you have to say in order to activate the plants or that we should have said before they were planted?" She nibbles on the carrot as she looks up at Leilani, raising her eyebrows.

"I don't think so," Leilani says. She speaks slowly as she thinks about her conversation with Nalani. "Nalani's grandmother didn't say there were any special words or prayers to say, and she would have told me if there had been." Leilani sits down at the island beside Aaliyah. "Maybe we were supposed to get them blessed?"

Glenn puts his coffee down and pulls out his cell phone to do a quick search on the matter while the girls continue to eat their dinner. After several minutes, Teddy joins them, looking more refreshed and dirt free. Glenn nods hello but continues to search for anything about a way to 'activate' the protection from the ti plants against the evil spirits.

Leilani lowers her mug and cradles it in between her hands. "All right, so how do we begin this investigation?" She picks up a carrot and munches on it while she looks between the three for answers.

Stan pipes in as he walks in from the other room, having finished setting everything up. "We'll turn all the cameras on and all the other equipment we use, then we can start asking questions to Tony and Tina. Hopefully, Roy will stay away tonight, and this session will be drama free." He glances at his watch. "We can start in a half an hour so that you all can finish eating. But while you're eating, I'm going to go back in and check and recheck to make sure that everything is working. I also need to make sure that the extra batteries are ready for use." Stan heads back into the dining room to check the equipment again.

Glenn watches Stan disappear into the dining room then leans in closer to Aaliyah, Teddy, and Leilani, lowering his voice so that Stan can't hear him in the other room, "Hey, does Stan look really tired to you?"

Leilani bites into her sandwich as she tries to picture Stan's face while Aaliyah nods. "He seems to have dark circles under his eyes."

"Stan told me he slept when he got home. He told me he worked on the computer but fell asleep at his desk. That's most likely why he wasn't here when we came back from breakfast and plant shopping," Leilani says. "He also had the food we brought him earlier, so he said he's not hungry." She finishes her carrots and sandwich before she stands in order to throw away her paper plate. She knits her eyebrows together when she turns to look at the others. "Do you think we need to worry about him?"

Teddy shakes his head. "If he took a nap, then I think he'll be fine for the investigation, but I would keep the coffee hot and the pot full just in case." He sips from the mug of coffee Leilani handed him earlier.

Leilani takes a sip from her coffee again before Stan sticks his head out to give them a thumbs up, letting them know they can begin the investigation.

Once Stan has gone back into the room, Glenn looks at the others and stands, taking his coffee and placing it by the pot to use later. "Well, are you all ready to get started?"

Leilani and Aaliyah get up and carry their coffee mugs into the dining room with Glenn and Teddy at their heels. Glenn snaps his fingers and spins back around, heading back inside the kitchen, only to reappear with the special leis. He places them on the table, picks up the first one, opens the container, and gently lifts it up from the plastic case. He lays it down gently on the table and does the same with the other four leis, being extra careful as to not harm them. Stan eyes the leis before he heads over to the nearest camera to turn it on.

Stan hits record on each video camera and joins them at the table. Leilani takes a deep breath as the nightmare she had earlier slips its way back into her mind. The images of the bloody bodies sit in front of her, staring at her with their dead gazes. She does her best to shove the images out of her mind as Aaliyah talks to the camera, telling the camera what they are about to do and what they hope to accomplish with the investigation.

Chapter Fourteen

R oy paces back and forth in the upstairs master bedroom, listening to the house as the group naps around him. He glares down at Leilani as she tosses and turns in her sleep, unable to get comfortable or relax fully. He smirks as he watches her struggle with her dreams, as she has done since moving into the house thanks to him. He stops pacing when Leilani groans and flops onto her back again as she pushes through the dark dreams that cloak her mind. Growing tired of watching the woman struggle with sleep, Roy walks to the door and opens it, leaving it open so that she will see it when she wakes up and grows increasingly scared before he heads over to the next bedroom. He opens the door and stares into the room at Aaliyah and Glenn, who are sleeping peacefully in each other's arms, their love for one another protecting them from him now. Roy looks disgusted as he backs out of the room and leaves the sleeping couple alone, turning to the next door.

Roy opens the next door, Teddy's room, and stops in his tracks. Teddy sits on the bed, fully engrossed in some book. He's lying on the bed, eyes glued to the page in front of him, his mouth slightly moving as he continues to read. Roy grins and takes a step into the room so that he can mess with Teddy, but as soon as he steps inside, a dark shadow materializes in the left corner, a shadow that he has never seen before. Roy hesitates as the shadow looms up beside the bed, too tall to be Tina or Tony, and Roy doesn't know of any other ghosts that are in the house. He monitors the shadow as it seems to grow darker and closer to Teddy's side. Not wanting to butt heads with the shadow until he knows who it is, he puts his hands up as if he is surrendering and slowly steps out of the room. He quietly closes the door, blocking the strange shadow from sight before he turns to go sulk downstairs. He stops halfway to the stairs when he sees Tony quietly closing Leilani's bedroom door and Tina quietly closing Aaliyah and Glenn's bedroom door.

He shakes his head and walks down the stairs, aggravated, "Fine, whatever." He shoves his hands into the pockets of the blood-splattered jumpsuit he wore the night he died, grumbling to himself because he hadn't scared Teddy. He wanders around downstairs, not sure why he feels so strange, so off, unlike this morning when he was ready to destroy the house and kill the people inside. He steps into the office and falls into the chair, growling up at the ceiling as he spins the chair as fast as he can.

Finally, after what seems like an eternity, the doors upstairs open and the occupants make their way downstairs, having woken up from their naps. Suddenly he hears one female let out a cry and he slips off the chair, hurrying out of the office wall to see Leilani has found Stan. Roy makes a face because he doesn't remember the front door opening, since he can hear everything that happens inside the house. And hadn't he killed that fool the night before?

Roy remembers sneaking up behind Stan as Stan saved everything to a USB drive and turned off the computer. Once the computer had gone black and the USB drive was set off to the side, Stan stretched and yawned widely as he readied to stand to get ready for bed. Exhaustion set in after a long day. He froze when he looked into the black screen and spotted Roy behind him. Roy's eyes narrowed in a sickening glare as he watched Stan. Stan breathed harder as he felt his heart pounding in his chest as he stared in fear at the menacing evil spirit that meandered closer. Roy seized the man sitting in front of him, knowing that he could take the man down easily. Without hesitation, Roy used his energy to slam Stan's face directly into the computer screen, laughing at the sounds of the glass shattering around Stan's face.

He pulled Stan's head back out of the glass, seeing the poor man's face cut up with blood seeping out of the cuts, a piece of the screen embedded deep inside Stan's left eye. Stan tried to let out a scream, but only a small pain-filled gurgle escaped his sliced lips, causing the cuts to open more. Roy snickered as he slammed the man's face back into the shattered and sparking screen. Stan's body spasmed as the sudden jolt of electricity shot through his damaged face and into his body.

Roy shakes himself out of the deliciously gruesome memory and watches as Stan walks into the kitchen with Leilani, talking and laughing. He hears Stan say something about eating the food that they had brought to him, and Roy scoffs. Dead people can't eat! But if Stan has eaten, then does that mean that Roy had only wished he had killed Stan? Had he daydreamed all of that and only watched Stan power off the computer and go to bed? Roy shakes his head again when he hears more voices and once again has to pull himself out of his own foggy mind to see the others have emerged from their rooms. He covers his ears, suddenly feeling as if the laughter is much louder as they pass him and enter the kitchen. He follows Teddy into the kitchen and listens to the chatter, flinching from time to time as the sounds of their voices grow louder, then get quiet and suddenly loud again. This has never happened before, so he doesn't understand what is causing the changes in the voices volumes or what has suddenly made him feel sick. He's a ghost and ghosts can't get sick. Right?

Roy looks around the kitchen to see if maybe he has missed something in the room that is making him feel this way. He can't see anything but he knows there is something wrong. He walks up behind Leilani and growls at her, wishing he could reach out and strangle her just to get it over with. But he has a plan to torment the group while they are doing their investigation. He would try to get them alone and murder them one by one. Roy thinks for a moment and remembers how fun it was to kill the family together. Maybe he should do the same with this group.

Roy coughs a little as he feels sick again and steps away from Leilani. She didn't look any different but he felt as if she is the reason he felt this way. He has to hide and regain his strength before he can put his plan to action. Tonight, they all die! But for now he slinks away like a wounded animal out of the kitchen and up the stairs. Roy slips into Leilani's bedroom and hides in the closet. He sits with his back against the wall and lets the blinding darkness cradle him. Roy lets memories of his girl walking out of the closet in new outfits find his blurry mind. He chuckles when they had hid in the closet once when her family came over to talk to her about the house and about selling it. They had found them but just sitting in the dark, holding hands made Roy feel like the richest man alive. He knew she wouldn't survive the cancer, but at that special moment, he felt as if she would live with him forever. Maybe that was why he always hid in Leilani's closet, because it reminded him of happier times.

Chapter Fifteen

Roy opens his eyes as sunlight streams through the closet doors. How long has he been in there? He stretches his arms and crawls out when he hears someone talking. But it didn't sound like Leilani or any of the others who have invaded the house. And why does he feel so heavy all of a sudden? He always feels light and free since he is a ghost after all.

Roy stares in disbelief as he stares into the eyes of the woman he loves, but how can that be? She passed away several years ago because of cancer, but now she is standing in her room, decorated the way she liked, and smiling at him.

"Tracy?" he whispers as he walks closer to her.

She smiles and takes a hold of his hands in hers, pulling him closer to her. "Roy, I have been waiting for you and aso happy to see you've made it." Tracy squeezes his hands and leans closer, kissing him gently.

Roy enjoys her soft lips against his, the magic he always felt with her kisses. Her kisses make his heart race and his spirits soar. He wraps his arms around Tracy, noting how she doesn't feel sickly. He lets himself smile, something he hasn't done in years. He breaks the kiss and just holds her, smelling her hair, feeling her breath against his cheek, and enjoying touching her again. Roy's body stiffens when he feels a change in Tracy. Roy runs his fingers through her hair and pulls his hand back, covered in her long black hair. He lets out a strangled sound as he lets her hair fall into a clump at his feet.

Tracy pulls back from Roy and looks into his eyes, her own emerald gaze dull as it had been before she passed. "Roy, will you always love me?"

Roy steps back as he watches Tracy's face sink in, her skin becomes pale, and her hair continues to rain down around her feet, just as it had when her chemotherapy had taken effect. Roy swallows as his happiness slips away and he watches in horror as the woman he loved wasted away before his eyes again. Roy closes his eyes as Tracy keeps asking if he will always love her.

Roy covers his ears until her voice disappears. When he opens his eyes again, Tracy is gone and he is back in the closet at night. He felt Leilani and the others downstairs and it causes his anger to bubble up inside of him. He has to get rid of the others. It was time he got Tracy's house back.

"Yes, Tracy, I will always love you," he whispers into the darkness of the closet around him.

Chapter Sixteen

Leilani sits nervously at the table, her eyes darting to each of her new friends, then to the instruments on the table in front of her. She has studied online what each instrument is, how they are used, and what they each catch during an investigation. Stan stands beside one camera just as he had during Leilani's nightmare, and it causes her to swallow hard as she places her slightly sweating palms down on the cool wood tabletop. She listens to Aaliyah talking into the tape recorder while Aaliyah explains the setup of the room they are in, which room they will investigate, and a quick back story about what had happened in that room twenty years ago. Glenn speaks up, telling the tape recorder what they hope to achieve with the investigation: ridding the house of Roy's evil spirit and contacting Tony and Tina again.

"Are you ready?"

Leilani blinks several times as she draws her attention away from the tabletop where she had been staring off into space and looks up to see Aaliyah looking at her worriedly. Leilani nods her head, picking up the thermometer so she can help with the investigation. "I'm ready," she assures the group, pulling a notebook and pen in front of her to take notes during the investigation. She takes the temperature of the room and writes it down to have a base temperature for the investigation. This way while they investigate, if there are any changes, they can note them. She clears her throat before she reads off her findings to the recorder.

Aaliyah smiles and gives Leilani a thumbs up and Leilani allows herself to breathe a bit more steadily, feeling better about the investigation now that she knows she can help them. She looks back down at her equipment, scribbling down the time and the temperature, not wanting to miss any changes. Stan steps behind another camera that reads heat signatures, and he raises his eyebrows when he notices a change. He points at the door, which makes Leilani instantly take a new temperature reading and write it down before she turns and aims the temperature gauge at the door.

Glenn looks towards the doorway and leans forward in his chair. "If there is anyone hiding in the kitchen, you are more than welcome to come join us."

"Tina? Tony? Is that you? Are you afraid to enter the room because of what happened here with you and your family?" Aaliyah asks, as she faces the doorway. Her voice grows quieter when she talks about the dining room and the sad events that took place there. "We have two chairs here and you are more than welcome to come sit and talk with us if you'd like."

Stan stays behind the camera and watches as someone peaks around the corner to look at the strange group in the dining room. The child shoots back behind the wall for a moment then reappears, this time accompanied by another child, who seems shorter than the first child. He grins as he glances over the camera this time, waving his hand to coax the two into the room, "Hey Tony... hi Tina."

Leilani hands her things quickly to Aaliyah before she jumps out of her chair to join Stan. Stan moves over so she can see what he is seeing through the camera screen. She smiles when she sees Tina and Tony slowly come out of hiding, standing hand in hand in the doorway. She raises her eyes to the door, excited that she is finally seeing the children, no longer afraid of them since she knows now that they are here protecting her from Roy. She looks back at the screen and waves, her excitement growing when she sees the children wave back at her on the screen.

Aaliyah watches Leilani's face light up and she knows that something remarkable has happened. Glenn and Aaliyah continue to take readings, writing changes that are happening in notebooks while Stan moves to another camera in order to make sure none of the batteries have died since Tina and Tony are most likely using the energy in order to appear.

"Dead battery," Stan says when he notices one camera has turned off and wouldn't turn back on. He moves to the next and chuckles, "Another dead battery."

Glenn slips out of his chair and kneels next to a giant black equipment bag, rustling through it until he finds the stack of extra batteries. He stands up and moves behind the two cameras that Stan had said needed new batteries and changes them while Stan heads to the other side of the room to check the last two other cameras. Leilani stares at Tina and Tony, still in awe that she can see them through the screen. Stan motions for Leilani to take her seat after he finishes checking the cameras and Glenn puts the dead batteries away in the bag's side. Leilani heads back to her chair and sits down, accepting the equipment back from Aaliyah, and returns her eyes to the spot where she last saw Tina and Tony.

Aaliyah gently pats two extra chairs, and she looks at the door, not knowing if they are still standing there or not. "We won't hurt you; we promise. Please come and sit with us." She visibly shivers when the air around the chairs becomes colder.

Leilani catches the temperature changes with her equipment as Tony and Tina walk past her and sit down in the chairs. Glenn takes his seat and passes Aaliyah the voice recorder so it is closer to the children to better catch their voices if they decide to talk.

Aaliyah places the voice recorder closer to the edge of the table and makes sure that the extra batteries and tapes are within reach when she needs to switch them out. She looks back at the chairs and smiles gently. "Tina, Tony, my name is Aaliyah. I'm Glenn's wife and friends with Teddy, Stan, and Leilani. Stan is the one behind the cameras while Glenn is sitting to my left. You already know Leilani, and Teddy is the one sitting on the other side of the table in front of me."

Leilani turns to face the chairs, smiling as she says, "Tina, Tony, I wanted to tell you how grateful I am how you two have been protecting me. And I also want to apologize for throwing away your toys. If I had known that you two were still here, then I would have never tossed them in the trash." She rests her hand on the table, her fingers brushing the lei, smiling. "I hope you can forgive me for that, and if you'd like, I can wash them and get them all cleaned up, so they aren't all dirty."

A shift occurs and one of the cold spots seems to rush out of the room, the cold coaxing Leilani to follow. Leilani glances at the others before she springs out of the chair, leaving the others. Stan clears his throat, catching Teddy, Aaliyah and Glenn's attention. He points at the chair where one child still sits so they can continue with the investigation.

"Remember using this box from last night?" Glenn asks as he turns on a black box and waves his hand in front of it. The sensor catches his movement and lights up the bulbs from green to red, emitting a sound. He takes his hand away, stopping the lights and sounds. "We would like to ask you some questions and if you could use this box to answer us, that would be amazing." He hands it to Aaliyah, who places it next to the recorder. The sensor points out towards the chair where the child sits, so it would be easier for the ghost to manipulate. "We will ask you yes and no questions. To answer the question with a yes, make the lights and sound go off, but to answer no, just leave the box alone. Do you understand?"

The box squeals to let them know the child understands and will answer their questions. Aaliyah flips her notebook to a new blank page so she can record the questions and the answers as they talk to the children. She dates the piece of paper and writes the first question that she would like to ask. She looks at the chair once she has scribbled down the question and clears her throat to let the others know she will ask the first question. "Are you Tina?"

The lights stay off and the box doesn't make a sound, so they know it is Tony who has stayed with them while Tina took Leilani somewhere else in the house. Aaliyah writes Tony's name, then sits ready to write the next question and answer.

"Tony, is Roy close to us right now?" Stan asks as he leans against the wall and looks over the camera at Tony's chair. Once again, the lights and sound stay off.

Aaliyah writes the question and answer before she writes the next question she wants to ask and talks as she finishes writing it. "Tony, is Roy upstairs somewhere?" She jumps when the lights shine all the way, letting her know the answer is yes. She shivers as she writes a positive yes next to the question and writes a new question. "Do you know where he is upstairs?" Again, the EVP recorder springs to life as Tony answers the question with a scary yes. She scribbles down the questions and answers in her notebook, feeling sick, but still wants to ask which room Roy is in upstairs. "Is Roy in any of the guest bedrooms?" She holds her breath as her hand floats over the paper after she has written the question, her heart pounding in her chest. The EVP box sits quietly, letting her know Roy isn't in the room where she and her husband sleep or in Teddy's or Stan's room. But she takes in a sharp breath when she thinks about the last bedroom and bathrooms that are left to ask about. "Is he in the bathroom?" Nothing.

Glenn senses his wife's reluctance to ask the next question they knew would be a yes and speaks up after clearing his throat. "Is Roy hiding in Leilani's room?" Without hesitation, the lights spring to life and the yes answer screams at them.

Stan straightens up and tilts his head back until his eyes stare up at the ceiling, slowly narrowing and shuddering when he thinks that above his head is Roy hiding in Leilani's bedroom somewhere. "Is he planning to come downstairs?" He didn't expect Tony to answer him, but a small whisper reaches his ear as Tony draws more energy so that Stan, Glenn, and Aaliyah can hear him say 'maybe'. Stan takes in a sharp breath when he hears the answer and looks down quickly at the other two, who exchange worried looks.

Meanwhile, out in the front entryway, Leilani stops and looks around, having lost the sensation of the ghost child being with her. She peeks in the office, but nothing looks out of place, nor could she sense anyone in the room. She takes a step back, ready to check the rest of the downstairs, when something catches her attention sitting near the stairs. She turns to see that Tina and Tony have found the toys and have set them up on the third to bottom stair for her. Leilani smiles and walks over to the stairs. She bends over and plucks the toys from the stairs but stops, her hands shaking, and suddenly feels dizzy. She blinks several times before she feels normal, squatting down and balancing on her heels for a moment so she can look around, wondering why she had felt dizzy. Leilani sees a figure standing at the top of the stairs, masked in the growing darkness. She hastily grabs the toys and steps back away from the stairs, not knowing who is watching her.

"Teddy?" She calls up the stairs at the strange figure, thinking it could be him, but she distinctly sees the figure's head shaking side to side. Her voice catches in her throat, but she squeaks out another name. "Roy?"

The shadow shakes its head again, then points back to the kitchen, as if telling her to go back to the others. But Leilani stands her ground, clutching the toys to her chest as she stares up at the shadow. She takes a step towards the figure on the stairs. "Who are you?" She feels like she has to know who the stranger is and that gives her courage. "Why are you here? We need to know! Are you working with Roy or against Roy?"

The shadow merely points to the kitchen a bit more urgently before it retreats into the darkness of the upstairs hallway. The sun has gone down by now and Leilani squints as she tries to find the shadow again but only sees darkness. Leilani sighs heavily and is about to walk away when one of the bedroom doors open and light spills out into the doorway and hallway. The shadow is gone!

Teddy appears behind her and Leilani jumps when he gently touches her shoulder. She glances back at him and then back up the stairs. "Teddy, there is someone up there."

Teddy looks at her worriedly and races up the stairs. He looks in each room, but he finds no one lurking in the shadows. Teddy returns to the top of the stairs and shrugs, "I couldn't find anyone in any of the rooms, Leilani. Are you sure it wasn't Tina playing a joke?"

"I am positive, Teddy. The shadow was much taller and didn't look like a girl. It looked more masculine and it pointed to the kitchen, telling me to go back to the kitchen."

Teddy shakes his head and shrugs. "Sorry, Leilani, but there is no one." He starts to head down the stairs, worried that she may have seen Roy.

Leilani sees movement behind Teddy when he is halfway down the stairs and watches in horror as Roy materializes on the top step, glaring at the back of Teddy's head. Before she can warn him, Roy leaps forward, and a scream splits through the silent house. Leilani wonders for a moment if it had been her screaming, but a little girl appears beside her, pointing up at Roy as she screams again. Teddy quickly spins around and tightens his grip when he feels his foot slip off the edge of the stair. His balance falters as his weight pushes him forward. Roy laughs as he finishes the job by collecting more energy and shoving the young man. He is looking forward to hearing Teddy's cracking bones as his body rag dolls down the stairs.

Everything instantly seems to move in slow-motion as Teddy does his best to hang onto the railing but fails, his hand unable to keep a good grip.. Roy laughs viciously, a red devilish glint in his eyes as he watches Teddy flail helplessly, teetering on the edge of the stair. Leilani stands frozen at the bottom of the stairs, the toys slipping from her hands and toppling to the floor. Tina's piercing scream rings out through the house again as she vanishes from sight, the sudden sound of someone running drowning out her voice, shaking the house to its core. For a split second, Teddy seems to float above the stairs when the air becomes thick and the lights in the upstairs hallway flicker on and off. Glenn and Aaliyah appear in the front foyer to see who screamed and why the air has suddenly shifted.

Shock and fear spread across their faces when they see Roy standing gleefully above a falling Teddy. Glenn cries out Teddy's name as he tries to race up the stairs in order to catch his friend and hopefully soften the inevitable fall on the stairs and the floor below. But before Glenn can reach Teddy, a shadow bolts down past Roy, shoving the maniac ghost hard backwards. This sends Roy reeling onto the floor of the top stair. The shadow seems to leap after Teddy, grabs the young man from behind, and pulls him safely back down onto the stairs. Once Teddy's feet are on firm ground again and he has his balance back, the shadow spins around and a deafening cry emits from where its mouth should be. The black pits where the eyes once were seems to glow angrily.

Roy leaps to his feet and snarls, leaping off the stairs at the mysterious shadow with his hands out, ready to grab the shadow's neck. The shadow lunges forward at Roy and they hit hard, the house rattling as if an earthquake had just hit. When the house shakes violently, Teddy loses his balance again, toppling into Glenn's arms, who drags Teddy down the stairs. This time both Tina and Tony appear on the bottom step, watching as the shadow tosses Roy roughly back up the stairs away from them. The kids cheer loudly, jumping up and down while pumping their arms up in the air. They root for the strange shadow as the shadow stalks up the stairs after the fallen Roy.

Leilani gently grabs onto Teddy's arm as she peers up the stairs at the fighting ghosts. The house shakes again as the two fall off the stairs, over the banister, and hit the floor without a sound. The two hitting the ground seem to resonate throughout the house, sending some sort of invisible shock wave that presses on the group from all sides. The group jumps when the ghosts fall, and they quickly move so that they can see around the stairs and into the narrow hallway that leads back to a bathroom. But once there, they see that the shadow and Roy have vanished. Teddy looks back at the stairs to see Tony and Tina have also disappeared, their toys abandoned at the foot of the stairs. The lights stop flickering and the house becomes still, growing dark as all the light bulbs die, a few even exploding. Glenn holds Aaliyah's hand, pulling her close and whispering low into her ear to help calm her down. Soon some lights slowly turn on, and the four turn to see Stan standing at the kitchen entrance, the lights still out, and a camera in his hand. He flips the lights back on in the kitchen with his mouth open a bit, scanning the room with the camera.

Stan closes his mouth and swallows as he looks at the group. "Wow! So, now there is another ghost in the house, and it looked like he or she was kicking Roy's butt." He stops recording and looks around before he looks back at the others. "Are Tina and Tony still out here with you guys, or did they vanish with Roy and the shadow?"

Glenn shakes his head, not knowing anything about Tina or Tony. He continues to hold Aaliyah close while they slowly walk together to the dining room. Stan hands the camera to Glenn as they pass. He's shaking and can barely hold the thing anymore. Glenn takes the camera, catching it as it slips out of Stan's hand. He looks at Stan, confused at his friend's weird behavior, and notices how pale Stan's face has become and how exhausted he looks. He is about to ask what's wrong, but Stan just smiles at Glenn and walks around the stairs to survey the spot where Roy and the dark shadow vanished. Teddy turns around to face Leilani, who is still hiding behind him, and he gently takes her hand, squeezing it lightly. Leilani pulls herself out of her trance and looks up at Teddy, feeling better once their gazes lock, letting out a quick breath.

"Let's go to the dining room and sit down, okay?" Teddy says, raising his eyebrows to soften his own frightened look.

Leilani nods and they leave Stan alone in the hallway where he is still trying to figure out where the ghosts have vanished. Leilani stops at the foot of the stairs and gingerly picks up the discarded toys. "I'll wash these in the morning for the kids," she mutters as she looks down at them. "Then they can play with clean toys." She allows Teddy to lead her into the dining room to join the other two.

Teddy leans against the back of Leilani's chair as he looks at the other two. "So, we know the kids are trying to help us, and now it seems someone else in the other realm has stepped in to give us a hand. I say we try to contact the shadow we just saw. I want to find out who he or she is and to thank them for having helped me."

"Do you think this new ghost will have enough strength to talk to us?" Leilani asks, as she turns in her seat and looks up at Teddy. "They had to have used a lot of energy in order to save you and to fight Roy."

Teddy opens his mouth to answer but quickly shuts it when the lights flicker for a moment and the EVP recorder sings out to them to let them know there is a spirit close by. All eyes turn to stare at the recorder, shocked by the sudden activity, their minds racing to who would try to contact them: the children, Roy, or the mysterious new spirit. They look up at one another in fear, hoping that it isn't Roy back for another round.

Chapter Seventeen

Roy gasps for nonexistent air, feeling as if he has been running for miles while under water with weights attached to his ankles. He almost feels as if his heart is about to explode inside his chest, but his heart hasn't pumped in years. He plops down on the floor, once again hiding in the back of Leilani's closet, tiredly glaring at the closed door and trying to wrap his mind around what has just happened. He is thankful for the cool darkness as it cradles him, but he still feels off, like he's hurt after the encounter with the strange new spirit within his domain. The new spirit is stronger, but Roy knows that whoever it is must be exhausted, like how he is feeling now.

Roy leans his head back against the wall, but his energy level is so low that he passes through the wall effortlessly and lies down with his head resting on the floor of the next room's closet. He groans as he sits up, feeling as if he's going to just melt away into the walls of the closet or the floor beneath him and he'll never pull himself free again. Maybe he should do that, just melt away into the walls and vanish from existence.

As soon as that thought crosses his mind, anger fills him once again, his promise to his woman slamming heavily against the front of his head and bringing him back to his old evil self again. It almost causes a sharp pain, but he can't truly feel pain, or can he? He pushes that strange thought out of his mind, not wanting to think about it because he has bigger things to worry about, such as a new ghost in his territory, helping the children protect that horrible woman, Leilani.

He crawls to the closet doors and peeks through the cracks, seeing if there is anyone in the room. He sighs in relief when the room stays still and he leans back against the wall again, this time not seeping back inside the wall as his energy returns. If his energy is returning, then he knows the intruder is regaining strength as well. He will have to work fast to stop them before they fully regain their energy. But what can he do? He knows if he wants to kill the group, he will need a lot more energy. But his energy isn't returning to him as quickly as it has in the past. He never had a problem with his energy returning until they had come back home after going out that morning, so what did they bring back that is different and affecting him?

Roy closes his eyes as he visualizes the group coming back from breakfast, going over in his head what the group had when they came home. All he can remember is some leis, potted plants, and food for Stan. But then he remembers seeing two of the group members, Teddy and Leilani, leaving the house for quite a while and when they came back inside, they were both pretty dirty, as if they had been digging in the dirt. But what could Leilani and Teddy have been adding around the house outside?

He shoves himself up from the floor and leaves the closet, his eyes darting here and there as he searches for any signs of the children or the shadowy ghost. He slinks over to the window warily and peers out through the blinds down at the yard, shifting this way and that to see if he can spot anything new they had planted. Not seeing what he is looking for, Roy slips out of the bedroom and enters each room to look out of the windows to see if he can spot anything new in the yard, but again, he can't see anything right away. He stumbles down the stairs as he continues to regain his strength, and hikes around the house, peering out of the windows until he finally sees something in the backyard, a new plant sitting in the farthest corner from the house.

He narrows his eyes and rushes out of the house, gliding to where the new plant sits. As he moves closer to the plant, a wave of nausea hits him, even though he should never feel this way, as he has no stomach or stomach acid. He stumbles a bit and stops a few feet away from the strange new plant, turning his head and gagging. The plant seems to cause how he is feeling. He backs away until he no longer feels like throwing up, but he still feels weak and sick to his stomach. Is this plant the cause of him feeling so out of sorts and weird for most of the day? Are they why he can't keep his energy or regain his energy quickly? And what about the leis? Are they also the reason he has felt so horribly? What kind of plant has that much power to cause him, an angry spirit, so much pain and suffering? *He* is the one who is supposed to cause the pain and suffering, not some silly little plant.

He grows flustered, which quickly turns to fury at the thought of a plant harming him, and he rushes towards it, his hands in front of him and a snarl on his face. He pulls energy into him so he can rip it out of the ground, roots and all. As he hurls himself at the innocent plant, he can feel his energy slip away and the nausea return with a vengeance. He fights through it and he gags as he grabs the plant. But to his horror, his hands burn, steam lifting from his palms where he holds the plant. Roy instantly lets go of it, jumping away before flames burst from the plant and onto his hands. He falls to his knees as his breathing comes out in sharp gasps, shocked at what has happened. Roy crawls away from the plant, dry heaving and wheezing, his arms shaking slightly as he creeps farther from the plant's strange magic.

After what feels like centuries, Roy has made his way back around the pool and heads towards the house to escape the evil plant. He stops to take a break, astonished that he feels as if he is sweating from the painful crawling. He has stopped dry heaving but continues to gasp for breath that he doesn't need. He glances back at the plant, glaring at it as his ghostly chest heaves and he struggles to stay sitting up. He scans the backyard, spotting in the other corner another one of those vile plants. He drags himself to his feet and wobbles back inside, sliding against the walls. He slips outside the front of the house, his eyes instantly looking for the alien plants that he had seen out in the backyard. He walks to the middle of the driveway when he sees to the left in the furthest corner another one of those ghastly plants. He turns to investigate the right corner and curses at the sky, throwing his hands up in annoyance as he stomps his way back towards the house.

Roy stands in the entryway and listens to the group in the dining room, his anger growing red hot in his chest. He doesn't want them out of the house anymore. Oh, no! He has decided that he wants them buried under the house, either alive or dead. It doesn't matter to him. But they wouldn't escape his wrath, and he was definitely the evil bastard to carry out this plan. He storms up the stairs to his sanctuary in order to plan how to rid the world of some annoying people. He glowers in the darkness, allowing his hatred to ride up and consume him, feeling his energy fill his ghostly body. He laughs; the laughing starts out low and menacing, but soon it bubbles out of his chest, louder and more dangerous. His face screws up into a snarl as he stands, doing his best to ignore the nagging power of the strange plants that sit in the four corners of the yard, steadily putting pressure against him as he rises to his feet as if they are trying to control his evilness.

The house trembles as it feels his anger and hatred seething from his ghostly form. He steps out of the closet in time to see Tina and Tony racing out of the room, obviously having been creeping around to see what he is up to. They are fleeing as fear grips them. Roy storms over to the door, still laughing like a madman as his eyes dart this way and that to see if he can spot where the two annoying brats have run off to, but they have vanished, hiding from him.

"Come out, come out wherever you are children," he snarls as he stands at the top of the stairs, looking down over the railing before he heads down the hallway to look into the other bedrooms. Not finding the nuisances, he walks back to the top of the stairs, feeling deliciously malicious as he takes a step down onto the first step. It is time to end the game and have the house back to himself, keeping it safe for his lover. He has grown tired of the company. And he knows that a gruesome murder is just the thing that will help him accomplish this plan, but he needs to kill them now. His fingers ache to start, tingling as if they have bugs crawling all over them, the same sensation he felt that night twenty years ago when he murdered the military family.

Roy heads down the stairs, his eyes on the prize and his mind reeling with plan after plan on how he will kill the group. The house shivers at the ferocity of the spirit's anger, trying its hardest to shy away but unable to escape. He feasts on the fear that seethes out of the walls, knowing that some fear he feels is from the ghost children and from the group cowering in the dining room. He continues down the stairs and heads into the kitchen, some lights flickering at him as if trying to scare him away from the group. He only laughs and stands in the doorway, watching the unsuspecting group. His eyes grow dark when he spies the leis sitting on the table, and he feels his strength fail him once again. He knows the leis are made from the same plant that is outside, and he takes a horrified step backwards, losing his edge.

Straightening his shoulders, he does his best to ignore it as he lifts his gaze from the wretched plants and stares at each person in the group. He counts the group but stops when he notices one is missing. He glances behind him, wondering where the one they called Stan was before he shrugs it off. He could kill Stan after Stan has called for help. That way, there would be witnesses quickly to the murders instead of taking a few days. After all, the sooner people saw the murders, the better for his plan to keep everyone away indefinitely. Yes. Stan would be the one to see what he had done to the others, then he'd choke the life out of him with one of the cords lying around.

Knowing how Stan will die, he turns back to the other four, a thoughtful expression crossing his face as he debates how he will kill them. He grins and narrows his eyes, ready to begin, but the smile slowly melts away when the lights flicker a bit, and their EVP recorder yells at them after he hears them ask about the shadow ghost he had fought earlier. He looks around to see if he can spy the shadow entering the room to talk to them, but the room stays empty of any other ghosts except for him.

Chapter Eighteen

"How do we know it isn't Roy who is making the recorder go off?" Leilani asks, fear in her voice as she looks around the room once the lights have stopped flickering and the recorder grows silent.

Glenn sits down, uneasy as he scans the room, not liking that he can't see anyone in the room except for himself and his friends. He jumps back to his feet and looks in the dark corners of the room for any kind of movement. He looks through the cameras but nothing catches his attention, so he returns to his seat and sits down. While he keeps his eyes on the dark corners, he shakes his leg up and down nervously.

Teddy rests his hand on Leilani's shoulder. "We will just have to ask questions to make sure that it isn't Roy." Still shaken from almost falling down the stairs, he gently squeezes her shoulder before he looks back at the recorder. He clears his throat and asks, "Is this Roy?"

The lights recorder stays off, allowing the four to breathe easier before they continue the EVP session. Teddy takes a seat beside Leilani, noticing that Stan hasn't come back yet, and he knits his brows together. He is about to go out and find Stan since they have a rule to never be alone during an investigation but stops when Aaliyah speaks up.

"Is this the shadow that protected Teddy when Roy shoved him down the stairs?" her voice quivers as she asks her question.

The lights all light up and the recorder screams a 'yes' at them. The group all talk at once, wanting to ask questions, especially a grateful Teddy. They all ask who the shadow is at the same time but stop talking when they hear one camera beep and the red blinking light on the front goes out.

"Dead battery," Aaliyah says as she stands so she can change it and continue the questioning. Just as she pulls out a fresh battery, the red recording light blinks again, and it makes the sound of the camera coming back on. "Wait, it's back on?" She steps away from the bag and walks behind the camera to see that it is indeed back on. To her surprise, the camera is also recording the group again. She glances over the camera at the others, shrugging her shoulders, completely confused at what has just happened. She returns to her seat, staring at the camera, half expecting it to stop working again as if something is playing with them.

Glenn leans over and picks up the voice recorder to check to see if the tape needs to be changed before they continue questioning the spirit. He nearly drops the recorder when he sees a small tape already labeled in a case next to it and a fresh new tape is already inside, ready to go. He grins as he carefully puts the still recording recorder down on the top of the table, "It looks like Stan is ahead of us still." His eyebrows furrow together as he glances around the room, just now noticing that they are missing their friend. "Speaking of Stan, does anyone know where he is?"

The EMF detector lights up and squeals an answer to Glenn's question, stating that whoever is in the room with them knows where Stan is located. Glenn grins and waits for the recorder to go silent before he asks the next question, "Is Stan still by the stairs looking for you?"

The lights stay off to let them know Stan has moved on from his own investigation by the stairs. Glenn leans forward on his elbows as he thinks for a minute, trying to figure out what to ask next to find where in the house Stan might snoop around for the ghosts of the children, Roy, and the mystery ghost. He snaps his fingers, causing the others to look at him curiously. "Is he in the restroom?"

They all look down at the recorder, expecting for the EMF detector to say yes, but it sits quietly on the table, causing them to worry more about their missing friend. They each ask the entity if he is in each room starting upstairs, but it still doesn't give them any answers.

"Office?" Nothing. "Upstairs bathroom?" Nothing. "In Glenn and Aaliyah's room?" Silence. "His room?" Still silent. "Living room?" "Backyard?" "Front yard?" "Getting a snack in the kitchen?" "In Leilani's room?" "In the downstairs restroom?" "Teddy's room?" They glance at each other since the only room left was the room they were currently sitting in, and they didn't see Stan enter, so where could Stan be if he wasn't anywhere in or near the house?

No one asks the last impending question, so Leilani clears her throat. "Is Stan in the dining room with us now?" She holds her breath even though she knows it will stay quiet. But to her horror, the lights all flicker alive, giving them a positive answer. "But how can that be? We don't see him here with us, and he's not a ghost himself..." She leans away from the device, "It's a trick! I bet this is Roy messing with us and Stan is still in the entryway looking around or is coming back to join us right now." She quickly pushes her chair back and hops to her feet, heading for the doorway where, unbeknownst to her, Roy is still standing, seething at the sight of them and preparing to attack.

Leilani stops before she walks through Roy and glances back to see that Teddy, Aaliyah, and Glenn have also left their seats in order to follow her so they can see for themselves where Stan is in the house. She turns back around but before she can walk again, she becomes frozen to her spot as Roy angrily reaches out to her and roughly grabs her by her arms.

Without warning, Leilani lifts off the ground and flies backwards, landing roughly on top of the dining room table, shoving the devices clear off to the other side. Leilani lays on the table completely stunned by what has just happened. Her arms feel freezing cold and tingle where she had just been grabbed.

Teddy, Aaliyah, and Glenn leap back when they see what happened to Leilani. Teddy tries to catch her, but it happens so fast that he misses. Leilani slowly sits up, moaning in pain, and looks around, confused. Glenn pulls Aaliyah back away from the entrance of the dining room, pushing her into what he hopes is the safety of a corner, and places himself in front of her to protect her. Teddy tells Leilani to go slow as she painfully scoots to the end of the table and slides off. Teddy holds out his arms in order to help Leilani stand, but Roy has other plans for the young man. The angry spirit rushes forward and slams into Teddy, sending the poor, unsuspecting young man away from Leilani. Teddy sails sideways into one camera, causing it and himself to crash into the back wall with a loud thump.

Aaliyah cries out when Teddy slides down the wall and crumbles limp to the ground, the camera still recording on the floor beside him. Glenn feels torn, stepping towards Teddy to help him, then moving back in front of his wife. He doesn't know what to do. Should he help Teddy and leave Aaliyah vulnerable? Or stay with Aaliyah and keep her safe? Though a ghost like Roy could just toss him aside like a rag doll. Leilani slips off the table, falls to her hands and knees, and slowly crawls over to Teddy's still body, checking his neck for a pulse.

"Teddy? Teddy!" She gently shakes his shoulder in order to wake him up, but he doesn't respond. She gently lays him down on the floor, checking for any broken bones and any blood on the back of his head where he had hit the wall with a hard force. Not seeing any damage, she leans close and talks to him in a low voice, hoping that it'll wake him up, her eyes darting from Teddy to the space around the room where she thinks Roy may be standing.

Roy hovers close to Leilani and the unconscious Teddy, debating on which to kill first: the girl or the boy. His eyes fall on the video camera that lies on the ground that is still recording beside Teddy's feet. He leans over and grabs the video camera and the mount, aiming the feet of the tripod at Teddy's chest. He stands, separating his feet to get a better stance so that he can slam the feet down into the unsuspecting Teddy. Raising the tools he will use to kill with high above his head, his hands gripping it hard, he's ready to slam the feet through Teddy. Leilani screams when she sees the camera's tripod floating dangerously over Teddy. She throws herself over him, knowing that with enough force Roy can and will kill them both, but she feels compelled to do something to protect Teddy from Roy's wrath. Glenn kisses his wife quickly before he rushes forward, plucking one of the leis from the table and as he bolts around the table to get to his friends. He throws the lei at the camera, hoping that the magic in the lei is real and can stop Roy from killing Leilani and Teddy. He is a skeptic about the stories and beliefs around the leis, but if it'll help save his friends, then he will do whatever it takes to save them. He comes around the table and even though there isn't anyone that he can see; he launches himself after the lei and tackles the camera and the invisible person holding it.

Roy hears movement behind him and turns to see what the other two are doing; instead, he comes face to face with a flying lei made from the dangerous leaves. He tries to move out of the way of the menacing lei, but it still falls too close for comfort, and he feels the camera growing heavier. Suddenly, Glenn crashes into him and the camera, sending the camera and its stand crashing to the floor and skidding away, broken. Roy watches as Glenn tumbles into the ground after the camera while sidestepping the lei, putting distance between him and its ungodly magic. He glares down at it as if it had shifted form and is now a snake rearing back, ready to strike and sink its dripping fangs into his leg.

Feeling as if it had bitten him, Roy walks backwards, turning his attention to Aaliyah, who is still cowering in the corner but is now unprotected. He walks backwards until he is at the entrance of the dining room, catching his breath, then darts forward, rushing at Aaliyah with a glint in his eye. He hastily looks down to see what he can grab easily in order to murder the unsuspecting woman. He is used to his victims being tied up and him in complete control, but he has to kill these four untied and it will be a challenge. His stride falters when nothing initially catches his eye that he can use to murder Aaliyah with until a cord catches his attention and he decides he will choke her to death. He leans down and uses his slowly fading strength to grab the closest cord, ripping it free from the wall, and pulls down the camera. The loud bang of the camera hitting the floor causes everyone to jump and scream.

Aaliyah sees the cord sailing towards her, and she quickly drops to her knees, cornered by Roy. She can't crawl away from him since he is in front of her and there is other equipment blocking a way to escape. Glenn leaps over Teddy's limp legs so he can run around the table to save his wife from the dangerous poltergeist. But before he can get close, the camera that Roy has just knocked over trips him, dropping him to the ground hard with a grunt and a gasp as air rushes from his lungs.

Roy stops in front of the scared Aaliyah as she crouches with her head down, her hands over her face, and her eyes squeezed shut. He glances to see Glenn struggling to get to his feet and decides that he has to go first, since he is more of a threat than the scared girl kneeling in front of him. Roy drops the cord after pulling on it to make it come closer to him, but Glenn's fallen body prevents it from coming any closer. He curses loudly, loud enough for the voice recorder to pick it up. Roy quickly strides over and kicks Glenn in the face to keep the man down before snatching the camera that he had knocked over, ripping it from its tripod with a loud crack.

Glenn groans as he looks up after having been kicked in the face by Roy and he stares up in fear as the camera drops to the floor inches from his face. The tripod floats up off of the ground, its feet pointing downwards like spears. He yells out when Roy appears, standing visibly in front of him, grinning like the devil himself, wielding his new weapon in glee. He tries to roll to the side, but the chair prohibits him from moving any farther away from the madman. He looks at Aaliyah, who is peering through her fingers; her face tormented by fear as she watches the tripod feet point downwards towards her trapped husband's back. Aaliyah's hands drop and she cries, shaking her head when she realizes Roy is going to murder her husband right before her eyes. Glenn puts on a brave face, smiling at his love, whispering that he will always love her, and closes his eyes just as the tripod jerks downwards with a loud crunch.

Roy laughs as he feels one foot of the tripod sink down through the man's sturdy back. Loud crunching mixed with Glenn's sharp yelp and Aaliyah's pleading for Roy to stop burn into Leilani's ears and mind. She turns her terrified gaze from the still limp Teddy to see Glenn's blood seeping slowly towards them from underneath the table, soaking the rug as it crawls. Glenn coughs and makes a rattling gurgle as Roy pushes the leg down further and twists until it breaks through to the other side of the man's ribs. The leg rests on the ground with some of Glenn's insides stuck to it, steading the wobbly tripod. To add injury to what he has done, Roy bends down, snatches up the camera, and reattaches it to the top of the tripod.

"Teddy! Teddy, you need to wake up now. Roy is here," Leilani says, her voice frantic. She shakes his arm roughly, sighing a bit in relief when Teddy finally stirs, his eyes twitching under his eyelids as he struggles to wake himself up.

Teddy hears a voice calling to him as he slips further away from...where is he again? He pulls himself back towards the voice, hearing the urgency and fear as they tell him about someone named Roy being there. Should he know Roy? Roy. Roy? Roy!

Teddy sprints towards the voice until he feels pain throughout his entire body, and he lets out a groggy groan as he opens his eyes, squinting as the lights filter through. He first sees Leilani's pale face, then the sounds of someone sobbing reaches his ears. He sits up and sees Glenn's dead eyes staring at him from underneath the table with one of the tripod's legs sticking through his body. Blood pools around him, mixed with his insides that the tripod's foot had forced out. He gags and chokes as he stares at the gory mess before he looks into the corner to see a devastated and broken Aaliyah curled up in a ball, her eyes staring at her dead husband's body, sobbing noisily.

"Teddy, we need to get Aaliyah, find Stan, and get the hell out of here," Leilani tells him, bringing him back to reality.

Teddy struggles to stand with Leilani's help and catches the table in order to keep his aching legs from buckling under him. He didn't want to crumble to the ground again. "Where is he? Where is Roy?"

Leilani looks around the room, clinging to Teddy's left arm to help him balance better. "I don't know where he is, but we need to leave now. He can have the damn house." She hurries around the table, carefully stepping around Glenn's lifeless body to reach the traumatized Aaliyah. She kneels beside the sobbing woman, gently placing a hand on her shoulder in order to catch the woman's attention and whispers in Aaliyah's ear, "Come on, Aaliyah, it's time to go."

Aaliyah raises her watery red eyes to Leilani's pale face and nods slowly, shakily standing up and gripping tightly onto Leilani's hand in order to gain her balance on wobbly legs. Together they walk around Glenn, Aaliyah nearly losing it again, and head back to Teddy. Teddy leans against the girls and they quickly head into the dark kitchen. They rush around the kitchen island, but a laugh behind them causes the group to freeze mid-stride. The group slowly turns around to see who or what is standing behind them.

Aaliyah lets go of Teddy and cries out when she sees a hint of light shine off the sides of kitchen knives of all sizes that float in the dining room doorway. Aaliyah turns back around and runs for the front entryway to escape. But she doesn't make it as the blades whiz through the air as Roy expertly throws them at the scared woman's back. Each blade sinks deeper and deeper into her back, with only a trickle of blood seeping down from the point of entry. But inside her body, the blades sever and puncture vital organs and nerves. Inside, blood pools, and her body twitches as the severed nerves cause her to lose control.

Aaliyah catches the wall, gasping for air as two of the blades pierce into her left lung, leaving her breathless. She inches her way along the wall, trying to keep on her feet even though they were shaking and threatening to give out from under her. She reaches behind her, feeling the hilt of one knife, the blade deep inside of her back. She whimpers and continues to slide across the wall for support, though she feels woozy.

Leilani and Teddy scramble to help Aaliyah. Teddy feels stronger after the slight rest, but they both jump backwards as Aaliyah, thinking that Roy is sneaking up behind her, spins on her heel. She swings at them to get away from her, tears running down her cheeks. Turning too quickly causes her to lose her balance, and she falls backwards up against the wall behind her, her arms wheeling as she tries to stop herself. She lets out a low grunt as the knives bite down deeper into her skin and organs, more blood pooling from the wounds inside and now on the outside.

She watches as Teddy and Leilani run towards her in slow motion, feeling suddenly exhausted from the efforts of trying to stay on her feet. She slides down the wall, the knives hilts scraping paint off the wall and creating a deafening scratching sound. Her eyes well up with tears as her body shakes in pain. Through the curtain of tears, she watches Teddy and Leilani kneel on either side of her with worry in their eyes. They call out to her and talk to her in faraway voices as they try to get her to stand up and go with them. But she is too tired to move.

As they continue to talk, she strains to hear them until their voices blend quietly, then vanish all together.

"Where are you going?" Aaliyah asks as they fade away right before her eyes. "I can't hear you either. Is everything okay?" She looks from Teddy to Leilani, squinting to see them better. "Teddy? Leilani?"

Leilani buries her face into Teddy's chest as Teddy closes Aaliyah's eyes, neither having heard a word she had said because Aaliyah was already dead before hitting the floor.

Teddy and Leilani quickly stand, glancing around them to make sure there are no other dangerous objects flying towards them. Both bolt out of the kitchen while holding hands so they don't get separated. They reach the front door without running into any trouble, their eyes darting around them for more flying objects or for Roy himself charging at them. Teddy reaches for the doorknob but as soon as his hand grabs onto the metal handle, his eyes open wide as a disgusting scorching smell quickly fills the air. He screams out and tries to pull his hand back, but the sudden heat has made it impossible as it has already melted his skin against it, trapping him. He lets go of Leilani's hand, using his free hand to grasp his wrist and pull his hand off the doorknob. But the attempt fails. His hand doesn't budge as his burning skin sizzles and causes him excruciating pain.

Leilani screams and grabs hold of Teddy, trying her hardest to pull his hand free from the knob as well, but she isn't strong enough to help him. Finally, with a sickening rip, his hand pulls free, leaving seared skin and some of his muscles from his hand on the handle. His left hand is nothing more than a bloody mess now. Teddy clutches his wrist and stares down at the bit of skin that still clings to his palm, seeing the fleshy and boney insides under the blood. The screaming dies down as Teddy stares down at his wounded hand and Leilani disappears in order to find something she can use to wrap around his hand. She peeks in the kitchen but doesn't see Roy lingering in the room, so she hunkers down and quickly runs to where she has some hand towels. From the dining room, she can hear the cameras making their usual clicking sound to let them know their batteries are getting low and will need to be changed soon. Keeping her head down, she makes her way to the oven where she slides open a drawer to find her hand towels, grabbing a few. She leaves it open as she crawls back out of the kitchen to Teddy.

Standing in the entryway with tears in his eyes and a throbbing hand, Teddy whimpers as he looks around for another way to escape. He spies the closed office doors, and he remembers seeing two large windows that face the driveway in the office. Maybe they can escape out of one of them. He looks back at the kitchen, doing his best to not cry out in pain to attract Roy's attention to them, and smiles through the pain when he sees Leilani crawling towards him. She stays hidden behind the kitchen island and hurries towards him with some hand towels in hand. She stops once she reaches the edge and peers around the side to see if she can spot Roy or anything that will show her where the psychotic poltergeist could be lurking. Her eyes widen when she sees the leis that they had bought floating out from the dining room behind her, Leilani scurrying around to the other side so Roy doesn't see her. She turns to face Teddy and motions for him to run and hide as Roy slowly makes his way towards the entryway. Teddy looks at her, confused, until he spots the leis floating towards him. His eyes widen and he stumbles backwards away from them, not knowing where to run and hide as his mind and body freeze in terror.

Chapter Nineteen

Roy watches in glee as Glenn takes his last breath, watching as the man stares at nothing and the blood seeps deep into the wood flooring of the dining room. He walks to the other corner, allowing Leilani to scramble past the dead body and to lead an unsteady Aaliyah out of the room. He taps his hand on his arm as he crosses them, letting the three retreat into the kitchen before he follows them.

Roy looks for his next weapon to use to kill the last three. He slides open the drawer closest to him, making sure that he is quiet so his victims don't hear him. He finds nothing fun he can use, so he opens three more drawers until he finds Leilani's kitchen knives. Without hesitation, he snatches up a handful of the knives and lets out a low, cruel cackle as he lifts his eyes to the group. He allows them to hear his laugh in order to distract them from escaping. He watches as they stop running and turn around to see the floating knives.

Roy stays hidden in the shadows, but he makes sure that Aaliyah sees his wicked stare. Vanishing from her view, he readies himself to throw the knives at her retreating back. He taps the end of the knives together, causing Aaliyah to separate from the group as he had hoped. He moves closer to the group, then throws the knives at Aaliyah's back. He had practiced knife throwing while alive and had nearly perfected his skills before he had been killed that fateful night.

He pouts when he runs out of knives to throw at her and stands watching the woman as she struggles to stand, feeling more of his energy slowly being sapped from his body by the leis still in the dining room behind him. He knows he has to get rid of them quickly if he wants to keep his energy from being sapped away completely, but he isn't sure how to get rid of them.

Glancing back at the drawers, ignoring the scene that plays out behind him, he rummages through the drawers. He finds a lighter and an electric charcoal starter, grinning. He grabs the starter, feeling the weight in his hand, while he stares at a lighter. He'll use them both. He knows he is going to use the lighter on the leis, but how will he get the plants to light and stay on fire?

He needs to buy himself some time so he can figure out what he will need to make his plan work. He looks down at the electric starter and tosses it up, catching it as he thinks. He clutches it and snaps his other fingers as an idea comes to him. He hurries past the three, Teddy and Leilani fuss over the already dead Aaliyah, and enters the entryway. He rushes over to the front door and places the BBQ starter on the doorknob. Roy watches as the starter heats it until it turns a deadly red. Once he is satisfied that it is hot enough, he takes the electric BBQ starter away from the doorknob and watches as the redness vanishes from the metal. He groans a little as he loses his strength, the starter dropping to the floor with a silent thud in front of the door. He pulls his arms close, breathing hard as he is forced to take a break from his hauntings. A few moments later, he bends down and grabs the BBQ starter, and stands. He takes in a sharp breath and turns, feeling someone watching him.

He looks up the stairs to see Tina and Tony cowering together, clutching their blood-soaked toys and shaking as they didn't dare rush down the stairs after Roy like they usually do. The house shakes from the anger and evil that has strengthened Roy, even with the special leis and plants that are supposed to ward off the evil energy. Tony and Tina cry out in fear as they see Roy glaring up at them with a smirk that could chill a ghost's blood.

"Once I am done with these two, I'll be taking care of you two and that damn shadow," Roy says, spitting out the words before he kneels back down and snatches up the starter, the item having slipped through his fingers after he turned. His fingers wrap around the heavy metal item, and he walks back into the kitchen, doing his best to hide the floating BBQ starter from Teddy and Leilani as they rush past him, leaving Aaliyah's body behind. He puts away the BBQ starter and picks up the lighter. He can hear Tony and Tina scampering off to hide while he looks for something flammable to add to the leis so they stay on fire.

He looks under the sink at the cleaning bottles, pushing through them until he finds a small can of lighter fluid. "Oh, this is perfect," he exclaims excitedly and puts the lighter down so he can muster up his energy to grab the can. "I need to get rid of those leis and the other plants if I'm going to get my energy back completely." He heads back towards the dining room, clutching the slipping lighter fluid can, already removing the top so he can spray it all over the leis.

He freezes mid-stride when he hears the distinct, beautiful sound of a man screaming in agonizing pain and the delicious sounds of flesh sizzling. Teddy has grabbed onto the front doorknob, trying to escape him. Everything is going well, but Roy is becoming anxious as he heads into the dining room, wondering when and where the dangerous shadow will appear to foul up his plans.

He stops in front of the table and uses the voice recorder to push the leis close together so he can use the liquid on all four without having to move too far. He pours the lighter fluid all over the four leis, making sure he empties the can. Roy drenches the plants with the flammable liquid, his eyes sparkling with excitement but grumbles when he sees the mess he has made over the table and floor and tosses the can behind him.

Roy feels a wave of sudden exhaustion come over him as soon as he picks up the leis. His stomach churns as he walks into the kitchen, the leis growing heavier with each stop, the liquid dripping below and leaving a trail behind him. Roy pulls on his anger to help give him the strength he needs to fulfill his mission. He passes the lighter that still sits waiting on the floor beside the sink cabinets. He stops just in the kitchen entryway to see Teddy running for the office, but Leilani is nowhere to be seen. Roy curses under his breath and moves faster, stumbling some as the leis continue to suck out his anger and evil energy. He stumbles again as if someone has bunched the rug under his feet and he sends the leis flying out of the kitchen.

The four leis land in a wet pile, the lighter fluid slapping the ground and spraying the back of Teddy's legs. Teddy stops and leans down to wipe away the strange liquid that has somehow splashed the back of his legs. He spies the leis on the floor and remembers that they can help protect him against Roy. He glances up to see Leilani is still in the kitchen, hiding behind the island. Teddy changes directions and grabs the leis so he can at least protect Leilani. Roy lunges forward to grab them, but Leilani motions for him to leave them and to run.

Roy notices Teddy looking behind him so he slowly looks around the island to see Leilani cowering around the corner. He watches as she motions for Teddy to run and leave the leis where they lay, mouthing for him to just go. Roy whistles a little through pursed lips as he takes his time, turning around and heading back into the kitchen for the lighter. He knows Teddy will ignore Leilani's request because Teddy wants to keep her safe. Roy grabs the lighter from the ground and walks back towards the entryway when the lighter falls to the ground and bounces away from him. He grabs a hold of the island in front of him to steady himself, but his hands slip through the island and he collapses to the ground in a heap.

Leilani hears something drop somewhere behind her and she freezes, her eyes widening in fear since she knows Roy was somewhere near her. She slowly turns around; afraid she will come face to face with Roy. Her breath comes out fast and her chest heaves as she turns to see no one is behind her, thankfully.

She slowly turns away and quietly crawls to the other corner, peering around it, still expecting to see his face glaring at her with a knife or something else in hand, ready to sink it deep inside her skull. But again, she sees nothing. She looks around, still breathing hard, to see if she can see what has fallen so she can grab it before Roy does, knowing all too well that it has to be a weapon of some sort.

Roy gags and coughs, trying to make the room stop spinning as he concentrates on trying to find where the lighter has fallen. He crawls a few inches, then stops gagging, feeling as if he is about to throw up food that he hasn't eaten in years. He shakes himself and continues to crawl as the floor topples this way and that, as if he were in one of those fun houses where the ground moves back and forth at a carnival. He closes his eyes for a minute before he opens them to see everything has settled, including his stomach. He pulls himself together, feeling his desire for death bubbling up through his body. He sees the red and blue lighter a few feet away and makes a move for it, but stops when he sees Leilani looking around. Her hands are brushing against the ground as she, too, looks for what he had dropped. He makes a face, unable to grab the lighter just yet because he knows if she sees what he is grabbing for, she can warn Teddy and ruin his plans. He crosses his arms over his chest and maneuvers himself so he can lean against the cabinets and watch Leilani search.

"Leilani?" a voice says from the entryway. "Leilani, where are you?" Teddy's head pokes into the kitchen, his eyes darting around the room as he searches for any signs of Roy.

Leilani stops searching and crawls back around the corner, out of sight of Roy, her eyes searching for Teddy. She slowly stands up when she sees him holding the drenched leis in his hands, liquid dripping off the ends of them and leaving pools on the floor. She doesn't know what the liquid is, but she has a horrible feeling that whatever it is, it is dangerous. She then remembers seeing them floating minutes before by an invisible hand and she gasps. "Teddy, Roy was carrying those just a few minutes ago. You need to get rid of them right away."

Teddy looks down at the leis, confused for a moment before he drops them into a heap at his feet, the liquid squishing on the ground. He wipes off his wet hands onto his shirt quickly. "All right, let's get out of here. We can try the windows in the office."

Roy grabs the lighter from under the island by his feet while they are talking. He stands back up, watching Leilani as she rushes around the leis and avoids the leaves from touching her shoes. Teddy looks around the kitchen one last time before he follows Leilani across the entryway to the office door. Leilani pushes the doors open, peering inside to see if she can see anything out of place that could tell them if Roy is in there. Roy steps into the entryway, playing with the lighter as he watches Teddy shifts his weight from foot to foot as he waits for Leilani to give him the okay to enter the dark office.

Leilani slips inside the office once she is sure nothing seems out of place and glances over her shoulder at Teddy. Something catches her eye behind him, and she slowly turns around, lifting her gaze over his shoulder to see one of her favorite lighters floating in the air. Her eyes widen as the flame bursts to life, then quickly dies, then shoots upwards again by an invisible hand.

Roy smirks when he sees Leilani's face fill with surprise as he flicks the lighter on and off from time to time. He glances down at the still soaked leis, wondering now how he will get these things to the other two and light them on fire, so he can burn Teddy and Leilani. He chews on his lower lip as he contemplates his options until he notices the lighter fluid has dripped all the way across the room and stops close to Teddy's feet. He shifts his gaze back up to Leilani's face as he lifts the lighter and shakes it so she can see what he has planned, flicking the lighter to life again.

"Oh my god," she whispers and grabs onto the door. "Teddy," her voice cracks as she tries to rush him into the office.

Teddy wrinkles his forehead as his eyebrows knit together at Leilani's sudden change in personality, turning to see what she has seen behind him. His eyes widen as he sees Roy materialize beside the leis with a lighter in his hand. Roy flicks the lighter on and off a few times and watches in amusement as Teddy's body shakes with fear while his eyes fall to the dripped liquid. Teddy finally realizes what the liquid is, and that he is in immediate danger.

Roy is about to drop the lighter on the pile of leis when the shadow springs out from behind him and tackles him to the floor, sending the lighter skittering to the front door. The flame disappears as it lands with a low clank and sits uselessly out of reach. Roy curses under his breath as he struggles with the shadow, rolling over so that he can get a better look at the shadow. Roy swings his fists at the shadow's face, wanting to land a few punches. The shadow grabs at his hands, shoving them aside, and gets in a few punches of their own.

Teddy watches the fight, frozen, his eyes trying to pierce through the shadow to see if the theories they had come up with of who the shadow is are true. But when the shadow finally kicks Roy away from them and looks at Teddy and Leilani, it isn't either Tony or Tina's mom or dad. They both gasp in pure shock as the face of their friend Stan stares sadly back at them.

"Stan?" Teddy croaks as he watches his friend give him a sad wave.

Stan points to the stairs. "Run now!"

Without hesitation, Teddy grabs Leilani's hand, pulls her out of the office and to the stairs. Roy stares at Stan in shock from where he lies and wonders how he can touch him if this man is alive. He stands up, facing Stan as Teddy and Leilani reach halfway up the stairs, his eyes never leaving Stan.

"How can you touch me?" Roy demands, not even moving for the lighter. He would go for it after he finds out how a live human can touch him. He has to know.

Stan takes in a deep breath as he sees Leilani and Teddy both stop on the stairs. The question, of course, gains their interest and they turn to look down at him. He doesn't face Roy but keeps his eyes on Teddy and Leilani, a heartbroken expression filling his face as he prepares himself to tell his friends the answer. "It's because I'm dead. What you and Glenn saw in the bedroom was real. Roy killed me, but somehow, I was pulled back into the house. Something is keeping me here in the house. It took a lot of energy to hide the gory scene when Aaliyah went into the room, but Tina and Tony helped me hide that, my car, and the food inside the fridge. They've been a big help, helping me in the short time I have been dead."

Stan sighs as he looks down, shaking his head. "I did my best to fight off Roy when he tried to kill you, Teddy, earlier in the bathroom, but I'm still not strong enough. I failed Glenn and Aaliyah." He balls his hands into fists, lifting his dangerous gaze to glare at Roy. "But I will not fail you two!" His voice rushes out in pure anger as he squares off against Roy.

Roy laughs and motions for Stan to come at him, now feeling gleeful. The welling of happiness in his chest mixes with his anger and it bubbles up inside of him, fighting the nausea from being so close to the leis.

Stan moves his neck to the side as if he is cracking it and speaks over his shoulder to his last two remaining friends. "Get upstairs and escape out the window over the porch. I've got this!" He grits his teeth as he rushes forward, crashing into the laughing Roy. They fall to the floor, threats flying out of their mouths as fists hit or miss one another. Both struggle to get on top of the other in order to pound the other into submission. As they roll and punch one another, Teddy slightly waves at his ghostly friend before he pulls Leilani up the rest of the stairs behind him, her eyes on the fight behind them.

Teddy lets her hand go as she runs into the room that Glenn and Aaliyah had been using. Leilani rushes to the window and opens it so they can escape out the window. Teddy leans over the railing, watching as Roy kicks Stan off of him and scrambles up to his feet, turning to face the fallen ghost. Stan hits the ground, then rolls before Roy can land on top of him or kick him in the chest. Roy punches the ground and hops back to his feet, facing Stan as Stan gets to his feet and places himself between the lighter and the raging poltergeist. Stan knows he has to keep the angry poltergeist away from the lighter.

"Come on, Stan," Teddy whispers as he watches Roy close in on his tired friend.

Stan snatches up the lighter and turns around just as Roy reaches him, reaching out for his neck. Roy grabs the young man's neck, wondering how he can kill another ghost so he can finally be rid of Stan. He tries to swat the other ghost's hand in order to make him drop the lighter, but Stan is quicker than he is and slips free. Stan sprints for the stairs to toss the lighter up to Teddy, but Roy, who is growing angrier and stronger, puts out his foot as soon as he turns to face Stan as the young man ran past him. Roy causes the young man to stumble and watches in glee as Stan tries to recover, but instead crumbles to the ground. The force of the fall nearly sends Stan through the floor since he wasn't ready and the lighter pops out of his hand, sliding away from him. Roy leaps over him and grabs the lighter. Roy curses under his breath as he feels a hand grab his ankle and causes him to lose his own balance.

Leilani pulls the window open after flipping locks and pokes her head outside, gasping when she sees Stan's car. Tears well up in her eyes as the realization that Stan is truly dead and is downstairs as a ghost fighting the evil Roy fully sinks in. She sniffles and angrily wipes away the tears as she steps away from the window. Wondering why Teddy isn't with her, she rushes out of the room in time to see Teddy racing back down the stairs.

"Teddy?" she yells as she races after him. "No, Teddy! Wait! We need to get out now. I got the window open so we can climb out and jump safely down to the ground below." She nearly trips but catches herself on the banister in time before she has a nasty spill down the stairs.

Teddy stops on the sixth step from the bottom and faces her. "Don't worry, Leilani, I'll be right back. I just need to grab the lighter away from Roy while Stan has him preoccupied."

Roy hears what Teddy has planned and spies the lighter just a few feet away from the bottom step. He turns into Stan's fist and loses his balance, falling to the ground from the force, but he quickly kicks Stan in the legs and makes the spirit topple to the ground beside him. Roy scrambles to his feet and pushes himself forward, his eyes trained on the lighter. Teddy, seeing Roy make a move for the lighter, hurries down the last steps, jumping off the last two stairs in order to reach the lighter before he can.

Man and ghost grab for the lighter, glaring at each other and pulling the lighter back and forth, trying to get it away from one another. Leilani continues down the stairs when two little hands grab her from behind and pull her to a stop. She looks down behind her to see Tony and Tina grabbing onto her hands, pulling on her gently back to keep her from going back downstairs.

"No, Tina and Tony, I need to help Teddy," Leilani gently scolds the two little children. "Teddy needs my help because Roy can kill him at any minute. Please let go of my hand."

Tina and Tony shake their heads and continue to tug on her hands, trying to pull her back up the stairs where they can hopefully keep the woman safe. Leilani sighs heavily as she goes back up two stairs in order to please Tina and Tony, but they won't stop tugging on her. They try to force her to climb up the other stairs to the landing above them. Not wanting to leave Teddy at the hands of Roy, she pulls her hands free from the two, causing them to sigh sadly and retreat up the rest of the stairs. They sit down, with their hands grasping the railings beside them and press their faces to the wood as they watch the fighting below. Leilani turns her attention back to Teddy and Roy as they continue to fight over the lighter while Stan struggles to his feet to join in the frenzy.

Roy stops pulling on the lighter and allows Teddy to pull it closer to his shoulder. Roy smirks devilishly as he watches Teddy's face grow confused, wondering why Roy has stopped fighting but refuses to let go of the lighter, allowing him to pull it closer. Roy, with the slightest movement of his finger, flicks on the lighter a few times, the lazy flame refusing to spring to life. Growling, he glances back to see Stan on his feet and rushing towards them. If Roy is to kill Teddy, his plan has to work, and that means he needs the lighter to work now.

Stan reaches for Roy's arm to pull him away from Teddy, but to his horror, the lighter finally listens and a flame bursts out of the top. The flame yawns and stretches, finally interested by the surrounding activity. The fire licks towards Teddy, tasting something delicious and wanting to devour every bit of the liquid that covers the man beside it and the floors below along with the strange plants that lay on the floor away from it.

Teddy's eyes widen when he sees the flames hungrily lap at his hands where the liquid from the leis still is present, even though he has wiped them off on his pants earlier. He drops the lighter and jumps back, but it is too late. In seconds, the flames jump off the lighter and devour his hands, lapping up the fluid and skin before the scared man's eyes.

Teddy drops the lighter and swats at the flames, but it only causes the flames to spread. Teddy spins this way and that, trying to escape the intense heat, but the fire doesn't let go, only growing as it reaches down to his feet where most of the lighter fluid has congregated. Once it touches the ground, it skitters across the floor, dancing around the trail that has been left by the leis that Teddy and Roy had carried around the front of the house. The fire reaches the leis themselves and causes them to burst into flames.

Roy laughs in delight and jumps up onto the second step as he watches Teddy spinning away from him as he hurriedly slaps at the fire while it devours his flesh. Roy claps his hands as the fire also destroys the leis, leaving only ash. The fire streams off towards the kitchen and dining room after it finishes with the leis. Stan rushes into the kitchen and returns with a jug full of water that he has found in the pantry. He rips off the top and pours it over Teddy while Leilani stands helplessly on the stairs, not sure what she can do to help. Teddy screams in pain as the fire rips through his flesh. She has to get more water to pour on Teddy, but Roy and the fire are blocking her way to get to the kitchen, where she can get more pitchers of water.

Roy looks up at Leilani and laughs even harder at her face, seeing tears sliding down her cheeks as she watches helplessly as Teddy's blood-curdling screams grow quiet as the fire destroys his vocal cords. Teddy collapses to the ground under the weight of the flames. The water gushes out of the jug over the body of Teddy once he is on the ground, but the water does little to stop the flames.

Stan yells angrily as Teddy grows quiet and still in the bloody skinless mess on the floor, the fire now devouring the man's insides, though the water has beaten back some fiery flames. Stan falls to his knees, dropping the empty jug beside the body, gritting his teeth and pounding his fists onto the ground angrily. He continues to punch the ground as Teddy's body continues to burn beside him before he springs to his feet and charges at Roy with a murderous gleam in his ghostly eyes.

Roy turns around just in time to see Stan rushing towards him and he readies himself as much as he can before Stan slams into him, taking them both down onto the stairs. Stan sits up and pounds his fists into Roy's face as he takes out his revenge for Teddy, Glenn, and Aaliyah's deaths. Roy laughs as his face keeps getting smashed by the enraged Stan, enjoying the man's anger.

Stan looks up at Leilani, taking a quick break from punching Roy. "Leilani, get out of here now."

While Stan is preoccupied with Leilani, Roy takes the moment to catch his breath and figure out his next move in order to stop Stan, then get to Leilani and the two brats. How can a ghost kill another ghost? He remembers an old movie where a ghost had a similar problem, and he quickly thinks of how that ghost had gotten rid of the other. He then remembers how the ghost had pulled out something from the other's chest, something he had called the anchor for the other ghost that seemed to hold the spirit to the earthly plane. The anchor helps ghosts finish whatever they need to finish before they can move on to wherever they go after they leave. Roy narrows his eyes as he looks over at Stan, trying to figure out what has kept this man anchored to the house. Roy remembers how Stan said he is going to do his best at keeping his friends safe.

Stan looks down at Roy, ready to pound the poltergeist into the ground, but he freezes when he sees Roy's eyes light up as he realizes something. Roy slams up into Stan, shoving the other surprised ghost off him and sends him backwards a few feet from Teddy's body. Roy was on him in seconds and Stan did his best to fend off the ghost, but he knew then that he was in trouble.

Stan swats Roy's hands away from him as he cries out, "Leilani RUN! Save... Gah!"

Leilani, already exhausted from the constant terror and crying, watches in horror as Roy slams his fist down on Stan's chest, pushing his fingers into Stan. She screams out, her voice raw and hurting from the constant screaming and tries to run forward to help, but her feet won't move forward. She prays her neighbors have heard the screaming or seen the fire and has called the fire department.

She watches Roy fish around inside Stan's chest. Stan tries to push Roy off of him, but Roy has grown stronger since the leis are gone and he can't escape. Stan gasps as he feels actual pain as Roy continues to dig inside of him. Roy's hand finally passes deep enough inside Stan to find the anchor, and he grins as his fingers close around something. Roy enjoys the delicious screams of pain from Stan as he slowly tugs upwards, his hand not letting the anchor go. He cackles as he tortures Stan. Stan no longer fights Roy, as the pain is too much.

Tina and Tony leap down the stairs to Leilani's side and drag the woman up the stairs. Leilani no longer fights the children, feeling numb and drained from all the events that have happened in the late night and early morning. She has lost everyone from the investigation team to the hands of Roy and she can't do anything. Except she can escape and warn everyone about the house to keep others from buying it and keeping others safe from the evil Roy's hands. She stops at the top of the stairs and turns in time to see Roy rip out a glowing ball from Stan's chest having grown;bored with playing with his prey.

Roy smiles as the ball shifts into a small camera, since Stan loves technology, and crushes it. He lets the small glowing bits fall onto the ground and watches it as it disappears once it touches the ground. Stan coughs and makes hacking sounds before he fades away, his anchor destroyed. He has nothing holding him to the house now. He looks sadly up at Leilani and waves before he disappears completely, his eyes urging for her to run while crackling fire spreads to the office behind him.

Leilani gasps as she watches Stan disappear after something that looks like a small camera has been ripped from his chest and crushed by Roy. Roy stands up, brushing his hands off in case there is still any residue from Stan's anchor lingering on them, and turns to look up at Leilani with a deadly smirk on his face. The flames create an eerie glow behind him that makes Leilani shiver and feel sick to her stomach. She leans against the railing as the floor shifts under her feet and she leans over, letting herself throw up onto the ground below for the first time since the crazy events had begun. She wipes her mouth and straightens up as Roy walks up the stairs, tapping his finger against the railing, licking his lips in anticipation of killing her.

Behind him, the fire eats away at the house, but he doesn't fear it. He knows firefighters will put it out, and he will have saved his girl's house. He keeps his eyes on Leilani, still tapping his finger while he hums a song he had learned years ago, a love song that reminds him of his girl, the song being called *My Girl*.

Leilani gasps and backs away as Roy quickens his humming and his steps up the stairs, knowing she needs to run, but her feet seem to move in slow motion as if she were walking through a bog. Tina and Tony see Leilani struggling and rush around her in order to do what they can to protect her from Roy. They put their little hands up in fists, ready to fight like their father had taught them to do when they were alive. Leilani trips over something, falling on her bottom with a rough yelp. She moves her feet out of the way so she can see what she has tripped over. She sees their toys laying on the floor, still covered in Glenn's blood. She kicks herself backwards on the landing, away from the toys so she can safely stand up. The commotion on the stairs draws her attention away from the toys and she hurries back over to the stairs, peering down from the banister. Her hands squeeze the wood as she watches the children trying to stop the grown man from getting up the stairs.

Roy growls as he fends off the able children as they throw punches and kicks at him, some even making contact and hurting. He finally catches a moment where he shoves the kids aside, rushing up the rest of the stairs. Tony and Tina scramble to get back up the stairs after Roy, the bottom of the stairs now ablaze and the sounds of sirens off in the distance quickly grow louder. Leilani backs away until she is against the wall next to the door where the window sits open. Roy is now on the top stair, panting and giggling like a maniac. He turns the corner and walks towards Leilani, cracking his ghostly knuckles, already enjoying the thought of picking her up and tossing her into the fire below. He steps on the old bunny and looks down at the ragged toy, raising his eyebrows, and an idea pops into his head. If Stan's anchor was his "heart" as a camera, then maybe the toys are the anchors for Tina and Tony. He nods his head and snatches the old toys and flings them over the railing into the fire below, laughing menacingly.

Tony yells out as his car falls just out of reach of his fingers while Tina stops running up the stairs and cries as she watches her favorite stuffed bunny fall into the fire. Instantly, the toys turn into ash, even before they are fully engulfed by the fire.

Tony and Tina turn away from their burned toys and look up at Leilani, sad expressions glued to their faces as they raise their tiny hands and wave. The fire engulfs them just as it has their toys. Then, in the blink of an eye, Tina and Tony vanish in two streams of smoke and with a low pop. Roy lets out an ear-splitting cheer that shakes Leilani to the core.

Leilani scrambles to her feet after having slid down the wall when she watched Tina and Tony disappear into nothing and backs away from Roy. She can't get to the window now, but she can get to another window to escape. It means she will have to go through Stan's bedroom, and since he and the children are gone, their power is gone, making the bloody scene visible.

Taking in a deep breath, she bolts to her left and into the room, slamming the door closed. She locks it, even though she knows it won't stop Roy. Her hands shake as she turns slowly around to face the horrors that wait for her in Stan's room. The stench makes her gag, and she nearly throws up again even though she has nothing else in her stomach.

The blood has dried, but the gore of the room still shocks her. She grows anxious, wanting nothing more than to get out of the room. Stan's dead body is forever embedded in her mind now and she rushes across the room with one of her hands covering her nose. She breathes out of her mouth as she struggles to get the window open, grateful once it opens and fresh air fills the room. She sticks her head outside and breathes in deeply, enjoying the sweet flower smells as they gently kiss her tear-stained cheeks.

Roy allows Leilani to run into Stan's room and waits, allowing her to see the disturbing scene she is bound to find, giggling at the aspect of her fear growing. He looks down at the fire as it continues to rage through the lower rooms in disgust, hoping the firefighters will get there soon so they can save the rest of the house. He strides towards the closed door, feeling a lot better since he destroyed the leis, and he gathers up his energy. He stomps while walking so Leilani can hear him, hoping to scare the girl more before he kills her.

Off in the distance, Roy can hear the sirens filling the early morning and knows he has to work faster since they are steadily getting closer. He didn't want her to escape, even though he knew they would think she had killed the others, just by the evidence left behind. She would either go to jail or be considered insane and locked away in an asylum for the rest of her life. Who will believe a story about an angry ghost murdering everyone except for her in the house? But either way, she could escape him with her life and he can't allow her to escape. No one can escape him. They must all die. He pulls his energy to him, then pushes it forward, ripping the door open, almost off its hinges. The door slams into the wall and creates an enormous hole.

Leilani jumps and screams as the door bangs open against the wall, the house shaking from the force, and spins around to face Roy. She covers her mouth as death closes in on her, making her gag. She tries to avoid looking at Stan's mangled body, but it is hard since it is everywhere in front of her.

Roy steps into the room, not letting her see him just yet, but allows his anger and hatred to fill the room. His emotions sweep over the entire room, causing Leilani to shudder under the overpowering emotions.

Fear fills her heart, causing it to beat faster and harder in her chest, almost feeling like it will suddenly stop from fright and kill her if she doesn't do something soon. She gulps in air, trying to calm her nerves, but it only causes her to grow light-headed. Her eyes dart around the gory room as she tries to find Roy in the mess.

Leilani places a hand over her heart as it aches from the fear and the extra pumping. She knows she has to get out of the house before Roy kills her, but she feels stuck to the floor, held down by the nightmare that she is living.

Roy laughs at Leilani's pale, terrified face and her reaction to the stunt he just pulled with the door. He enters the room, a bit of relief washing over him when he sees the mayhem he had left behind is real. He stares at Stan's body, still sitting in front of the broken computers as he had hoped. He takes a moment to look around at his handy work when the sounds of sirens coming up the street pull him once again out of his thoughts. He curses at himself for allowing himself to become once again distracted when he is supposed to be killing Leilani before the firefighters, ambulance, and police make it to the house.

Leilani hears the sirens, and she turns to climb out of the window, relief rushing over her. If she can get outside and onto the street, she can escape Roy and keep others away from the house. She needs to warn Nalani about the house, about Roy, and tell her that no one can move into the house. She is almost out of the window when she feels strong hands grab her roughly around her ankle and yank her back into the room. She screams but her scream comes out as silent breathing since she no longer has a voice. She pulls on her leg, scrambling to grab onto anything that will help her stop Roy from dragging her back into the house. Her nails crack and break off as she grabs at the tiles that make up the roof of the house's patio. Tears stream down her cheeks as she feels her ankle pop as Roy continues to yank on her. Leilani does her best to twist her ankle out of Roy's hand, but Roy only grips tighter and squeezes.

Roy grabs onto her ankle with both hands and twists hard, causing Leilani to yelp as she feels her ankle bone resist the twisting. She yanks harder to free herself, her knee and leg popping in protest. She inhales sharply when suddenly her ankle makes a horrible cracking sound and pain shoots up through her body, letting her know her ankle is broken. No more tears leak out of her eyes as she has cried them all away earlier, but they clench tightly closed as Roy now twists her broken ankle this way and that, causing her more agonizing pain. The hands move up and soon she is crying out hoarsely as Roy uses his ghostly strength to break the rest of her leg, Leilani whimpering as she continues to struggle to escape. She turns to be met with a nasty grinning Roy as he works on breaking and moving her broken bones around inside of her limp leg; the leg growing numb with each twist.

Roy waits until Leilani is pulling away from him again, then lets her broken leg go abruptly. Roy letting her go sends Leilani tumbling out of the window with so much momentum that she can't grab anything to slow herself down or stop herself. She tumbles off the small porch roof, spilling over the edge to the ground below. But before she hits the ground, she tumbles and hits her back on the railing below. No words or hoarse screams emit from her mouth as her back snaps and she collapses to the ground in a heap. Roy leans out the window and watches as Leilani falls onto the porch railing. He sighs happily when he hears the satisfying crack of her back when she hits,. the railing splintering under her weight from the force of her falling body and scattering all over the porch.

Leilani closes her eyes, groaning as she tries to move, but her body doesn't cooperate. Roy pulls himself back inside and slowly saunters through the disgusting room, down the stairs, through the fire that is slowly making its way up the stairs and out the front door. He shoves his hands into his torn jean pockets and leans against the porch railing that hasn't been destroyed, looking down at Leilani. He whistles at her broken body, seeing some blood seeping out of her arms and legs where the splintered porch has cut her. Leilani opens her eyes and stares up at Roy, her mouth moving, but no sound comes out. She tries to move, but her body won't respond to her mind telling it what to do, and she narrows her eyes at the spirit.

Roy pushes himself off the railing and heads down the stairs so he can stand over her, feeling sick because of the outside plants that he couldn't destroy. He looks around for something to use as a weapon, his eyes falling onto the splintered wood, a smile crossing his face as he looks for the biggest and sharpest piece.

He grins at the terrified Leilani as he bends down and picks up the sharpest looking piece he can find, touching the tip and pretending that it pricked his skin. Roy picks up a few other pieces so he can make it look like she had been impaled when she fell. Leilani tries to move again, but her broken back refuses to respond. She can do nothing but watch as Roy picks up the sharp pieces of broken railing, knowing this will be her end.

The sirens blast in the air as two fire trucks turn into her driveway, nearly slamming into hers and Teddy's car. Leilani looks at the fire trucks upside down and tries to yelp out for help as soon as they stop, but her voice is gone and only a small squeak comes out. Roy looks up and grumbles as an ambulance turns into the driveway, moving up behind the fire trucks, the fire trucks now shoving the cars out of the way so they have more room to fight the fire. He drops the railing pieces quickly so the strangers don't see them floating over Leilani and melts back into the shadows as he watches the firemen and women quickly unravel the hoses, hook them up to the water supply, and spray the fire.

The EMTs hop out of the ambulance once they have parked and rush over to where Leilani lies, assessing the situation of her broken body and other wounds. They gently place her on the gurney after clearing away the broken pieces of railing and strap her so that she doesn't fall off. They quickly roll her towards the back of the ambulance as quickly as they can so that they can rush her to the hospital to get her stabilized and to see how extensively her back is broken. Leilani sighs in relief as soon as they place her in the back of the ambulance, feeling safe since Roy has retreated to the house after everyone arrived. Roy lowers his gaze as the water rains down around him and the fire finally dies out. His job's done for now, but he will have to stay and keep others away from the house. He glares after the ambulance as it backs out of the driveway and turns to speed down the street to take Leilani to the hospital, carrying her away from him.

Chapter Twenty

Nalani stands in front of the badly burned Victorian house, her hands resting on the handles of Leilani's wheelchair, and her eyes watering with tears. Leilani stares up at the house, still sensing the evil present in the house, but she can't see if Roy is staring down at her from upstairs where the house didn't burn. The story has been all over the news and in the papers. They call her crazy for believing an evil spirit murdered the paranormal team and had tried to murder her, but the ghosts of the two children had done whatever they could to help her escape.

The police questioned her while she healed in the hospital, but they hadn't believed her, only taking notes and nodding their heads, but their eyes told her everything. They arrested her once she was released from the hospital two months later, but they released her after the trial because there wasn't enough evidence that would convict her of the murders.

After being released from jail, they then committed her to an asylum, the judge who committed her, saying she needed a break. She lost her job while she was in jail, but Koa fought for her and nearly lost his job as well. They released her from the asylum after only having been there for a month thanks to Nalani and her family, the only people who believed her about Roy and what he had done.

Now, six months later, Leilani sits staring at the dilapidated home, her dream home, with nothing but hate and resentment in her heart. Nalani stares at the house that is now empty since she had hired a moving company to move everything to a new house quite a few miles away. She tried talking Leilani out of coming back to the empty shell earlier that morning, but Leilani insisted she had to see the place one last time.

After being released from jail and the asylum, she withdrew into herself, staying in her room at the new house. She would only talk to Nalani a bit when she would get some food, though she still needs help since healing from the surgery that fixed her broken back keeps her in a wheelchair. Nalani tries to get her out and do things like they used to, but Leilani always says no and leaves it at that. Nalani could tell that her friend has changed, and she doesn't know how to help her or get her back to her old bubbly self again, even though she tries every day.

"I want to go inside," Leilani says suddenly, surprising her best friend.

Nalani jumps at Leilani's voice, not really hearing what she has said, lost in her own thoughts about that day and seeing the house in such a horrible state. "What was that, Leilani?"

"I want to go inside," Leilani repeats herself slowly as she looks down at a black bag sitting on her lap. "I want to put the flowers inside and... and I want to be alone for a few minutes so I can say goodbye and apologize to them."

Nalani had agreed to stop by a store and pick up a few beautiful bouquets of flowers for those lost in the house, but she hadn't agreed to Leilani going inside of the crumpled house alone. She is about to argue, even though she hears the pain in her friend's voice. She knows Leilani blames herself for the deaths of the paranormal investigating team. When Leilani pushes herself forward, Nalani's hands slip off the handles. Not wanting her friend to hurt herself, Nalani quickly grabs the handles and gently pushes it forward in order to tell Leilani that she'll do it for her. Leilani lifts her hands off the wheels and lays them back gently down on the bag, smiling to herself, her eyes never leaving the front of the house.

Once Nalani has pushed the wheelchair to the porch steps, Leilani gingerly stands up and grabs the railing, ambling up the stairs to the front door. She had to have several surgeries on her back and leg after the fall from the upstairs window and she was slowly making progress in her walking. Nalani sighs as her friend, while carrying the bag, heads to the front door, unlocks it, then looks back at her. Nalani hears some strange sounds from inside the bag, but she ignores it. Nalani puts on a smile and gives two thumbs up, letting Leilani know she is there with her.

"You can go back to the car, Nalani. I have my phone, so I can text you once I'm ready to leave and need your help with my wheelchair." She walks inside, closes the door behind her, and quietly locks it.

Nalani, not hearing the lock, shrugs, and grumbles to herself as she heads back to her car, wheeling the wheelchair in front of her. She locks the wheelchair next to the passenger side of the car and slips in behind the wheel. She turns on her radio so she can listen to music while she waits for Leilani. She pulls her phone from her back pocket and sets it down on the passenger seat so she can see and hear when Leilani texts her for help.

Leilani drops the keys by the door and walks into the burned kitchen, placing the heavy bag on top of the island, and unzips it. She pulls out several small cans of lighter fluid and a few lighters that she has been secretly collecting. She heads into what is the rest of the dining room, carrying a few cans of fluid, and pours them out on the ground and into the kitchen. She leaves a trail so the fire can find its way. Leilani opens the gas oven and turns it on before she grabs the rest of the cans of fluid, hobbling her way out of the kitchen.

As she walks, she continues pouring the fluid until the downstairs is covered. She makes sure she doesn't leave a single corner dry before she heads up the stairs; the fluid trailing behind her, splashing everywhere. She knows Roy is close because she can feel his anger, but she doesn't know where he is hiding right now. Leilani wonders if he is more dangerous now or if the plants outside are still sapping out his energy, making him a bit more docile. Ignoring the feeling, she keeps pouring can after can, dropping the empty cans wherever the last drops fall, and popping open a new one.

She stops from time to time to catch her breath before she moves slowly around the rooms upstairs, emptying her cans. She has to return to the kitchen a few times to get more fluid before she has covered the walls of each room upstairs. She leaves the bedroom where Stan was brutally murdered for last. She stands in front of the closed door for a moment, taking a step backwards as she almost loses her nerve to enter. But she can still see and hear her friends' deaths at the hands of the madman, or should she call him the mad ghost? Thinking about Teddy, Stan, Glenn, Aaliyah, and even Tina and Tony and their family gives her the strength she needs. She shoves the door open and pours out the last can, glad that she had hidden so many cans to get the job done right. She remembers seeing Roy killing Stan by pulling out the man's 'heart' from his chest and by killing the children by burning their toys, so she thinks if she burns the house completely, Roy will die and finally go to hell where he belongs. It was her dream home, but it had become a nightmare, and she has to stop the nightmare before it happens to someone else.

It is a suicide mission; she knows this, but it has to be done. Roy must be stopped, and she hopes her plan is what will stop him. She can feel Roy stirring somewhere in the house, most likely feeling her presence now, and she knows she has to act fast before he can get to her. Pulling out her cell phone, she types out a message to send to Nalani and her other family and friends, apologizing for what she has to do and telling them that she loves them very much. She re-reads the message, satisfied with it, but doesn't hit send just yet. She wants to wait until the fires begin and after Roy sees she is the one starting them.

Leilani pulls out one lighter she has brought, flicks it to life, and quickly chucks it into Stan's room, watching as the flame leaps off the tip of the lighter and eats away at the room. She waddles down to her old bedroom, her legs growing tired from the walking, and grabs another lighter from her pocket, tossing it alive into her room, followed closely by another lighter to help spread the fire faster. She slowly walks over to the stairs and takes a seat on the top stair, exhausted.

Roy bursts out of her bedroom angrily, his eyes searching for the one who has started the fires unexpectedly. His dangerous gaze falls onto Leilani, sitting on the top stair, and his voice echoes through the house, "What in the world are you doing to my house?"

"I still own it, Roy, but I've decided that it all needs to go," Leilani says as she plays with the fourth lighter in her hand. She flicks it on and off, the same way Roy had done months ago before killing Teddy. "I know this place anchors you to this domain, Roy. You see, I've done my own research after watching you re-kill Stan and the kids. So, it's time to say goodbye, Roy, to this world and this house." She smiles at him over her shoulder while she throws the lighter down the stairs, then she quickly tosses three more after it, all the ones she had brought.

Roy screams, rushing down the stairs to catch the lighters before they can hit the ground. The smell of lighter fluid is strong, and he knows if he doesn't stop the lighters in flight, he'll be in trouble. Roy catches one lighter, but the others slip through his fingers and hit the ground, instantly lighting the place up. He screams out in rage once more, his screams mixing with the hungry cracking of flames and Leilani's crazed laughter.

Tiredly, Leilani leans against the railing as she watches Roy's attempts to stop the fires from escalating. She listens to the fire spread behind her and flinches a little when she hears something fall somewhere in the house. Picking up her phone, she smiles down at the list of names that appear in the mass text before hitting send. Then she sets the phone back down, leaving it.

Roy glares up at her as the fire races towards the kitchen and the gas that calls seductively to the flames. Leilani hears the crackling as the fire spreads faster behind her and she looks down at Roy, who stares up at her. She waves at him as the fire hits her from behind, her laughter now a cry of pain that is silenced as soon as the kitchen explodes.

Outside, Nalani hears her phone go off, and she picks it up, expecting to see a text from Leilani saying that she's ready to leave. Instead, it's a long text telling Nalini to sell her things, that she loves her, and goodbye. Nalani drops her phone and scrambles to get out of her car, but something in the backseat catches her eye and makes her stop. The bouquets sit all lined up on the seat, the last being made of Leilani's favorite flowers. It's one she didn't remember purchasing when they went to the flower shop before. She jumps out of the car as the smell of fire and smoke hits her nose and she turns to see the upstairs is already ablaze. Seconds later, an explosion rocks the neighborhood and Nalani tumbles back into her car.

Car alarms and dogs barking fill the air as she struggles to get out of her car to see the house now fully engulfed in fire. There's no way for Leilani to escape. She screams Leilani's name as she falls to her knees in front of her car, sirens already blasting not too far off from the house. Someone has already called 9-1-1.

As she watches the house burn through her tears, she sees an angry-looking man through one window glaring out at her. Then, just as quickly as she sees him, he's gone. She gasps when the next figure she sees is Leilani, joined by Teddy, Aaliyah, Glenn, and Stan in the windows of the office. They wave to Nalani before they turn and walk back into the fire, vanishing. Nalani does a small wave, then laughs, knowing her friend is at peace. She wipes away her tears as she stares at the ball of flames that had once been a house.

Nalani answers the police officers' questions while firefighters work on getting the fire under control. A sense of calm floats in the air along with the smoke and a few flower petals from one of the nearby trees. The flower petals land at Nalani's feet, bringing a tearful smile to her face. Plumeria was Leilani's favorite flower. Nalani takes it as a sign that Leilani is at ease with her decision and is happy she has ended the horrific hauntings of the evil spirit named Roy. Nalani turns her attention back to the police officers as the firefighters put out the last of the flames.

The house has burned down to nothing but rubble and ash.

ACKNOWLEDGEMENTS

I cannot believe I am sitting here writing this page for a book I have written. I have struggled so much in my writing life, having thought of giving up on more than one occasion. But thanks to a lot of amazing people in my life, I continued writing and finished the book. Then the struggle to self-edit and find someone who believed in me and my book enough to publish it began. I cried, I laughed, I screamed my head off... inside my head. Then I met someone who believes in me and my book enough to take it, help me mold it into a better story thanks to having an amazing editor help me, and now will publish it under their publishing company.

Stacy, thank you for believing in me and allowing my book to be published under your publishing company, Hear Our Voice, LLC. It truly means the world to me. I cannot express my joy and excitement enough to have found you. And I look forward to publishing more of my books with you. I am proud to be your author with your publishing company. And thank you for introducing me to Holly M. I loved working with her.

Holly, thank you for being my editor. I feel that my baby, my first published book, has become our baby. You have helped me so much through your editing skills, turning my vision and writing into a stronger book. I hope we get to work together again soon. I had a great time learning from you and am glad we stay in touch. You are an amazing editor and am proud to call you a friend.

Yvonne H., my friend who, if it weren't for you, my book would be nameless. I put out a cry for help for a unique and perfect title, and you answered that call. You gave me the best title for this book and

not only the title, but you also broke it down for me, so others will say it as well. I am truly grateful to you for helping me the way you did. You are amazing!

Sarah S., thank you for putting up with all of my messages to you, and asking for help with this book and other books. Whether it was to ask you about how something sounded or even to help me write this page, you were always there for me. I am so glad to have you as my friend and in my writing corner. You will always be my writing partner in crime, and I can't wait to write the children's series with you in the future.

Kat F., Eric F., Sara L., Sheena C., and Katie J., my truest and best friends since high school. You have been there for the difficulties of my writing and always pushed me to never give up. When I was really excited about my writing, you told me to keep going. When I was sad about my writing, you encouraged me. You all are the best friends a girl could ever ask for, and I thank you from the bottom of my heart.

Mom, Dad, thank you for instilling in me the love of reading, even though I read when I wasn't supposed to like when I was supposed to do homework. But without my love of books and becoming a huge bookworm, I wouldn't be where I am today with my writing. My reading opened a door to a whole new world and turned into a passion for stringing words together to form this book and many more books to come in the future.

I couldn't have done it without the streamers I watch on Twitch, too. PreyStalker, JordanKGames, ReAnimateHer, BigSeanLive, novelist_crim, Pyro33, Deafgirl_gaming, and so many more. You all are always asking me how my writing is going and making sure I stuck with it. A lot of you even help me get more inspiration for other books or blogs through our talks during streams. None of you laughed at my dream of becoming a published author.

You all pushed me and now, thanks to you, we are here. Also, thank you so much for the friends I have made in the streamer's chats. You all have cheered me on, and now I am where I want to be.

And to the most important person in my life, the one man who would never let me quit writing. To my best friend and my husband, Ryan, I may have written this book for me, but it's also for you. You've helped me prove to myself that I can write and to not stop writing. On days, I stopped believing in myself. You never did, and you pushed me to keep writing. Those days when I broke down because I felt like I was the worst writer in the world, you took me in your arms, held me, and told me to stop thinking like that because you knew I could write. Those days when I was frustrated because I couldn't get something to sound right, you looked, read it, and helped me find those words. You told me you would always believe in me, and that keeps me going. Ryan, you mean the world to me, and I couldn't do this without you. Thank you, love, for believing in me, my writing, and my dream of becoming a published author. We're published!

To you, dear reader, thank you for taking the time to read my first book. I know it may not be to everyone's liking, but I am still grateful to you for buying it and taking the time out of your day or night to read it. I hope you enjoy it, though. But if not, then I hope you will give me another chance and read other books written by me. You may find one you like. Keep reading and believing in yourself and your dreams.

ABOUT THE AUTHOR

Lacey Gordon is an avid writer in many genres, most notably horror and paranormal. This Southern Californian native's enthusiasm for writing took hold in high school and she hasn't put the pen down yet. Even though her love of horror is her first passion,

 Lacey enjoys writing books in several genres, including children's stories. This accomplished writer has written several published stories for language tutoring companies. At this time, she relishes in writing with Reading Gate Co., Ltd. Lacey's creative talent doesn't end there as she is also an avid blogger and posts numerous stories on her website, bloggingwithcrazdwriter.com.

Her biggest fans are her loving husband and two daughters. A former Navy wife, Lacey eagerly planted her roots in Tennessee after years of being on the move. Her family

continues to grow with the addition of 2 cats, 1 service dog, 6 ducks, 23 hens, and 2 roosters, for now. She still loves to travel and can't wait to travel more with her husband and girls.

As a final note, don't get too attached to her characters, as their fate is always debatable if they meet a gruesome death or live to see another day!

CPSIA information can be obtained
at www.ICGtesting.com
Printed in the USA
LVHW032227230922
729162LV00002B/223